**AERIK FRANCIS**
I identify as Black and Latinx. My father is a Bla...
New York City; his parents, my grandparents, in...
the US from Jamaica and Panama. My mother...
woman from Colorado with family roots indigenous to the
Southwest US/Mexico.

**ALTON MELVAR M. DAPANAS**
I am of Filipino (Higaonon and Waray), Spanish
(Castilian), and Chinese (Shanghainese) heritage.
My people are from the southern Philippines.

**ANDRÉ O. HOILETTE**
My people are from Jamaica and China.
I identify as Jamaican.

# INFINITE

•

# CONSTELLATIONS

**KENJI C. LIU**
My people are from Japan, Taiwan
and New Jersey.

**BRIAN K. HUDSON**
I am a citizen of the Cherokee Nation of Oklahoma, and
my people are from northeast Oklahoma.

**JUAN J. MORALES**
I am/identify as Latinx, and my people are from
Ecuador and Puerto Rico.

## LUCIEN DARJEUN MEADOWS
I am a writer of mixed Cherokee and Euroamerican descent, and my people call Shaconage/the Great Smoky Mountains home.

## DANIEL JOSÉ OLDER
I am a son of islands and exiles, a crossroads of multiple diasporas; my people are Cuban, Jewish, Santeros, Catholics, warriors, poets, and nerds.

## GEORGE ABRAHAM
I identify as Palestinian american and my people are from Ramallah, Al Quds, and Nablus.

## MARY LOU JOHNSON
I identify as Black, Black Seminole, and American.

## KENZIE ALLEN
I identify as Oneida and Haudenosaunee, as a descendant of the Oneida Nation of Wisconsin.

## MELANIE MERLE
Chickasha Saya. I am Chickasaw. My people come from the Mississippi Valley, and from Oklahoma by way of Removal. I identify as "mixed," both First Nations/indigenous and as the grandchild of immigrants.

# INFINITE CONSTELLATIONS

## AN ANTHOLOGY OF IDENTITY, CULTURE, AND SPECULATIVE CONJUNCTIONS

### EDITED BY KHADIJAH QUEEN + K. IBURA

TUSCALOOSA

FC2 is an imprint of the University of Alabama Press

Inquiries about reproducing material from this work should be addressed to the University of Alabama Press

Book Design: Publications Unit, Department of English, Illinois State University; Director: Steve Halle, Production Assistants: Emily Fontenot and Kylie Hagmann
Cover image: Sergey Nivens/AdobeStock
Cover design: danielle c. miles
Typeface: Adobe Caslon Pro

Library of Congress Cataloging-in-Publication Data is available from the Library of Congress.

ISBN: 978-1-57366-198-0

E-ISBN: 978-1-57366-900-9

# CONTENTS

## SPECULATING US

## The Editors, Khadijah Queen and K. Ibura

> to even write *apocalyptic* is to assume a certain immortality, a boundlessness.
>
> —George Abraham

> To assume: to presume: to guess: to risk error
> A boundlessness: infinitude: without constraint
> Immortality: unending life: everlasting: timeless

> assume the empirical formula of ancestors
> —Ruth Ellen Kocher

When we started reading the many offerings for this anthology, we expected to encounter time travel, outer space, parallel dimensions, technology, magic, the apocalyptic and post-apocalyptic, worlds familiar-strange and wildly imagined. And those speculations exist here, vibrantly. But what we didn't expect, what enthralled and surprised us: the attention and care with which the authors in these pages depict human relationships, the sentience and preciousness of animals and nature, the deep honoring of memory, and the rootedness to place(s) alongside the centering of culture.

> To what can we return when we turn time / toward sequence
> —Jennifer Elise Foerster

> There are always multiple realities, and to create and maintain one story is what takes
> childish self-deception.
>
> —Cindy Juyoung Ok

Constellation: pattern: grouping or relative position of the stars
Speculate: hypothesize: meditate: reflect: wonder

Wrapped in the familiar, we might miss the unusual. We might miss the messages in our dreaming. We might fear remembrance, mistrust our own voices, avoid what we observe and cannot explain.

if she looked in the right direction she could know.
—Lynn C. Pitts

The dream can only end with my waking.
—Melanie Merle

What is the vibration of a voice unfettered by wounds?

I knew as I was speaking that it was the scorpion again, crawling from its burrow, but the words had already escaped my lips.
—Shreya Ila Anasuya

I throw my head back and scream.
Maybe this time my voice will carry.
—Yohanca Delgado

The writers in this anthology mirror, instruct, bind and unbind, myth-make and myth-invert, transform and transmute, make us belly laugh or hum our understanding or gasp or whisper gently or remember that sometimes we need to holler and fight as we grieve. Any dangers herein, imagined-observed in poem and story, transport us: theoretical / possibility grounded in the near real, moving from latent to extant, then unleashed.

I felt those tambores radiating through my body, whispering their secrets.
The guitar let out an ocean of notes, dancing with me
—Daniel José Older

I hear her song vibrate off the cliffs: *People have as their names, their rivers, their rivers.*
—dg nanouk okpik

As children of musicians and writers, as writers and artists ourselves, we know a jazz composition banks on a balance of expectation and surprise. Notes build on inspiration and improvisation via cool and skill. We know a painting blends color and line, texture and invented pattern to create a visual narrative. We feel in the music of this work, in its order and arrangement, an opening conversation made complex by its keening awareness—sharp, tender, pained, confident, luminous, delicate, a power measured in accumulated sentences and in where lines choose to break.

I was a thunderous woman, built tall by the engine of my great-grandmother.
—Thea Anderson

her smile radiates up from her mouth to her eyes, through me and across
—Brian K. Hudson

A "her" is sometimes addressed. But also, any pronoun, or none, or earth, or space, which unfold as themselves, unburdened by categorical impositions.

dreams aquamarine needled
—Aerik Francis

looking into the night / under infinite stars
—Mary Lou Johnson

This work does not presume; it presents—its presence a constellation of appearances, a symphony of belonging.

we love like / No other blooming.
—Lucien Darjeun Meadows

And a presence, where? An appearance, to whom?
Everywhere, us.

I want all proverbs to be legible
—Sarah Sophia Yanni

Us is a topography, a shifting landscape defined by many different connections and circles of relatedness. We-ness can turn on a glance or a word. Some of its spokes are unbreakable.

liminal / the state of / being on // a threshold
—Wendy Chin-Tanner

I no longer return to the forest alone.
—Kenzie Allen

In these pages, the living earth is metaphor and mimesis, model and solace. Actions and definitions drive the narratives and reflect back what we know. Beauty layers us, feeds us, is us—

I look behind the sun and under one of its thick, red rays
—Juan J. Morales

Meanwhile, the sun set a god and rose a moon goddess
—Ra'Niqua Lee

Odes to the dear and imperfect.

adorned / with duranta leaves.
—Alton Melvar M. Dapanas

*Ocean,* / from Greek *ōkeanos*, the great river that / wanders around the earth.
—Kenji C. Liu

A limitlessness within imposed limits: an ease, in avoidance of expectation.
Free from: free of: free in: prepositions interchangeable according to circumstance.

in seconds too small to measure
—shakirah peterson

Watch for the organic flow of imagining, the kinship links, the friendship both familial and chosen, long-lived and new-instant. This is a grounding, not just in the worlds we create for ourselves on the page, but in real life. A space where truth is not a tool for manipulation, but one for building and threading, connecting realities that enhance and empower and strengthen. Directing multivalence with an intentional, object-constrained freedom. In this dimension skipping through and around is not chaos, but participation in meaning-making, expansion, and witnessing.

go-where-your-finger-lands / when-the-spinning-stops
—Soham Patel

Refuse to remain lost
—Shalewa McCall

We exist between layers of desire and ambition—physical, intellectual, emotional, spiritual. We thrive in intimacy and kinship as we delve into ourselves and surrounding lands and waters, surpassing anything surface, reaching for an encompassing language.

Cothilda used the skin suit to travel / the sunlit hours.
—André O. Hoilette

Expansive sentience, the kind of knowing that powers its own intuitive collation: music as place, place as music, music as haunting, haunting as self-memory, memory as dimensional and material, time as self-measure, waters as names—

Bedazzled / with everything I love about myself
—Tonya Liburd

Unhurried in some cases, urgent in others, the spectrum between languor and alacrity harbors persistence, crafting worlds with an evolved relationship to time.

The album spins and spins, scarab wings furling and unfurling.
—Sheree Renée Thomas

In collecting this work, we felt humbled by the love threaded throughout the voices speaking to us in stories and poems that vault beyond expectation and settle in our consciousness as an expansion of what's possible when we tend to one another with intention. We felt lifted, held aloft in these arrangements of language. We hope that as you read each story and poem, you will find the same sense of empowerment and celebration that we know has sustained us over countless generations, and in their beauty and humor and intelligence and complexity, continue to enrich us still.

# INFINITE CONSTELLATIONS

# OSKʌNU·TÚ

## Kenzie Allen

transl. "deer"

*"they tell me the word carries with it
the meaning of 'peace'
and you cannot pull those things apart
or sift out the animal from the state
of being or vice versa,"*

—Brian Doxtator, as taught by Tom Porter

For a few more moments, it is ours.
            You are not that kind of wolf who would devour the
world.
I no longer return to the forest alone.
            No-face doll, water lily—

I look for myself in every lake mirror,
            suspended in briar,
the tilted back throat and howl.
            In the overgrown, river-dappled,
I don't know what it looks like,
*peace*, I say, except
for the outline of where it's been.
I feed her peaches. She licks my fingers
            almost clean. Velveteen

of newly grown, the strawberry
                        trail into cinder cone
I made my haunt, a thicket
clover-charmed. An island
where we all are well fed
                        a roadside warning. Soft supple
meat. We never can go back
to listen for the soundless. My stomach
                        ripe for arrow and
                        so unsettled. We would be better
fur-lined, to slip through snow
smoothly, if headed
                        in the right direction.
If I could become it, quivered
skin fit to leave my bones
past,
gaze tied
                        to the hunter, headlights,
                        this body I can't bear
into exile,
that time of year our antlers shed.

Kenzie Allen

# SHE SANG TO ME ONCE AT A PLACE FOR HUNTING OWLS

*Utkiavik*

## dg nanouk okpik

I wade through the nesting ground, fitted like a fingerprint. You say it's a place of speckled day owls with golden eyes. You and I traveling together, following the caribou at the entrance of *Quunquq* River, we see caves in old sod houses which belonged to reindeer herders. Our dogs start barking, whining. We follow the whale-rib steps up to the ridge, leave tobacco. We keep hiking up the mountains where there live many Dall sheep, we set camp. I dream of a snow bird with pearlescent plumes, a horntail, and a spiked crown. She brought me a lens to use in the echo chamber. When we come upon *Okpikrauq* River, I hear her song vibrate off the cliffs:

*People have as their names, their rivers, their rivers.*

# THE SWAN

## Lynn C. Pitts

Two-twenty. Her light snore—she hoped it was light—shook Joy awake. She looked around warily. The whole "open office–floor plan" made the midday nap a relic of the aughts, back when creative directors at ad agencies had offices. She needed a power nap and there was no point in fighting it.

Joy strolled to the ladies' room and made a beeline for the spacious wheelchair-accessible stall, where she carefully laid three layers of the paper liners on the toilet seat. A quick fifteen-minute nap while perched on the paper-covered toilet was enough—she could sleep anywhere—but first she had to handle normal bathroom business. She pulled her underwear down and there, in the crotch of her lacey La Perla splurge panties, was a snowy white feather the length of her middle finger.

Joy picked up the feather and stared, amazed, slightly amused.

*Obviously it's a feather from your down pillow that was stuck in a pillowcase and ended up in the laundry bag with your panties.*

But the La Perla splurge panties were a hand-wash only item.

*

Hot Trainer stood over her smiling with demented pride. "You did great today!"

Joy gazed up at him from the gym mat, gasping for breath and wondering if her arms and legs would ever forgive her.

"So, today was the last session in your package." Hot Trainer said in that syrupy tone she found so . . . compelling.

Joy sat up and pushed her face into a smile. She couldn't afford another package of sessions, and her reason for booking with him in the first place belonged on the long list of bad decisions she'd made about men. But then he smiled the smile that, back in the spring, led to the one-night stand that led to the too-expensive, crack-of-dawn workouts she despised.

"Yup," she heard herself saying. "I'll stop by the front desk and get another package." *Why are you saying that? We're not doing that, are we?*

"That's awesome, sweetheart. You're doing great."

Hot Trainer strutted off to his next appointment. Joy took a deep breath and willed herself to her feet. No, maybe her legs would not forgive her. As she tugged her T-shirt over her hips she felt something flutter between her thighs. She twitched at the sensation and pulled at her leggings. What would it take to find comfortable underwear?

In the gym locker room, Joy headed to one of the little-used private changing areas. The Manhattanites who belonged to this particular brand of upscale gym saw the locker room as an opportunity. Who wanted a private changing room when one could peel off one's Lululemons and display a body slimmed and toned and strengthened by Spin and Barre Burn classes, weight lifting and burpees, the gym's twelve different kinds of yoga? The private changing rooms were always available.

The tiny room didn't have a door, only a curtain that didn't reach the floor. Joy pulled the curtain shut and slipped out of her workout gear. When she pushed her panties to her knees, a small clump of pale feathers fell out of the leg opening and landed unceremoniously at her feet. She dropped her towel on them and hoped no one saw. Her heart raced at a rate that would have made Hot Trainer happy.

Joy stared at her naked self in the changing-room mirror. All the experts said you couldn't change your body if you didn't love your body. It sounded like the kind of shit people said when they never had to shop in the plus-size section of stores or had never been called a big ox in front of everyone at their cousin's tenth birthday party. *Not that it matters, because we're over that.*

She looked down at the towel, the clump of feathers hidden beneath it like a telltale heart.

*

Joy decided she was overreacting. There had to be a logical explanation. In fact, she felt as though there *was* an explanation, just out of reach, that if she looked in the right direction she could know. In the meantime, the feathers increased in size and frequency. By the end of that first week, she wanted to believe she was having a reaction to underwear. After all, she didn't wear underwear to bed and she wasn't finding feathers in the sheets. That was kind of logical. That Friday she went commando.

She got on the B train for her morning commute feeling confident; she'd worn her favorite navy-blue linen pants (slimming and less wrinkle-y than the typical linen pants). Then, halfway across the Manhattan Bridge, as she admired the sparkle of the morning sun on the waters of the East River and New York Harbor, Joy felt two feathers slip down the leg of her pants. The train was packed. A woman with a thick Caribbean accent was shrieking about Jesus. No one except a wide-eyed toddler noticed the feathers slide across Joy's sandals. Her belly went cold, a stone at her center.

At work, she hid out in a huddle room for most of the morning, declining meetings, saying she needed time to focus on some radio scripts. She hid the feathers in her notebook. At lunch she went to Duane Reade and purchased a pack of Fruit of the Loom underwear. Throughout the day, the reality of it all dawned on her again and again, shocking her anew each time.

*

At home, Joy slumped across the bed and considered this alien evolution. She imagined the feathers shifting inside of her, quivering like dandelion fluff between her legs.

Maybe the feathers were her Rubicon, the plot point that marked her life transformation from potential to actuality. "After the feathers," she would write in her journal, "there was a great tidal wave of creative energy.

I was no longer pained by the unfinished screenplays and the comic-book idea that waited in stasis on my laptop."

*But you don't journal, remember? So that lil' fantasy sounds like a reach. Maybe you should be figuring out what you did to cause your VAGINA. To Issue. Feathers.*

She'd never been consistent or even interested in journaling, but now she wanted nothing more than to reverse-navigate the recent course of her life. What wrong turn had led her here? Why did it feel as though the answer was just there in the peripheral vision of her mind's eye?

Joy woke up in the middle of the night, disoriented and still fully dressed in her linen pants and Duane Reade underwear. Then she remembered that she was a woman whose vagina issued feathers. She reached for her phone, stopped. There had been enough Googling for one day. None of her searching had yielded anything helpful except for the disturbing theory that syphilis had jumped to humans from livestock, "possibly sexually."

Her own sex life in the past year had been unremarkable, very close to nonexistent. Her annual pap smear in the spring—post the one-night stand with Hot Trainer—had been pristine. Still there was that feeling that the answer waited in a blank space in her mind, just out of reach.

Through a space between her window shades, a nearly full moon glowed above the Brooklyn skyline, its light spilling across her duvet in all the clichéd ways that moonlight does. Her friend Nicole once said that moon-bathing was replenishing. Nicole was into that sort of thing. Joy reached her hand out to a moonlit section of the bed and waited to feel a difference.

\*

Two weeks after the first feather, there was something new: a pins-and-needles feeling in her groin and along her belly that intensified all morning. Joy left work early, saying she felt a migraine coming. This was not completely untrue, especially when she undressed in front of the full-length mirror in her bedroom and her reflection revealed small, delicate white feathers all over her mons pubis and spreading upwards. It was one thing to have feathers falling, but quite another to have feathers growing. She pulled at one. It hurt as though she were pulling at a firmly rooted part of her body.

"Okay. Don't panic."

*Nah, bitch. PANIC.*

She took deep cleansing breaths like the teacher in candlelight yoga class taught her.

Then she padded naked to the kitchen, got the vodka from the freezer, and poured herself a generous shot. She took a gulp, walked back to the mirror, and looked again. Yup. She was growing feathers.

Joy started to cry.

She'd been on the floor sobbing and blowing her nose for nearly an hour when she decided she could no longer soldier through alone. It was time to call in her girls.

Carla was a journalist on the health and medicine beat. She wasn't a doctor but could speak with great authority on a variety of health issues, especially when it came to women's body parts. Normally Joy found this kind of annoying, but the current circumstances absolutely called for Carla.

She also needed Nicole, who, in addition to being a part-time life coach, dabbled in various spiritualities, and was heavy-duty into birding. Joy texted them both. Then she threw on a loose-fitting cotton caftan with no underwear—the pins-and-needles feeling had intensified and she couldn't tolerate anything touching her—and sat on the sofa to wait for her friends.

*We've managed to get through three-plus decades on the planet without contracting any STDs—well except that one time—only to end up with feathers growing out of—*

"Stop it. That's not helping."

*

"I'll be gotdamn," Carla said.

Joy lay awkwardly on her sofa, holding the caftan up while her friends peered, aghast, at her feathered nether region.

"Dear Goddess." Nicole gasped and covered her mouth with her hands, making her heavily bangled and braceleted arms clink and sing. "Please tell me you have some sage."

"The kind you burn or the kind you cook with?" Joy asked, sitting up and pulling the caftan down.

"What we need," Carla said, "is vodka."

Nicole and Joy stared at Carla.

"Don't you bitches think we need a cocktail?!" Carla snapped.

"I'll get the glasses," Nicole said.

"Vodka's in the freezer," said Joy.

Drinks were poured. The fading blue light of the summer evening seeped through the windows while they sipped. "Okay, Carla, you're sure you've never heard of any STD that causes feathers to—"

"I've never been so sure of anything in my life."

Nicole had drained half her glass and was calmly scrolling on her phone, nodding to herself as she looked from the screen to the open box of white feathers on Joy's coffee table.

"Joy, honey, you gotta see a doctor," Carla said gently. "I mean, maybe we just need to go down to Atlanta. I've got a friend who works for the CDC and . . . "

"Swan!" Nicole shouted. "I knew it. These are definitely swan feathers." She looked up wide-eyed and nodded vigorously. Nicole had recently shaved the sides of her hair and dyed the remaining mohawk a deep blue, and Joy couldn't help but think that she looked like a bird herself.

Carla looked from Nicole to Joy. "Your vag is turning into a gotdamn swan."

"Well, fuck." The feathers were real. They were the feathers of a real, actual, alive-on-this-plane-of-existence bird.

"So, I have to ask this," Carla said. "You been doing any kind of freaky shit with animals? You know? Dabbling? No judgment—"

"Are you asking me if I've been fucking swans?"

"Gir . . . yes. I'm . . . That's the question at hand."

"It is a relevant question," Nicole said softly. "People are doing all kinds of things these days to reconnect with nature. The ecosexual movement, for instance, is very real and people are—"

"Nic. Do not start talking about tree fucking—"

"Gimme a break! I'm just trying to create a safe, sex-positive space for Joy!"

"Both of y'all stop! No, I have not been having sex with birds!"

"Okay. Calm down. Getting your pressure up is not gon help right now. Let's just focus on your recent sexual history."

"Well that's easy. There is none. Recently. Not since the trainer back in April."

"I can't believe you fucked a personal trainer."

"Carla." Nicole gave her a stern look before turning back to Joy. "Are you sure, sweetheart?"

"This is the longest walk across the no-dick desert I've ever taken. Trust, I'd know if I'd stumbled 'cross a damn oasis. And I've had a checkup since April."

"Wasn't there someone back in . . . ?" Carla frowned and chewed on her bottom lip. "Why do I feel like we're overlooking something?"

*Exactly! We feel this way too!*

Joy stared at Carla, the pins-and-needles feeling rising between her thighs, up her belly. "That's weird," Joy said. "So do I. Every since this started, I've been feeling like I know something . . . or that I forgot something. You know?"

"Now *that's* strange," Nicole said.

"Oh *this* the part that's strange for you?" Carla laughed. "But then you are Wiccan or some shit these days, right?"

"I'm currently in between spiritual modalities, Carla. But your forgetting does make me think of something." She fiddled with her bracelets. "There's a guy we should go see, but it might be a little weird."

"Bitch, we way past weird."

\*

The three women stood on the sidewalk across from Fort Greene Park, Joy and Carla staring up at the glowing windows of a stately brownstone, Nicole tapping away on her phone.

"Okay, Nic," Joy said, taking deep, candlelight-yoga breaths in the hopes of calming the pins-and-needles feeling racing up her belly. "Why are we here?"

"So, I know this witch—"

"We're in crisis and you think Harry Potter is the answer?" Carla hissed.

"Would you stop interrupting me with all the negative—" Nicole was interrupted by her phone buzzing. She walked a few feet away, speaking in urgent whispers.

They all jumped—Joy felt as though her feathers all stood on end—when the outer gate to the garden level creaked open and a short, wiry brown man with close-cropped salt-and-pepper curls stepped out. "You'd better come in."

Joy and Carla looked to Nicole, who was already making her way down the stairs, and then to each other. "Look more like a leprechaun than a witch," Carla muttered.

*

Ernesto was pleasant enough, though his apartment was unsettling. Every surface was covered in a dizzying array of books and icons of varying religious origins. Joy identified battalions of Buddha heads, an army of Virgin Marys, dozens of Jesuses—one that appeared to be covered in red velvet—Ganeshes, Kalis, and Durgas, a massive Isis above the fireplace mantle, a herd of Anubises, eyes of Horus blinked back at her. So many Hands of Fatima raised in greeting. Or caution.

" . . . So, Joy has this situation," Nicole was saying. "Without going into painful details—"

"Please don't," Joy interrupted, snapping out of the bric-a-brac-induced haze.

"I wasn't going to tell him about—"

"We need to remember something that happened," Carla interrupted, giving both of her friends a look. "Joy and me. We think something happened. We can feel it, but we can't remember it. I know that makes no sense."

"I understand," Ernesto said, chewing on his bottom lip.

"You do? Because I feel like I fell down the damn rabbit hole," Joy said.

Ernesto stood abruptly and dug through the overstuffed drawers of a desk creaking under the weight of dozens of crucifixes and a large reproduction of the *Pieta* covered in silver sequins. "Here we go." He turned back to them, holding two strands of rosary beads.

Carla sighed. "Papi, I don't think a novena is the answer."

"Me either," Ernesto said. "The rosary beads are just a device to help you focus your mind. A bead for each day, starting with yesterday. Go through every detail of each day you can remember. Eventually you'll get to the day this thing happened, whatever it is."

"Then we'll remember?" Joy asked.

"Maybe, maybe not. But you'll remember the circumstances around the thing. The place, the people. And the missing piece will be this obvious chunk of empty space in the day, or maybe a feeling like an itch that desperately needs scratching. It will get you closer than you are now." Ernesto dropped a rosary into Joy's outstretched hand. The beads were cool and smooth in her palm. She clutched them tightly.

"What if this don't work?" Carla asked. "You got a magic spell?"

Ernesto smiled.

\*

They sat in Joy's living room all night, she and Carla with their phones open to their calendars, drinking vodka sodas and saying the novena of that summer's days. By the time they arrived back in early June, they were drunk and nearly incoherent, Joy wondering if she really had fallen down the rabbit hole and found her very own feathered-vagina wonderland.

June 9. Steve and London's wedding.

Every unnatural feather on Joy's body made itself known. She winced.

She'd never gotten so sober so quickly. "Carla," she said, grasping at the dark space in her head, her voice drowned out by Carla and Nicole's laughter. The darkness had a shape, a man-shaped space.

*

On June 9, Joy and Carla had gone to a wedding in the Catskills, on a farm refurbished to rustic hipster elegance. The ceremony took place a ten-minute walk into the woods, surrounded by old-growth trees and a sea of ferns as far as the eye could see. Though Joy was allergic to mosquitoes and some thirteen varieties of grasses, even she was not immune to the beauty of the setting, the sweetness of the ceremony. She wiped away tears as the party strolled back through the woods, to the barn where the reception was being held.

He fell in step with her, offered her a handkerchief. "Breathtaking, wasn't it?" His accent was vaguely foreign, but she couldn't pinpoint country or culture. Not that she cared. He was the most beautiful man who'd ever flirted with her. Tall, dusky, broad chest, full lips, square jaw, piercing eyes, the color of which seemed to flicker and shift in the dappled light of the woods—medium brown or golden brown or brownish green—the whole package. She guessed some Afropolitan mix, but it hardly mattered.

He focused intently on her, though there were plenty of single, more nubile women focused intently on him. He fetched her cocktails and rearranged seating so he could have dinner next to her. He coaxed her to the dance floor, though she warned him she wasn't a great dancer.

Late in the evening he walked her to a little clearing in the woods and put his bespoke suit jacket on the ground for her. They lay on their backs and he pointed out every visible constellation, of which there were many in the clear night sky. There was no outdoor lighting at the hipster farm. The heavens showed out.

Cocktails plus wine with dinner plus the Milky Way providing mood lighting plus the forest whispering some ancient love ballad. She most definitely had sex with the Hot Afropolitan on his bespoke jacket among the oak and hickory and beech trees. The next day she couldn't recall his name, no matter how hard she tried. She looked for him at the Sunday goodbye brunch, but he didn't show. Carla and the others remembered him from dinner, but no one remembered his name. Joy described him to the bride and groom, but they had no idea who he was.

*

*I'll be damned.*

"How could I have forgotten . . . " Carla rubbed the bridge of her nose. " . . . that you fucked a strange guy in the woods without a condom?"

"Can I just say . . . " Nicole was busy pouring a round of soda sans vodka. " . . . If having sex with this man caused her vagina to grow swan feathers, I'm guessing a regular ole condom wouldn't have done the trick anyway."

"Thank you," Joy said, gulping her soda.

"I mean, no judgment," Carla said. "But how we gonna find the hottie from the wedding? He's clearly no ordinary nigga. Look what it took to even remember he existed."

"This is definitely supernatural," Nicole murmured, making the sign of the cross.

"Girl, stop. You haven't been Catholic since the 90s."

Joy's phone buzzed and she looked down annoyed, wondering who'd be texting her at that hour. It was her cousin in Louisiana, sending a picture of their uncle, who'd caught a giant turtle in the bayou behind his house. Her feathers quivered with excitement.

"Obviously," she said.

"What's obvious?" Carla asked.

"Phones. Remember they asked us not to take pictures at the ceremony? But everyone had their phones out at the reception. Somebody got that guy on camera."

*

Emails and texts were sent. The next day exactly two people had managed to find images that captured the elusive Hot Afropolitan.

One image had a shot of him from behind, doing the Cha Cha Slide. He was flailing, facing the opposite direction from everyone else. Joy's face was distorted with laughter, her full cheeks pushing her eyes to little crescents. For half a second, she didn't recognize herself, lamented the fleshiness of her chin, but she remembered the feeling. It came flooding back in a rush that made her feathers quiver, the thrill of him, the way it felt to be the center of his attention, of everyone's attention because she was with him and it was very difficult to not look at him and whatever he was doing.

The second picture was of the wedding guests all looking toward some happening out of frame, maybe the first dance. Hot Afropolitan was headed in the opposite direction, striding out of the open barn doors. Something or someone caused him to look back over his shoulder and his profile had been captured. Semi-wild 'fro. Neat beard. Classical-statue forehead and cheekbones. One hand in the pocket of slacks that hugged his tight-enough-to-bounce-a-quarter ass.

That was it. None of the other twenty-two people they knew at the wedding could find a single picture that contained Hot Afropolitan's face.

The second part of the plan involved taking the case to social media. Joy and Carla concocted a "missed connection" story for Facebook and Instagram and posted the picture. *Hey fam. Anybody know this guy? Met him upstate. We got a whole Cinderella/Prince/disappeared at midnight situation. Help a sista out. You know what it's like in these dating streets.*

For the rest of the weekend, the only thing her posts generated were quippy comments.

*Too good-looking. Probably on a weekend furlough from the psych ward. You dodged a bullet.*

*Married for sho.*

*That's the ancestors protecting you. Dude that fine will definitely mess up your FICO score.*

*What's for you will be for you.*

Joy resisted the urge to cuss out everybody who quoted a cliché.

*

Joy spent most of Saturday and Sunday in front of the mirror, cycling between despair and fascination. Her layer of white feathers thickened and spread across her hips and stomach. A soft, downy cluster formed at the small of her back. A faint, bright line shadowed her spine.

Monday morning she called in sick and lay in bed listening to her heart pounding in an unnatural way. She'd read that avian hearts were larger, relative to body size, than mammal hearts. They had to work harder and faster to meet the metabolic demands of flight. Would her bigger heart have a greater capacity for love? And disappointment?

*How are you gonna explain this to mommy?*

She forced herself out of bed. Wallowing was tempting, but her pulse pounded a furious drumbeat and urged her on. She needed to be out there, finding Hot Afropolitan, even though she didn't know what she'd do when she did.

In the mirror, she took in the progression of white feathers across brown skin, feather against flesh, alien and self. *We have feathers.*

Tears gathered in her eyes, but she didn't feel like curling up on the floor like she had before. She ran her fingers through the alien growth. They gleamed in the morning sun, smooth and plush to the touch, the softest thing she'd ever felt, softer even than Hot Afropolitan's lips, which, at the time she encountered them on various parts of her body, she had declared the softest thing she'd ever felt. She let the panic wash over her in waves and then recede. In truth, the feathers were beautiful.

*Yes, feathers are beautiful. On birds. And on couture dresses. Not growing out of our body!*

"I mean, I haven't worn white in years, not on these hips."

*They* are *beautiful against our skin.*

"That's all I'm saying."

Joy wondered: If the feathers kept growing unabated, would she still be herself, still human? The feathers pulsed at their roots, aquiver with possibility.

*Unless you go full bird, you'll never be able to fly. Homo sapiens is too big, human bones are too dense.*

Was she too fat to fly regardless? Would she remain rooted to the ground no matter what, the feathered human equivalent of an ostrich?

*

That afternoon her phone vibrated with a Facebook Messenger notification.

*Hey, it's me. Saw your post. Let's meet up. Um, also, could you take the pictures down? It's kind of a thing.*

Her feathers began to throb.

*

"Has it occurred to you that this guy might not be . . . safe?" Carla said, pacing Joy's living room.

"I already had sex with him in the woods in the middle of the night. If he was an ax murderer, I'd be dead."

Carla and Nicole nodded. It was hard to argue with that.

"My instincts tell me this guy is the key," Nicole said. "Especially since he wants to meet on the lake in Prospect Park—where the swans live. I mean . . . "

"All right, well, my instincts say this muthafucka could be crazy. So we coming with you." Carla put her purse on her shoulder. "I borrowed my cousin's stun gun."

*

Standing on the Lullwater Bridge, Joy watched the day fading while Carla and Nicole settled in on a bench a little ways away. Joy tried her best to look nonchalant. The summer evening was golden and languorous, the air thick with humidity that everyone tried not to notice because it'd all be gone soon and the short, cold days of the long winter would be upon them.

And then he was there, striding toward her, his burnished brown skin, wild afro, and sometimes-gold-sometimes-brown eyes catching fire in the summer light.

*GotDAMN.*

Joy's feathers shivered and throbbed, a sensation part sensuous, part alien racing up her belly and spine. The world turned bright and sharp, the edge of everything crisp. How was it possible that she'd forgotten a single detail about him?

"You bring me Joy . . . " he whisper-sung a line from the song in his smooth tenor as he gathered her up in a hug that smelled of seawater and sandalwood. "You good, love?"

And just like that his name came back to her, as though she'd never forgotten it: _____.

"_____. You just disappeared."

"Apologies. It's . . . complicated."

She took a deep breath and willed her heart and hormones to settle. She tried to ignore her throbbing . . . feathers. "Listen. The Facebook post was just me trying to find you. I'm not looking for romance . . . I mean I'm not *not* looking for romance . . . but that's not what's important right now . . . "

"Romance is always important . . . "

"Uh-huh . . . Well, no, I'm not good. I need to ask about your health." The words all came out in a rush. He stared at her for a moment, looking puzzled. She took a deep breath and prepared to launch into detail when an "oh shit" expression distorted his beautiful face.

"Aw, man!" He dropped his head back, eyes closed, and sighed. "Feathers?"

"Um. Yes."

He wore a large silver ring, finely wrought in the shape of a mermaid, and he began to rub it nervously. "I need you to keep an open mind."

*

"So, you're a . . . god."

"Technically, depending on who and what you are, I'm a god-seed."

"Like, a baby god?"

"Close enough—look, I know it sounds absurd."

*It's fucking ridiculous.*

Joy looked toward the bench where Carla and Nicole sat watching. He followed her gaze.

"I promise you're not in danger. And I'm not crazy. Just . . . stick with me for a bit."

Joy decided right then that he was completely insane. But then she remembered she had feathers growing on her body. Maybe it wasn't magic. Maybe it was insanity, contagious insanity. Carla and Nicole had seen the feathers too. Had she passed the crazy on to them? Was it a plague of crazy?

"Look, I get it. You think I'm insane. I've been around long enough to know there's nothing I can say that'll convince you. So . . . " He looked around. There were a couple of joggers, a few pairs of lovers, a lady reading a book, Carla and Nicole on the bench a little ways off. _____ sighed, shrugged, raised his index finger to the sky and crooked it, like he was beckoning someone from across the room.

For several long, awkward moments there was nothing except the hum of life in the park. Then that hum receded beneath the whistles and tweets, honks and calls, splashes and flaps—a great wave of sound rising from the park.

*Girl, run!*

But she didn't run. She knew she needed to know. And after the first moment of panic, she didn't think she could run away, even if she wanted to.

The fading light deepened as a vast, motley flock of birds descended from the dusk. Canada geese and ducks, hawks and robins and pigeons, crows—or maybe ravens—and swans, a vast assortment of small, feathered bits she couldn't identify. They landed around Joy and _____ on the bridge, covered the boathouse, splashed down on the Lullwater.

Somewhere behind them voices yelped in fear. Running footsteps retreated. A distant scream.

Joy's feathers vibrated powerfully. Her body strained toward _____, and in her bones she knew she could not resist his summoning. Her eyes filled with tears, her chest with awe. This was magic and it was scary. "Shit," she whispered.

The biggest swan she'd ever seen rose from the water below. Joy took a step back. It flapped its great wings in _____'s direction. He held out a hand to it, a sad look in his eyes. The creature responded with a vicious hiss and released its bowels at his feet before returning to the Lullwater.

Joy turned toward Carla and Nicole's bench, where they sat open-mouthed, staring at their friend and her one-night stand, the godling.

\*

Our understanding of gods is limited. Deity-kind contains innumerable pantheons of beings whose existence and power may or may not be rooted in human belief, powered by prayers and offerings, or enticed by adoration. They are a vast, unknowable constellation stretching across time and reality that, on a few occasions, intersects with our mortal world.

These assorted pantheons rarely interact themselves. Not for the ludicrous reasons humans separate themselves, but because all of deity-kind are manifestations of some extraordinary power. Interactions could lead to dangerous and unpredictable reactions, like crossing the proton streams in *Ghostbusters*. Among some pantheons there are actual rules of a sort, discouraging mingling or creating hybrid deities, and so forth. These rules are mostly for the protection of the less powerful beings.

Take a certain Greek god; his name is not so important. Once, many ages ago, he went exploring. This god, who was not as potent as he imagined, found himself dazzled, as so many were, by a powerful goddess from a Nigerian pantheon. She is called many things among her human worshippers: Mami Wata, Yemaya, Yemoja, La Sirene, Mother of Water, Mother of All. All the gods of her pantheon emerged from her womb, as did the waters of the Earth. Her loins were nothing to sneeze at. She was an elemental, a creature who existed long before there were humans to believe in her and who would carry on long after.

The Greek glimpsed her first in one of her human forms, Black and naked and glistening beneath a full moon, luxuriating in the caress of the sea-foam on a beach near what would one day be Lagos. He checked the offerings that surrounded her and made one of his own. He transformed into a spectacularly large white swan, scattered pale blue jewels and pearls and silver beads among his plumage, and descended, shimmering, onto the surface of the ocean.

Yemoja explained, quite clearly, that she required absolute fidelity from her lovers, that the consequences for infidelity would be dire, and, most importantly, that he was to never even look in the direction of her sister, Oshun. Yemoja was so luscious and her face so enchanting and her manner so gentle, the Greek couldn't fathom being drawn from her side or that it was possible to stir her to anger. She was undulating waves, fresh salt on his tongue, a blue as deep as the mountains were tall, sea-foam in the moonlight. He dove in without a second thought.

All you need to know about the eventual outcome is written across the face of history. The Greek empire crumbled. The Greek pantheon of gods shrank to a sort of irrelevance on the fringes of deity-kind, dependent upon human fictions and scholars for their continued existence. All of their temples lie in ruins. And to this day, there is no species of swan to be found anywhere on the African continent.

But Yemoja and the Greek did have a son.

*

Joy, Carla, and Nicole watched him pace before them in the shadows of the boathouse terrace, explaining things as best he could.

They were all trying to be inconspicuous while he told the story, hiding on the side of the boathouse, away from the crowd of people his little display of power had attracted. The birds were slow to disperse because, as it turned out, the godling had mastered summoning birds but hadn't quite figured out sending them away.

Which was the crux of the problem: he didn't have full control of his powers. His loving, patient mother had banished him to the human realm for a thousand years after what he said was a minor indiscretion.

"So you're just out here . . . practicing superpowers on unsuspecting women?" Joy asked, incredulously.

"Not . . . exactly," he said, head cocked to one side. "Because when you put it like that it sounds terrible. And among my kind, I can assure you, I'm definitely not terrible."

"Well among my kind you're completely fucking terrible," Joy snapped, her feathers and her irritation rising. "How many women have you fucked into swans? Because I'm assuming that's what's happening to me . . . "

He struggled to form words, which, for Joy, verified the worst possible news.

" . . . I'm actually turning into a goddamn bird! That big swan on the bridge, the one who tried to shit on you, that's one of your exes, isn't it?"

Nicole rubbed her back and whispered gently: "Could he be dangerous? Should we be yelling at him?"

*She's got a point.*

The godling held out his hands for calm and eased toward Joy. "Listen, I never meant to harm you," he said. "I really thought I had the whole transfiguration thing under control. It hasn't happened in decades. I swear."

In spite of herself, Joy felt a powerful sense of calm washing over her. The delicious scent of him suddenly rolled across the terrace.

"And, yes . . . I'm not gonna lie . . . you are turning into a swan—"

Nicole gasped.

Carla cursed: "Muthafucka."

"—but I'm *this* close to figuring out how to undo it. Really. I've already almost succeeded on a number of . . . my lovers."

"What does that mean? *Almost* succeeded?" Joy spat.

His fragrance intensified.

"And stop wafting your damn cologne or whatever that is over here!"

"Okay, yes, my natural scent is also a calming agent. I'm just trying to make this as easy as possible. But listen . . . here's the upside: when you're transforming you stop aging. Great, right?"

"What do you mean?"

"I mean, while I figure this whole mess out, you'll basically be kinda immortal."

"But you've figured it out, right?"

"Almost. I'm almost there."

"Uh-huh. And how far away is almost?"

He bobbed his head a bit, looking up as though counting to himself, the whole time twisting the mermaid ring. "Well, I'd say, roughly . . . about . . . seventy, eighty years. Give or take. I mean, transfiguration is not something you want to rush."

Joy felt her legs give way. Nicole caught her before she hit the concrete. The godling stepped forward to assist, which is when Carla tased him with her cousin's stun gun and he collapsed in a beautiful heap at their feet.

"I didn't think it would take him down like that," Carla said, looking at the stun gun. "Impressive."

*Fuuuuck.*

"Fuck," Joy gasped. "Did you just tase a god?"

"Baby god," Carla said.

"I have a thought," Nicole said.

"I think we're very open to suggestions right now," Joy said, looking around to see if anybody was watching. The godling's bird stunt had everyone focused on the Lullwater.

"The mermaid ring," Nicole said. "It's a symbol of Yemoja."

"His mama," Carla said.

"Right. And it's clearly important to him. He touches it almost constantly. What if . . . and, okay, this is crazy, but stay with me. I think the ring could be a link to her, Yemoja. What if we asked her for help? Cause we need help. We could make an offering . . . and you know, tell her what's happening?"

The other two women stared at Nicole.

Joy's legs still shook a bit. She tried to form words but could not. Finally, she took a deep breath, squatted, and grabbed the ring—a finely carved silver mermaid, her tail winding around the godling's finger. "Why not?" Joy said. "Why the hell not?"

Nearly two hours later they stood barefoot on the beach at Coney Island, a shopping bag at their feet. Joy turned off her ringing cell phone. The godling had been calling nonstop. Apparently, his powers didn't extend to tracking. She struggled to stay focused. This was not a time to stumble through in a haze. She wanted to remember every detail, to hold on to who she was. Her feathers shivered, reminding her that she hadn't been who she was for weeks.

"Maybe it's all bullshit anyway," Joy said. It felt briefly comforting to say this even though she knew it wasn't true. "What kind of god gets taken out by a stun gun? Maybe he's making it all up."

"There are feathers on your vagina."

"You don't have to keep reminding me of that!"

"Okay you two," Nicole said, reaching down into the bag. "Let's get on with this before we get mugged."

Joy and Carla watched as Nicole arranged all the items on a scarf on the sand in front of them. "You still got the ring?"

Joy held up the ring she'd pulled from the godling's finger. Nicole's idea had seemed . . . as plausible as anything, all things considered. Nicole had flirted with Ifá for a moment years before, so surely she knew what she was talking about. It seemed brilliant, especially since there were no other ideas on the table.

But now that they stood at water's edge, a makeshift offering of fruit and flowers piled at their feet, Nicole preparing to read some incantation she found on the Internet, Joy found herself drowning in fear and doubt. Her feathers shifted with nervousness. The whole thing needed more thought. Her boss would say the idea was very, very surface.

*Now's not the time to doubt yourself. We've got to DO something.*

"Nic, I think let's skip the incantation from the Internet," Joy said.

"That shit was corny," Carla said nodding.

"Probably for the best," Nicole said.

"Okay." Joy took a deep breath and looked down at the ring, heavy and cold in her palm, gleaming in the light from Nicole's cell phone.

"At least the moon is full," Nicole mumbled nervously.

"Well," Joy said, her feathers shivering so intensely she had to clench her teeth. "Let's jump right in. Right?"

She looked from Carla to Nicole, who answered in tandem. "Let's do it. Yes."

"Yemoja!" Joy called, in a voice she hoped sounded appropriately reverent. She looked to Nicole. "Am I pronouncing it right?"

"You're doing great."

"Okay. Yemoja!" She clutched the ring tightly. " . . . Um, great one, Mother of Waters, sorry to disturb you. I know we're not doing this properly . . . " Fear filled her belly but the more she talked, the better she felt. She felt her voice rising. She barely recognized herself.

" . . . I really need your help. Your son—" She paused, searching her mind for his name. She'd just said it an hour ago. She looked to Carla. "Why can't I remember his name?"

"What? His name is . . . " Carla's brow furrowed as she strained, her mouth working around a word that wouldn't form. "Dammit. More magic shit. His mama know who her problem child is. Keep going."

"Right. Yemoja, your son has been . . . turning women into birds. Swans to be specific. It's happening to me right now. He says he's trying to fix it, but it doesn't sound like he's got a handle on this. I'm asking for your help. I believe . . . I believe . . . I'm worth saving. Please." She looked to her friends. They nodded and smiled their encouragement.

Then the three women waded in as far as they dared and carefully placed their offering on the retreating waves. They watched as the flowers and fruit bobbed on the dark water.

Joy kept the ring clasped tightly in her hand, its weight the only thing keeping her from floating away.

*

An hour later they sat damp and uncomfortable on the sand, still waiting.

"I'm starving," Carla declared, breaking the silence. "How long you think we got to wait?"

"I don't know, Carla. The last time I summoned a goddess I didn't keep track of the time."

"Girl, I'm too hungry and too sober for sass."

"You know what I feel like eating?" Nicole said. "Fried fish from that place way up in Harlem. We used to go there all the time when Carla lived on Edgecombe."

"Mmmm, Famous Fish," Carla said, closing her eyes with the memory.

They were suddenly filled with the cravings of seafood from meals past, got lost in a debate about Gulf Coast or East Coast oysters, when Joy noticed the ocean at their feet had gone quiet, dead calm. Gulls landed around them and all along the shoreline, white feathers shining in the moonlight, not one of them shrieking or calling. The sounds of the board-walk boomed unnaturally loud, no longer muffled by the rush and retreat of the sea. Joy's feathers flexed and stood on end, pulling painfully at her already-tender skin until she gasped in pain, her eyes filled with tears.

"Something's happening," she mumbled.

*Well, damn. You did it.*

And then *she* was there, the goddess Yemoja, tall and Black and powerfully built, walking out of the stilled waters of the great Atlantic into New York harbor, trailing clouds of sea-foam. She wore an exqui-sitely tailored white linen suit, the jacket open to reveal she had nothing on beneath it except her gleaming, dark skin and long strands of pearls and silver and blue jewels draped over and around her body. Her long locs, studded with more pearls, swirled atop her head like turbulent wa-ters. The scent of seawater and roses rolled over the three women, filling their lungs and noses until they thought they would suffocate.

"First of all, give me my ring." She looked pointedly at Joy, who got to her feet, shivering with the pain of the hundreds of tiny feathers on her body pulled taut, as though they would be ripped from her skin. She held up her hand, the ring in the middle of her palm. The goddess reached for it and when her fingers brushed Joy's, the shock reverberated throughout her body. Dark spots swam in her vision. "This better be good," the goddess said. "I hate New York in August."

Joy lowered her dress, and the goddess rubbed the bridge of her nose and sighed deeply.

"Can you help me?" Joy said. To her ears, her voice sounded small and far away. The presence of the goddess was as loud as it was beautiful.

"I'm afraid not. He did this. He has to undo it. He has always struggled with . . . consequences. I banished him to this realm hoping he'd learn, but—"

"You sent your powerful, irresponsible son here, to practice on us? Because we're disposable?" Joy could feel her feathers pulsing along her belly and spine. Her voice rose in volume and she could not keep it back.

"Um, maybe don't yell at the goddess?" Nicole whispered.

"I don't care! What more can happen?" Joy screamed, feeling as though her voice would split her in two if she didn't let it out.

*Yes, honey. Tell 'em why we mad!*

"Plenty," said the goddess, enunciating every syllable. "Watch the way you speak to me. Child." The deity's anger filled up the space between them and all three human women grew as still as the ocean beneath the goddess's feet. "You are walking around in your life carelessly, wearing your need like a crown. Your need is a summoning for those like my son— human and deity alike."

"But you can't fix the swan thing?" Joy said, her voice tamed, her eyes lowered respectfully.

"Look at me," the goddess demanded. Joy looked up and swallowed. A moment or two of looking directly at the entity was merely uncomfortable, sort of like staring into the sun. But gazing upon her for longer took Joy to a place where she could see her own self as the goddess saw her, a fleshy, be-draggled, desperate creature, huddled at the water's edge. A thing deserving of pity and maybe something more. Was this what she was? Joy blinked and shook her head, turned her gaze away from the goddess. Beside her, Carla vomited. Nicole began to cry. Joy wondered what they had seen when they looked in the face of the entity.

The goddess just nodded. "Well. As I said, I can't undo my son's actions. But I can help slow your transformation." She reached up and plucked a pearl from her hair and held it out to Joy, who took the jewel, careful not to touch the goddess as she did so.

Joy stared down at the pearl as though it would explode. She wondered if whatever it was going to do would hurt, how soon she'd start to feel normal again. "Thank . . . you? How does it work?" she asked, glancing quickly up at the goddess, who seemed to be getting taller. Joy rubbed her eyes and looked back down at the pearl.

"Return to this place on a full moon, with the pearl, and submerge yourself in my waters. It will temporarily reverse the transformation and protect your human essence until my son can figure things out."

"How often should I return?"

"Everyone's different," the goddess said.

"How will I know?"

"The feathers will tell you. Consider them a summons."

"And if I don't . . . " Joy glanced up at the goddess again. "I'll just continue to change?"

"You will transform, as all the women before you have. So you see, it will be up to you to save yourself. Definitely do not lose the pearl." Her voice faded to a hum, a vibration that emanated from the goddess in waves and brought the women to their knees.

Joy tore her gaze from the face of the goddess and put herself back together. She held the pearl tighter than she'd ever held anything and was finally able to get to her feet. She reached out to Nicole and Carla and pulled them to their feet, clinging to their hands longer than necessary.

The goddess really had been getting taller. She stood nearly ten feet and was so magnificent the human women didn't dare to do more than squint at her and turn away. The goddess lifted her face to the sky in ecstasy. "Can you smell the moonlight?"

Joy forced herself to look up at the face of Yemoja once more. In that moment, the goddess's body collapsed in a burst of sea-foam that swept over them and settled along the boardwalk as far as Brighton Beach.

In the wake of Yemoja's dramatic exit, Joy gasped to see a version of herself stretching forward and away from the present.

There will be years of watching the feathers grow and recede, seeing how far she can go without a trip to Coney Island with the pearl—which she will have set into a custom bracelet with a lock that she never takes off (it drives TSA workers crazy). She becomes obsessed with living by the sea, but refuses to move to Coney Island. She will move to a hamlet on the Long Island Sound, to be on the water. Carla will tell her not to because she will hate it, and she does. The great real estate crash everyone who is not rich had been waiting for will happen, but she will land a job working on a liquor account because no matter how dim the world gets people will not stop drinking, and she will come out on the other side of the Last Great Recession okay. She will buy her dream condo and move back to Brooklyn. She will fall in and out of love with her feathers, with herself, with men with whom she can't bring herself to share her secret. She will never marry. She will make a smart stock pick. She will sell a screenplay. She will take a sabbatical, travel. The whole screenwriting thing will not work out. She will curl up in her condo in despair and listen to old Adele songs. She will let the feathers grow and grow until it's almost too late. She will get over it and throw herself back into the life of the city. The godling has told the truth about one thing—she will age very slowly. She will explain it away by citing melanin and good genes and healthy living. She will replace her crown of need with an aura of arrogance and wisdom that certain types of men find sexy but, to her great amusement, by that time, she will not care. She will have a lot of sex anyway. She will declare herself celibate. She and her friends will laugh at this and she will end that experiment in less than four months with, believe it or not, a personal trainer. She will drink a lot of vodka sodas. She, Nicole, and Carla will buy houses near each other upstate and create a compound and hold one another together through marriages, divorces, lovers, a surprise baby (Nicole's), aging parents, and breast cancer. Finally, one day she will feel that excruciating, undeniable pull she felt on the Lullwater Bridge so many years before. She will get in her car and drive, following the pull further upstate, until she arrives at a house in the woods on a lake. He will be waiting for her. He will still be too beautiful, but different. He will be humming with power that lends an air of wisdom. "I'm ready," he will declare. "Took you long enough," she will say.

# ANTI-CONFESSIONAL, AGAIN

*in the voice of Juta Kamainen*

## George Abraham

> "No, I can't explain . . . I loved him. That's all. That's enough."
> —Juta Kamainen, from *The Subtle Knife*, by Phillip Pullman

Despite the truth of us, I wished you this whole world &
     another. I cannot give you

anything but this: my every city, the sound
     -less coast & all the worlds disappeared

in you. Less a window than a one-sided
     light. There was never an eternity in me

to reject. My expectation
     precedes you, love. There's a heart

in my chest & a heart
     in my sky, a thousand miles south

of anywhere, back
     when anywhere had meaning—when you

could see me not as daylight's every
     border. And am I not the most backwards notion

of *angelic?* Crown me halo's
        antipode. Thorn me, Dust

-luster & lust
        -less fiend. You were prettier

when I last imagined you, love
        -less &, land torn, I pity

that I could almost forgive
        you in this othered dusk. This

being my final
        faithlessness: to dis

-remember your elsewhere, wishing
        you no more than this rough &—edgeless,

I carve a universe
        in your fluttering

chest with a blade of tremble
        incarnate. Languageless, it wasn't

you I wanted
        to split, the small

of your every *every*: particle
        to shadow, dust to Dust—of the failed

God between us—of all the worlds
        you did not end in me.

        George Abraham

# PLINK

## Yohanca Delgado

I throw my head back and scream. Maybe this time my voice will carry. Wishful thinking, I know, to imagine the sound swirling and spiraling up and beyond the white porcelain wall like a smoke signal. Scaling the walls is impossible. Among my long list of regrets is the wardrobe for pretending. Flouncy regalia, impossible to move in, decadent and toothache sweet. How I rue these velvet slippers, the hue of raspberry sugar-dusted fruit candy, the kind 12 dancing princesses must replace each morning. I slip even in pacing. And this gossamer gown, with its embroideries of curious fawns and flirtatious butterflies, all that is tender and rendible, layered thick over heavy skirts of taffeta, acid green and firm as a cheesecake when it meets the fork. But had I not always complained, at least once a day, that I could lose a little weight?

I walk the circle again, humming to keep myself company, and the lullaby helps. But then there's a distant galloping, and an earthquake topples me to the ground as the sky darkens. In the circle of sky, an enormous eye appears, the large doe-brown eye of my daughter. Her lashes are as thick as tree trunks.

She's here! I twirl my dense skirts to catch her eye. I leap and run across the floor, slipping and sliding. I am on a deserted island, waving to a distant ship. *I'm down here*, I shout. *Get me out!*

Now that my daughter is a giant, her voice is tectonic and deep. I press my palms against the white porcelain. *It's tea time*, she says, and the curved wall vibrates with her toddler's lisp. The eye blinks slowly, then is replaced by the enormous, volcanic spout of a teapot, tremulous and looming.

The spout emits a slow stream of liquid and my horror subsides when I realize it is tepid water from the tap. Ever-careful—even at four, she is afraid of spilling—she pours a swelling current that lifts me up in slow, lazy swirls. My skirts float up around me, and I'm surprised that Penny still does not see me. I must look, from above, like a small green bloom, floating in the water.

I wave my arms as the water brings me closer. A flowering up and up to see the world I knew before: the nursery we painted pink as the inside of a rabbit's ear, and filled with fluffy things. Can you keep a fragile life from breaking by wrapping it again and again in the softest blankets?

The water stops coming and the eye returns. This close, her iris looks like unexplored land, a brown velvet topography with flecks of gold and black. I wish I could live there. The rim is almost within reach and I begin to swim for it, but my daughter says, *Tea color!* And I see, in her pudgy hand, my bottle of Shalimar.

I scream myself hoarse as she carefully unscrews the top and tilts it slowly into the teacup. Just a few drops and a dense fog of bergamot, ambergris, and vanilla nearly knocks me unconscious. *Smells like mommy,* my daughter booms to herself. *Looks like tea!*

*Don't drink it!* I scream but my daughter doesn't hear. She's gone away again. I start to swim for the edge as hard as I can now, but she returns and drops in a sugar cube from the kitchen. It lands with a heavy plop and ripples me away from the edge. I turn toward the shimmering iceberg and use every ounce of the strength I have left to hoist myself onto it, dragging the weight of my waterlogged skirts after me.

I lay flat on the glittering sugar cube and spread my arms and legs out, to make myself as visible as possible, though I am no bigger than the crescent on one of her fingernails. How afraid I was, when she was new, to clip those scythe-sharp half-moons!

I stare up at my giant baby and gather my strength. I pray that she will see me. In a few moments, I will strip off this water-soaked dress and

Yohanca Delgado

swim for the rim; maybe there will be a way out from there. Maybe she'll swallow me whole and the roles will be reversed. Maybe I will live in her stomach this time.

With a toddler's chaotically careful hands, my daughter lifts the teacup and the whole world tilts one way, then another. She holds the cup up to her face and at the smell of the perfume, her nose twitches. Penny's eyes graze blindly over me, the asterisk on her cube of sugar.

A thunderous sound rattles the perfumed waters around me and I brace myself flat. She is humming, I realize. She is humming a song I taught her. The melody thrums through me. Under my wet cheek, the rough grains of sugar begin to melt.

# DREAM OF A SPACE TATTOO

## Juan J. Morales

Inside a dream within a dream, my dad sits next to me, telling me about a new tattoo he got to instruct us where to go. I lift his sleeve and look at his left shoulder. Instead of the faded green bird, there is a fresh spaceship, housed in a vertical rectangle. The nose of the ship is outlined in black and colored with brilliant reds and yellows. Where there should be white is his flesh. Toward the bottom, I study the Roman numeral XI and celestial coordinates telling us where to meet. My mind is traveling galaxies and dark frontiers where I hear whispers of time travel. I'm crying because I lost him four months ago, and I wake up repeating, "He knows where we have to go." Everyone in the room pauses conversations to look at me. I'm pointing to my vanishing father, still poking at his tattoo.

# CARVILLE NATIONAL LEPROSARIUM, 1954

*For Dad*

## Wendy Chin-Tanner

and this was
the shame of
the body there

amid the
pecan trees
spanish moss

myrtle and
jasmine rot
down by the

river you
were a boy
between a

column of
live oaks and
birch trees white

skins peeling
surrounded
by barbed wire

liminal
the state of
being on

a threshold
in between
one thing and

another
leper and
boy a fence

is not a
fence but mir-
rors its maker

Wendy Chin-Tanner

# HELLO, GHOST

## Soham Patel

As you trace your finger over

the globe your uncle gave you

the year you were born,

you remember how he used

to call it your baby earth.

It has raised and indented

relief. Your finger trembles

when you spin it fast. Fast

like the metals spinning

past the mantle at the core.

But on this 12" replica

of where we are—with its

white-like-parchment antique

ocean—only synthetic resins

and textile fibers can reside.

You remove a line of dust.

Rolling fingerwide waves.

Recall this isn't like those

go-where-your-finger-lands-

when-the-spinning-stops

destiny kind of games.

This is for remembering

the dust trail you're always

leaving behind and the one

you aim at errantly

like a bewildered scout.

If language can only offer

a reduction of things—

why is it years

later when you notice

it still says Ceylon, you say

nothing and keep spinning?

# THE SACRED INTERRUPTED
*Excerpt*

## Mary Lou Johnson

### Note and Cast of Characters

The actors are delivering a story rather than performing one. In this sense, the actors are able to weave in and out of each other's dialogue while maintaining their own stories and presences.

The staging is two chairs. A table in the corner with a vase of vibrant flowers can be placed in each corner of the stage.

Woman 1/ American of African descent, late 20s to early 30s

Woman 2/ Of African descent, mid 30s to early 40s

*(Both women walk onto the stage and sit down without acknowledging each other)*

One time when I was five
I snuck downstairs/while they were watching some TV drama about rich people with poor lives.

My father in his green recliner—feet up with his "green glass" on a side table Forbidden to look at never mind touch
My mother on the couch, pillow behind her head, feet up, with her own special glass, always in hand
So engrossed with JR and Pamela and Bobbie/
I crept up like a 5-year-old ninja and snatched that glass/
Brown liquid with ice cube bobbing,

A cold sweat against my warm hand
A strange vapor stinging my eyes but/
Never mind/
/ the warning those vapors were telling me/
Not today, little one, not today.
I took a deep breath and the largest swig I could/
Thinking/ "Ahh gotcha"

That swig swung back.

Ahha-gotcha too

As careful as I could/ with shaky hands and tear-filled vision/ I placed
the glass back on the coaster/
And crept back upstairs.
My heart and head pounded/my tongue felt delirious and alive/ with
Sleep passing over me like a breeze/ hovering above/ and about to rest
*downdowndown*
on top of my shivering body/
when I heard melody of/
My mother's generous bosoms/ closed mouth ***hahahahahas*** In symphony with my father's gap-toothed ***kikikikikis***
As my parents lived through the shenanigans of the Ewings.
At least this was my chosen thought
And with burning ears and burning throat/my eyes made heavy/ my
head slightly spinning/
    I smiled/ the first of small victories/ live long in an impish mind,
    Of being with them/ in their little world/ with not a care in the
    world . . . stolen moments of
                  simplicity and love . . .
and it was the sweetest moment ever.

*(Singing in a gospel call and response style:*
*Woman 2: Slow down slow down sloooowww doownnnn*
*Woman 1: I remember I remember I remember)*

My mother/ in my father's chair
Reclined, I could see very little/
The top of her head moving back and forth, slight moans escaping against her will My father's knees were all I could see until he shifted and I could see the bottoms of his feet
Splayed out in reverence, moving back in forth in concert with the sounds of moans and a sigh
So terrified in the not knowing/
I gasped

And then silence . . .
This moment here/
the sacred interrupted/
What has been undone can no longer be
My father's eyes meet mine
A hand, dripping wet/ beckons me forward.

Shamefully, head low, shoulders lower, I come and see . . .
My mother's feet, soaking in a tub of/
my father's hands dripping with/
Water
And now my hands follow his/
Massaging/
Rough heels and toes and in between toes and the top and the bottom and over and over we work in union
Rubbing out the pain
And the sadness and the struggle and the damage and the lies Carried around/ the added weight of us in this world/
We work in silence, my mother smiles.
We touch her instep, her laughter becomes a moan/ too weary to do much more from parted lips
We dry her feet with a towel, and he takes lotion that smells of peppermint and life

And we massage it—Life
back into her soles, her toes, her ankles . . . we work in silence until the
only sound we hear are her snores.
He covers her in a blanket and turns out the light.
We place everything away and he turns to me and smiles.

> *Woman 1 or 2 begins to beatbox . . . it fades out and Woman 1*
> *(either say or sing): Breathe breathe breathhheeeee*

Death is that beyotch who comes to the party uninvited/
Empty-handed/
But wanting to taste everything/
Thirsty/
Flirting with everybody/
And never alone.
Always with a plus-one/
Coming in with a bullet, or a car, or rope, or a razor, or a pill or cancer.
and after two years, it comes.

My father/
He wanted to die at home.
My mother/ his wife, the nurse/ prepared us as best as she could. From
pediatrics to geriatrics, she knew/ Death did not care about the who
why when what or how/
Death was coming and she was prepared.
An Ensure every few hours
Chocolate tastes better than Vanilla/ Banana is very sweet/soon it will
be Ice cubes and cool lemony swabs/
Catheter in/ Catheter out/ watch his hands/ it will be reflexive/ he
won't feel it because Morphine/
This button/ push when moans and twitches come quickly
Careful/ watch what you say/ he can still hear you/ he is listening He
Just

Can't

Speak

Gathered in a room made smaller with that Beyotch hovering around/
sucking time/ warping the tick tick ticks/ we wait.

Minutes feel like seconds but last longer than hours.

Then years.

We had waited and time/ and chemo/ and love/ and prayers couldn't
stop it. There is no escaping this moment

It reaches into you deep and twists your mind to play games of What
if . . . What if . . .

What if . . .


It could have been caught earlier?

And not spread so fast

And not even happened



And . . . and . . . and . . .

We play this game in silence. We have to be there for each other, ourselves, our father and our mother, his wife, and now the Nurse.

We wail inside/

No one ever wants this moment/ especially when the moment is now.

    *(Woman 1: An improv of What if . . . in which the actress mentions*
*random thoughts . . . ex. What if I start laughing at the funeral because my*
      *uncle will be singing off-key and doing his shimmy shake dance*
                *About five examples)*

I felt cold/

He must have felt colder/

I placed the blankets tighter around his feet/

They were like ice.

I looked at my mother, his wife, the Nurse.


She knew, I knew, he knew, we knew and all we could do was wait

Tick tick tick
His feet, so cold, were no longer with us.
So I massaged his hands, so warm
Life is so fleeting, is fleeing
My mother, the nurse, held his other hand, fingers over pulse we waited,
until He smiled/
the purest, most beautiful smile I had ever seen/
We had ever seen—my mother, his wife, no longer the Nurse—for it
was in a flash and it was gone.
What comes after the smile, is a grimace. A grunt then nothing . . . ex-
cept In between those moments, I felt something, a piece of him, going
through me.

To feel a soul move through/ close your eyes/ take a deep breath/ and
imagine How you felt/ the first time—

You saw snowflakes falling from the sky/ or walked into the ocean/ flew
on a plane/
or fell in love when kissing someone who loved you/
The first time/
You bit into a juicy sun-ripened peach on a hot summer day/ or smelled
the head of a newborn baby/
Or heard the unbridled innocence of children's laughter/ or music that
made your feet move all by themselves.
It feels like/ looking into the night/ under infinite stars/ and grasping
how precious is this experience/ so fleeing/ so fleeting/

He left/ with a gift, an energy so divine and peaceful and intimate and
tender and love.

*(Music: uplifting operatic-inspired*
*melody of call and response*
*Between Woman 1 and 2)*

Mary Lou Johnson

# DIGITAL MEDICINE

## Brian K. Hudson

"Kaw-naw-nay-sgee," the old woman enunciated carefully, pronouncing each syllable for me as she squeezed my lips open with her strong, bony fingers. This intimate moment was happening in spite of the fact that I had only met this woman a few moments ago. Awkward. Peggy Sixkiller (or Peg, as she said her friends called her—so I should, too), the strange old lady who was now squishing my face as she sounded out the Cherokee word for "spider," seemed to be my polar opposite in terms of personality. She was clearly an extrovert; me, not so much. In the few minutes before I became the puppet for Peg's ventriloquist act, I had introduced myself. Peg had been expecting me. Before long, she asked the question I was waiting for, cocking her head with a mischievous, inquisitive smile.

"So, what'd a sweet, young girl like you do to get in trouble?"

I looked at the ground. "I was arrested for being a hacker," I mumbled.

"A hacker, huh?" she asked.

"A hacker," I repeated, this time more distinctly. "A computer hacker. I accessed computers without permission," I clarified.

There were different types of hackers: malicious black hats, goody-goody white hats, and the more complicated gray hat hackers, the kind I was, or, at least, the kind I wanted to be. That's the reason I had dyed the rest of my hair gray after shaving the sides short. But that was TMI, so I kept my mouth shut.

"So, you snuck into someone's house and got on their computer machine?"

"Nooooo," my eyes widened. "Nothing *that* bad. I just access computers on the web . . . the Internet."

"How'd you do that?"

I told Peg how I compiled programs to crawl the net through my modem, looking for hidden files, access points, bugs or glitches, anything worth exploring. I didn't tell her about the incident at school, which had been my biggest hack to date. The security on the school's system wasn't all that great, but I felt the data I had found would have given me some bragging rights on the hacking forums I liked to read, if I were the type to brag.

"So you crawl around the web looking for bugs?" she asked.

"Yeah. Basically," I answered.

"Why?" she asked.

"Um. I don't know . . . " It was a good question. It took me a few moments to come up with an answer. "Curiosity, I guess?"

"Hmmm." She narrowed her eyes and gave me a slight nod. Apparently she was cool with my explanation. "I'm going to call you Spider, because you crawl around the web looking for bugs." She gestured, making her right hand crawl like a spider across her upraised left arm to illustrate her point. "Yup, you're a Spider all right." She smiled.

It was crazy-accurate because *spider* was another name for *web crawlers,* which referred to the type of program I coded. Bots, crawlers, spiders: these were all names for code that scoured the web for one thing or another. I was considering whether or not to explain to Peg the significance of her word choice when she interrupted my thoughts.

"Jaw-law-gees Hee-woe-nee-sgee?"

I stared. "Huh?"

"You speak Cherokee?"

"I can say hello, but that's about it."

"Kaw-naw-nay-sgee. That's how you say your name, Spider, in Cherokee." That's when she reached her bony hand up to move my mouth as she repeated the syllables of my newly given name. In fact, Peg never used my real name. She called me Spider, either in English or Cherokee, for the rest of my sentence. It wasn't a particularly feminine name, but then again, I wasn't hella-girly like those Rah Rahs jumping around for the crowd at the basketball games.

*

Late the next morning, the weather was already climbing toward hot and sticky, just like most summer days in Tahlequah, Oklahoma. I slipped into my beat-up Doc Martens and drove my Jeep up to the trailer on the hill at the outskirts of town. I wondered what type of work Peg would have for me. Cooking, cleaning . . . those were my best guesses. I knocked and was greeted by Peg and a blast of cold air as she opened the front door. She stood there in a yellow housedress smiling at me.

"Oh-see-yo, Kaw-naw-nay-sgee," she said.

"Hi, Peggy, um, Peg," I said.

"Kaw-naw-nay-sgee," she repeated, more slowly this time. "That's what you are."

"Kaw-naw-nay-sgee," I repeated, but my mouth fumbled over the unfamiliar syllables. I hoped that my delivery was good enough to avoid her grabbing my face again.

"Uh-huh," she nodded, happy enough, I guess, with my pronunciation. "Come on in here to the couch. I have some work for you."

I sat down on the light-brown tweed couch, tucking my skirt underneath me, and tried to be discreet as I looked around Peg's spotless living room. Across from me, hanging upon the wood-paneled wall, was a framed photograph. I peered at the picture. A woman who looked like Peggy wearing her Sunday best stood next to a younger version of herself. Two children, a boy and a girl, stood before the two women, who each rested a hand atop a child's shoulder. All were smiling for the camera, but Peg's smile extended to her eyes and seemed more real, more sincere somehow, as though she had been smiling even before the photographer had asked them to do so. The frame was free of dust, and the glass protecting the photo looked like it had just been polished. No cleaning for me, I guessed.

"You want something to eat, Spider?" Peg called from the kitchen. "I got eggs and wild onions, still warm."

"No thanks, Peg," I called back. I guessed I wouldn't be cooking, either.

"Suit yourself. You're probably full from eating all them bugs," Peg said. I could hear her chuckle at her own joke. I smiled to myself.

Peg shuffled back into the living room, carrying coffee for both of us. Peg ducked behind the tweed recliner across from me and reappeared with two pairs of concentric wooden hoops, holding them up as if I would understand their significance.

"Cross-stitch," she said, answering the look on my face which probably had *huh* written all over it.

"Oh." It was all I could manage in response. What was cross-stitch?

"Here. I'll show you," Peg pulled several large squares of white fabric out from a basket behind her recliner. She unrolled them and stacked the fabric on the coffee table in front of me. They each had a hand-drawn pencil sketch of a barnyard animal on top. Sketched beneath each drawing was what I assumed was the Cherokee word for that animal. But the names of the animals were in actual syllabary, writing I had seen but never really understood. Peg placed one wooden ring on the table and centered the penciled chicken on it. She then pressed the other wooden ring over it, making the cloth taut between them. "You just follow the pencil marks making little X's with your thread, in and out, in and out. Like this. When you're moving down the line, come from the bottom like this. That's a backstitch." She had started the thread down one of the chicken's legs.

"Okay," I said, cautiously taking the hoop from her and continuing the pattern of the chicken with the red thread.

"Jee-taw-gaw," she enunciated.

"Jee-taw-gaw," I blurted to avoid those bony fingers.

Peg picked up the design of the pig and started working on the cross-stitching with me.

"What are these for?" I asked, falling into the rhythm of the task: pushing the needle up through the fabric, making an X, turning over the hoop to make sure it didn't snag, and finally pulling the thread tight.

"Pillows for the kindergarten students. They use them for nap time," she said.

"Oh, yeah? That's cool. Do you make much money selling them at the school?" I asked.

"Money? Nah," Peg said, waving her needle hand to dismiss my question. "What do I need with money? The trailer's paid for and I have plenty in savings."

"Oh. Can some of the kids not afford pillows for school?" I asked.

"Possibly. But that's not why I make 'em," Peg answered.

"Then why?" I asked.

"It gives me something to do to pass the time." She paused for a moment as she completed and then inspected a stitch. "But the main reason I make these pillows is . . . well, curiosity. I guess."

"Curiosity? I don't understand."

"Most Cherokee kids, at least here in Oklahoma, don't speak their own language. I thought these pillows just might spark their curiosity in learning to speak Cherokee." She smiled. I smiled back, and we continued cross-stitching in silence.

After a few hours, I was happy to see that we had almost a whole farm full of barnyard animals spread across the living-room table.

"We're making good time, Spider," she beamed at me. Peg began to sew the pillows together after handing me a blank cross-stitch hoop. "Make whatever you want," she had instructed me. "Let your imagination go wild." Half an hour later, after she had finished a few pillows, Peg confessed that she knew how to spell more animal names in Cherokee than she was able to draw.

"I can't draw, either, sorry," I said, "but . . . you could print clip art from the web."

"Clip art?" she asked.

"Yeah. You can print all kinds of pictures, animals, patterns, lots of stuff, and then trace them onto the fabric. But you'd need a computer and printer for that." I paused. "Maybe the library will give you access to print them?"

"Hmm. Maybe," Peg agreed. "What you workin' on over there?"

"Just finishing up," I answered, holding up my hoop for her to see. I had stitched the following sequence of numbers into it with bright-green thread:

01010000

01000101

01000111

"What on earth is that?" Peg asked.

"I made it for you. It's your name, Peg, in binary code. Computer language. How computers talk to each other," I explained.

"I love it." Peg's eyes lit up. I felt a warm glow in my chest.

\*

The next morning, I found myself waking up earlier than normal, feeling eager to see Peg again. I showed up to her trailer earlier than the mid- to late-morning times I had been arriving at for the last two days. The lyrics "she is on the run" were blaring from my Misfits CD. It didn't occur to me until I reached the last bend in the rutted road that led to her house that she might still be asleep. I turned my stereo down and was relieved to see the lights burning bright inside her trailer as I pulled into the drive. Peg opened the door, beaming at me as I made my way up the steps. She stood at the door in a light-blue nightgown. This time, I took Peg up on her offer of breakfast: scrambled eggs with wild onions and black coffee. After breakfast, we walked into the living room. I sat on the tweed couch, feeling full from breakfast and ready to start working. The cross-stitch binary code that I had made for Peg was framed and hanging on the wall next to her family photograph. When I turned back to Peg, she was facing me and standing with her hands clasped in front of her.

"I have a surprise for you," she grinned, and then walked into her bedroom. She returned holding a blank pillow in her right hand, which she rotated like she was Vanna White revealing the final letter of the puzzle to display a striking design on the reverse. The expert stitching depicted a spindly gray spider standing in a white web with the syllables:

which looked as if they were woven into the web itself. The stitching was much more intricate than the simple technique Peg had taught me for tracing the outlines of the animals on the kindergartners' pillows.

"Oh. Wow. That's beautiful, Peg."

"I want you to have it." She smiled and handed the pillow to me.

"Aww. I love it!"

Peg stood there smiling and I felt I should hug her, so I awkwardly moved closer. She clasped me, along with the pillow, so tight that I lost my breath for a moment. When I regained access to oxygen, the only thing I could smell was her Youth Dew perfume: spicy and sweet. She held me at arm's length for a few seconds, peering up at me with a smile. Finally, she let go. "Time to get to work." She patted my right shoulder and turned to walk toward the front door. She took a ring of keys from a hook near the door and handed them to me. "I got some boxes in the trunk. I need you to bring them in."

"Sure," I said. I took the keys and headed outside toward a big blue Chevy Caprice. I thumbed through the keys, finding the round trunk key, and opened it up. I was surprised to find three large boxes that contained all of the components for a personal computer. It was a Compaq Pentium II—not quite top-of-the-line, but Peg still must have spent a grand and a half on it. Four hundred and fifty megahertz of processing speed was probably more than fast enough to do anything that she would want. I snickered to myself, thinking of the unlikely possibility of Peg becoming a hardcore gamer and needing to upgrade to a custom tower with a top-of-the-line Pentium III processor and a graphics card with its own processor for quick pixel rendering. *As if*, like the Rah Rahs would say.

"Where do you want them?" I asked as I was bringing in the first box, sweat already forming on my brow.

"You can set it up in the kitchen. Thanks," she replied.

It took longer to lug the boxes into the trailer and unpack them than it did to connect everything to the back of the tower and plug it all into the power strip. When I was finished, I stood back to look at the system. The whole thing took up most of Peg's small kitchen table. Peg peeked around the corner from the living room, fresh from working on pillows, just in time to see my handiwork. "Oh-sda!" she exclaimed, adding, "That means 'Good.'"

I repeated the affirmation to her in Cherokee. No bony fingers.

"Welp. Go ahead and power it on." She motioned toward the screen.

I hesitated. "Um, actually . . . the judge ordered me not to access a computer. So I don't think I should, like, actually boot it up." My eyes scrolled to the floor.

"And he also told you to help me with whatever I need, right?" she asked.

"Yeah, but—"

"Tell you what," she said as she sat down in front of the keyboard, motioning for me to pull a chair up beside her. "What if you just tell me what I need to do and I'll sit in the driver's seat? Thataway it won't be you accessing the computer. It will be me."

"I guess that would be okay."

"Good. Now show me them patterns," she grinned. I walked her through booting up her computer. When the Windows 98 start-up sound hummed through the speakers, she looked at me in wide-eyed anticipation. Her lips were pressed tightly together and she hunched her shoulders up in excitement. It had to be the cutest grandma face I had ever seen. I stifled a giggle bubbling up inside me.

"Click here," I said. Her hand was on the mouse and I placed mine over hers to show her how to click on an icon. She picked up how to double-click quicker than I expected, and I directed her to the America Online icon because the software was already preloaded. I helped her sign up and she dialed up to the Internet for the first time. She made that same cute excited grandma face again when the screech and the *ping-ping* of the modem handshake connected us to the rest of the world.

After spending the afternoon printing clip-art animals for her cross-stitch patterns, Peg and I stayed up late into the night drinking coffee and exploring the web. Sites that I had already grown bored with were new and exciting to Peg, and I recited several URLs to her just to see how she would respond to the sites. Peg's most animated reaction was in response to our visit to the Hampster Dance page. She put her hands to her face and squealed with delight when the animated GIFs of various hamsters and rodents danced around to the looped "Dee da dee da dee da doh." It was still all I could do to keep from spitting out the gulp of coffee I had just taken when Peg *eek!*ed at the monitor full of dancing vermin. At two a.m., the caffeine finally reached the limits of its powers and I started to crash, nodding off at the table. Peg told me that I'd better just sleep on the couch and that a blanket and pillow were in the hall closet. She didn't want me to drive home half-delirious from lack of sleep. I asked Peg if she could log off the Internet so that I could call my dad. Even though it was late, I didn't want him to worry when I wasn't home in the morning. When I went to the closet to get the blanket and pillow, I heard the *ping-ping* of the modem handshake again and saw Peg wide awake, her face bathed in the glow from the monitor.

*

"I want you to teach me how to be a hacker," Peg said, looking down at me, chipped mug of coffee in one hand and bowl of yellow puffs of cereal in the other. I had just opened my eyes and these were her first words to me of the day, like she had been standing there waiting for me to wake up.

"You . . . what?" Why was an elderly woman wanting me to teach her how to hack? It was too early in the morning for me to understand something this weird.

"I want to be a hacker like you," Peg repeated.

"Did you even sleep?" I responded, still foggy.

"Nah," she shrugged at me. "I'll sleep when I'm dead." She placed the cereal and coffee on the table in front of me as I sat up and pulled my hair back into a ponytail. Peg sat down on the edge of her recliner. I spooned a couple of bites of Cap'n Crunch into my mouth and tried to process what Peg was asking me.

"Why do you want to be a hacker, Peg? I mean, what do you want to do?" I asked.

"I'll show you after breakfast." She stared in silence at me for a few minutes, then asked me, "What computer did you hack off to get into trouble, if you don't mind me asking?"

"It's just 'hack,' and I don't mind," I answered. Over the rest of my cereal, I explained to Peg how a few of us at the high school had suspicions that one of the coaches who taught geography was favoring his jocks and the most popular cheerleaders. So I hacked into the grade system, printed out everyone's names and grades for all their classes, and stapled the list to the corkboard in the hall. The data showed a sharp uptick in GPA for basketball players in geography class. I circled those parts to draw attention to the discrepancy. Unsurprisingly, it had caused quite a bit of drama.

"Oh. Is that it?" Peg sounded a little disappointed. "I thought you maybe hacked into the FBI or something."

"Whoa, nothing like that. The feds would have gotten involved for something that big," I said. Instead, the tribal court had handled my case and sent me to Peg for community service.

"Then how'd you get caught?" she asked, still literally sitting on the edge of her seat.

"It was stupid, really," I said. I then went on to tell Peg how a single piece of paper had caused my downfall. I had been so careful. I masked my IP so that it looked like I had accessed the school computer from China and I used rubber gloves to carry the printout just in case they dusted for prints. My printer jammed, however, on the last page, so I just reprinted it. I took the jammed paper—here is the stupid part—and just crammed it into my backpack. So when they searched the belongings of everyone under suspicion (that is, the handful of computer geeks at Sequoyah High School) they found the partially-printed page in my possession. Busted.

"Mmmmm." Peg contemplated for a moment, then stood up and darted to the kitchen. I followed, carrying my coffee mug. Was she disappointed in me for what I'd done at school? Or maybe she was disappointed that I wasn't a better hacker. She walked directly to her computer, leaned over to the back of the tower, and unplugged the printer cable. She turned to me and grinned. "No paper trail."

"No paper trail," I echoed back to her.

*

It turned out that what Peg had in mind wasn't really hacking. Well, at least not at first. What she wanted to do was to make a version of the Hampster Dance web page that featured characters from the Cherokee syllabary dancing around the screen instead of animals. So I showed her how to download the Microsoft GIF animator and a Cherokee font. I convinced her that we should start small, working with just one syllable at a time. After several tries bent over the long-stemmed microphone, Peg recorded herself pronouncing the first Cherokee character—D— to her satisfaction and saved it as a .WAV file. A little while later, we got the pixels of the syllable to bounce just the way she wanted them to. Then I showed her how to use Notepad to write the few lines of HTML needed to make a simple web page. She typed "<title>First Syllable of the Cherokee Language</title>" after the opening <html> tag. After that, all we needed was a little bit of code to display the animated GIF in the center of the page and play the "Aw" sound on a loop in the background. I could tell by the look on Peg's face that she was pleased.

"Your first web page, Peg. Congrats!" I cheered, causing her to blush.

"This might be enough to spark someone's curiosity, Spider, what do you think?" Peg asked.

"Sure. I'd definitely be curious if I came across this." Another idea struck me. "Maybe we can add a link to the entire syllabary and a short bio of Sequoyah?"

"How do we put it up on the Hampster Dance website?"

"Uh . . . " was all I could manage in response. Peg wanting to hijack a popular domain totally caught me by surprise.

"That page has millions of visits. I saw the counter at the bottom of the screen."

I struggled for a moment with how to let Peg down gently. "Yeah. That's not so easy, though. We'd have to figure out the admin password to the site. And even then, it would only be up until they caught the problem and changed the password."

"Good. Let's do that."

And that's how I started teaching Peg how to hack—well, crack, to be more accurate. Cracking is the art of breaking into a system by guessing the password. I explained to Peg that cracking software basically tried every possible combination of the available 128 ASCII characters. Because of all the possible combinations, it took a long time to crack a password. We could write that program together, I said, like we did her web page, but I already had a cracking program that I had modified. It was the one I had used to bust into the school's grading system.

I ignored the voices in my head warning me that this wasn't a good idea. I showed Peg how to download and install HyperTerminal and directed her to dial into a Linux box that I kept as a mirrored backup of my files at a friend's house. She downloaded the bash shell script and I showed her how to modify the code. I explained how it ran through a proxy server that masked our real IP address. I also told her that after every few attempts, we would need to change the IP address that it attempted to log in from.

"All this IP hopping will basically help keep us from getting caught," I explained. Well, I hoped.

"No paper trail," she said.

"No paper trail," I responded.

"Let's get to cracking," Peg said with a mischievous smile as she interlocked her fingers and pushed her palms outward, popping several of her knuckles.

*

I went home early that evening, leaving Peg to her own devices. It was highly improbable that the program would crack the password to the Hampster Dance site overnight. Even if it did crack the site, it would take several months. I figured she'd get bored with clicking after half an hour and go back to a more innocent activity like downloading clip art for her cross-stitching patterns.

When I showed up to her trailer the next morning, Peg answered the door in the same blouse she had worn the night before. Her eyes were blood-shot and she held an empty coffee mug in her hand. Instead of offering me coffee or breakfast, she gave me a quick "hello" and went straight back to the computer.

I followed Peg to the kitchen and sat beside her. "Did you even sleep last night?" I asked.

"Ahhh," she waved a hand at me, "I'll sleep when I'm dead."

"I've heard that one before, Peg. You need some new material," I teased.

"How 'bout this for new material?" Peg pointed to the screen. I was looking at someone's email inbox: chet@chetcornmaker.com.

"Who is Chet Cornmaker?" I asked.

"I guess you don't keep up on Cherokee politics, huh?" she asked.

I shook my head. "I don't really keep up on any politics." She looked disappointed.

"So this guy is a politician, a Cherokee politician?" I asked.

"He might become *the* Cherokee politician—as in, the chief—in the runoff election on the 25th," she explained.

"Oh yeah . . . " I said. I realized a moment later what this all meant. "You mean you hacked into the email of the guy who could be the next chief of the Cherokee Nation of Oklahoma?"

"Yup," she said.

"But how?" I had helped Peg set the parameters of the cracking program to use FTP protocol in order to gain illicit access to websites. I hadn't expected her to crack email with it.

"The program you gave me had options for cracking email." Peg scrolled down to a section of the code where several lines started with hashtags. I knew that hashtags meant the programmer was commenting on her code. Her cursor landed on the heading #CRACKINGEMAIL. "I just followed the directions there. It told me how to find the company that holds Chet Cornmaker's website."

I nodded. I knew she meant "hosts," but didn't correct her.

"I didn't understand this other stuff here," Peg pointed to lines referring to Post Office Protocol and Simple Mail Transfer Protocol. "So I just
searched for the company's telephone number and called them. They were
overseas, so it was daytime there. I just asked them for these settings—"
she scrolled down and pointed to the information the program needed to
crack emails. "I told them that I needed to set email up for my boss on
his new computer. I said I had the password but needed the other information, and they were very helpful and gave me everything I needed," she
said with a crooked grin.

"That's brilliant, Peg!" I said.

"Oh, yeah?" she said. "Well, I guess I'm a real hacker now, huh?"

"Yup. You sure are." I said.

*

The next morning when I knocked at Peg's front door, I didn't get an
answer. After a few minutes, I started to worry, so I let myself in to check
on her. As I closed the door behind me, I could hear her talking on the
phone in the kitchen.

"I understand you're very busy, Margaret. I just thought it would be
nice to see you and the children this summer . . . I know it's a long trip,
but you know I can't travel in my condition . . . Yes, okay . . . but could you
at least put 'em on the phone? Oh, swimming lessons? That's nice—Have
'em call later, then? Oh! Or they could send me electronic mail. I have
this new computer—Oh, you have to go? Well, it was nice to chat for a
minute. I'll try to call when you're not so busy."

I knew that I shouldn't have stood there eavesdropping for so long.
The conversation was winding down quickly, so I darted back out the
door, making as little noise as possible. I waited another few minutes
before knocking again. Peg took longer to open the door than usual, and
when she did, her shoulders were slumped and her eyes stared listlessly
right through me.

"You feeling okay, Peg?" I asked.

"Oh, nothing serious." She didn't look at me. "I think I might just be coming down with one of them summer colds," she said.

"Need me to get you anything?" I asked.

"No. I'll be fine. I just need some rest. Tell you what: why don't you go home and I'll call you when I'm feeling better. I might be contagious and I'd hate to get you sick, too," Peg said.

I drove home and sat by the phone in my bedroom, watching TV. Peg didn't call that night. Finally, in the late evening, I started cleaning my room because I had nothing else to do. In a pile of neglected papers on my desk, I found a registration receipt for a college-prep class I had forgotten that I had signed up for.

I tried calling Peg a couple of times the next morning but kept getting a busy signal. Later that day, I was sitting at my desk leafing through a stack of *Cherokee Phoenix* newspapers that I had borrowed from my dad, looking for a picture of the guy whose email Peg had hacked. Just as I found a few pictures of him, the phone rang and startled me. I jumped up and grabbed the phone, dragging the coiled cord with me back over to my desk.

"Hello," I said.

"Spider?" It was Peg.

"Yeah, it's me, Peg. You feeling better?" I asked.

"Much. You'll never believe what I found. Get over here quick!" she said.

"Sure, okay. Be there in a few," I said, hanging up the phone. I left a note for my dad.

*

When I got to Peg's, she was standing in the open doorway as I walked up to her trailer. Peg looked like her old self again, her energetic smile extending to her eyes. It was hard to believe that she'd been sick just yesterday. She didn't say a word. She just turned around, swooshing her yellow dress, and I followed her straight to her computer in the kitchen.

"Take a look at that," Peg said, standing beside the computer and pointing at the monitor.

I sat down in the chair and looked at the screen. It was an email from Chet Cornmaker's sent-mail folder. I skimmed the contents.

"'Abolish term limits for executive positions.' What does that mean?" I asked.

"Cornmaker is planning on being chief for life!" she said.

"Wow. That's jacked up. Would that even be legal?"

"It's legal if he gets a law passed saying it is," Peg answered wryly.

"So, what do you think we should do?" I asked.

"Well, the runoff election is in a few weeks. Maybe if we can tell enough people what Cornmaker is up to, they won't vote him in," Peg said.

"So, like an article in the *Phoenix*? Wouldn't we get in trouble for cracking his email?"

"I got a better idea," Peg gave me her mischievous grin again. "We make a web page about it to replace Cherokee.org." She slapped her hands together for emphasis.

Hacking the Cherokee Nation's official website was going to be just as hard as hacking the Hampster Dance page, but I didn't want to discourage Peg. She was so enthusiastic about the idea. I spent the rest of the evening helping Peg code a simple web page for the task from scratch. I told her how to set up a plain white background and add a large, centered .JPG close-up of Cornmaker we had copied from his website. Above his smiling picture we entered the phrase "CHET CORNMAKER WANTS TO BE KING" in big black font. Below the picture, in equally large font, read: "WE DON'T NEED A KING." Below that, in a smaller font, we placed a hyperlink with the words, "If elected, Cornmaker plans to abolish term limits for chief. Click here to read his incriminating email."

Then I helped her modify the cracking program to run a simple script that would send the site files to the public_html directory once it was cracked.

It was getting late and I had held off telling Peg about my college-prep class long enough. "So . . . I signed up for a college-prep class a few months ago. I forgot about it until yesterday. It's starting tomorrow but it'll only be for one week. I can cancel if you want me to. It's no problem," I said.

"Nah. You need to go so you can get good scores and get into a good college. Besides, you'll probably like hanging out with people your own age anyway," Peg said.

"People my age are boring. I'd rather hang out with you. But I already paid for it, so I guess I'll see you in a week," I said.

"Knock 'em dead, kiddo," she smiled, and wrapped me up in another one of her oxygen-depriving, perfume-infused hugs before I left.

\*

I spent the next week ignoring the fact that I wasn't legally allowed to operate a computer. Alternating between studying for the mock college exams and sitting in the computer lab at the high school listening to the teacher lecture about mind-numbingly basic computer skills made for an uneventful week. The pace of the course was slow enough that I could surf around a bit while the teacher wasn't looking. I knew it could take months to hack into the Cherokee Nation website, but I couldn't help myself from typing *cherokee.org* into the browser and hitting refresh every so often just out of curiosity. On Thursday afternoon, the teacher was showing us how to make a simple family budget in Excel spreadsheets. I had already finished and was waiting on everyone else to catch up, so I typed the address of the Cherokee Nation website into the browser again. I gasped aloud. Instead of the official Cherokee Nation page, there was the page that Peg and I had made, exposing Chet Cornmaker.

"Are you okay over there?" the teacher called out. I forgot I wasn't alone.

"Sorry. My bad. I'm fine," I mumbled. For the last two hours of class, I couldn't concentrate. All I could think of was rushing over to Peg's and celebrating with her.

After class finally ended, I sped over to Peg's trailer, only stopping at the supermarket along the way to pick up a chocolate cake for us to share. It seemed appropriate to celebrate Peg's newfound hacking abilities with chocolate. When I pulled into the driveway, I saw a car parked next to Peg's blue Chevy Caprice. I knocked on the door and a strange woman answered. She looked familiar, but I'd never met her before.

"Thanks," she said, taking the cake out of my hands as if she expected me. She turned toward the kitchen. "Come on in."

The family photo on the wall reminded me that this was Peg's daughter.

"Peg must have been very lucky to have a neighbor like you. You must have heard the ambulance last night," she called from the kitchen.

My heart sank as the words "must have been" echoed in my head. I had a few seconds to compose myself before the woman came back from the kitchen.

"Margaret," she said, extending her hand.

I shook her hand. "Spider, uh, at least that's what Peg calls me."

"She always did love to give people nicknames." She managed a small smile. "Mom had a million for me until I finally convinced her to use my real name," Margaret told me. "Would you like something to drink?"

"No, thanks," I said. I sank into the familiar tweed couch. Margaret sat in Peg's recliner.

"She really shouldn't have kept coffee in the house. This wasn't her first heart attack, you know. The doctor said she had a problem with metabolizing caffeine and it could be genetic. That's why I never touch the stuff. But Mom did what whatever Mom wanted, regardless." She shook her head.

"Oh. I didn't know about the coffee," I said, my head still swimming.

"Say, you're young . . . Do you think you could do me a favor?" Margaret asked.

"Sure," I said.

"I thought since you were younger you might know something about computers. Mom has one in the kitchen," Margaret said.

"Yeah, I know a little bit," I said.

"Well, could you reset it? I mean, wipe out the personal information and reset it to how it came out of the box?" She explained, "I'm going to sell it to help pay for the funeral expenses."

"Yeah, sure," I said. Margaret went to the bedroom and I collapsed down into the kitchen chair facing the computer monitor. It felt strange to be there without Peg "in the driver's seat," as she put it. The computer was already booted up. I pulled up a browser and dialed in to check the Cherokee.org page again. The admin must have caught the hack quickly because the home page was already back to normal. Well, a couple of hours was better than nothing. I searched the computer for the hacking script but didn't find any code left from her hack of the Cherokee Nation site. I even checked the recycle bin. Good for her, no paper trail. Then I searched for files I wanted to keep, ones that reminded me of Peg. I took her first web page, the one with the Cherokee letter bouncing around, and the one we had built together yesterday, and moved them into a new folder on the desktop. I looked around the hard drive for anything else worth saving, and that's when I noticed the text file on the desktop named "tospider.txt." I double clicked the file:

*Spider,*

*I realize that I never told you the Cherokee story about Spider. You'll probably find different versions, but this is how my grandma told it to me.*

*In the beginning times, it was very cold because no one knew how to start fires. But there was one fire, an old burning sycamore tree, on an island in the middle of a big lake. A group of animals decided that they needed to get the fire to help keep everyone warm. Bear went first because he was the biggest and strongest. He swam to the island, but when he tried to carry a hot coal back in his paws, he just burned all his hair black. Snake went next because he was the sneakiest. He swam to the island, but he too couldn't carry the hot coal. When he tried to put it on his back, the fire burned all his skin black. Spider spoke up and told the other animals that she could bring back the fire, but they all laughed at her, saying that she was too small. Crow went next because he was the fastest. He flew to the island and put a small burning stick on his wing, but it burned all his feathers black before he made it back to land.*

*Again, Spider told everyone that she could get the fire back to the shore. They still didn't believe her, but they decided to let her try anyway. Spider said she needed a ride to the island, so Crow told her to jump on his back, and they flew to the island. Spider had learned some technology from watching the dirt daubers build their mud nests. She gathered a little mud and made a small basket just big enough for a tiny ember. Once it had dried, Spider put the ember in the basket and flew back to the shore on Crow's back. The ember was still glowing and hadn't burned through the mud basket. All the animals cheered for Spider because she had figured out how to get fire from the island. Since then, because of Spider, we have always had a way to stay warm.*

*I thought I'd type this story out just in case I forgot to tell it to you next week when you come by.*

*Keep a fire,*

*Peg*

*

I read and reread Peg's note with tears streaming down my cheeks. When I finally wiped my face dry, I moved "tospider.txt" into the same folder where I'd saved the web pages, dialed into the Linux box at my friend's house, and transferred them all. Then I rebooted Peg's computer.

"No paper trail," I whispered before typing *format C: /s* and hitting the enter key. I reinstalled Windows 98 from the CD, shut it down, and boxed up the computer, monitor, and printer. I said goodbye to Margaret and told her that I was sorry for her loss before driving away from Peg's trailer for the last time.

I still don't know how Peg managed to crack the Cherokee Nation website. Chet Cornmaker won the runoff election for chief later that month, but that didn't really matter. It didn't take away from Peg's accomplishment. It had no bearing on what she meant to me. I wish I could have told her about Cherokee being added to Unicode a few months later so that every computer in the world could display the language. I wish I could have shown her my college application, where I'd listed "Cherokee and Binary" under the languages I had studied. But most of all, I wish that I could have seen her smile one more time. Sometimes I dream that I'm with Peg at the moment she finally cracked the password to the Cherokee Nation website. I see her holding her coffee mug and her smile radiates up from her mouth to her eyes, through me and across the whole room. That's why I upload this readme.txt file to every server I crack, either manually or through one of my bots. I was lucky to know Peg Sixkiller. I think she would have gotten a kick out of knowing her story is out there crawling through the Web.

EOF

# REFLECTION ON SPICES

*Excerpt from "reflection on spices, in three parts"*

## Sarah Sophia Yanni

I move through smell, at least in my mind, and by this I mean: the smell of salt and chile de arbol and bay leaves in black beans takes me to abuela's kitchen. I blame this on two distinct things—first, science tells us that smell is linked to memory, we know this. it's biology. secondly, though, when my mother cooks in our san fernando valley kitchen, she cooks out of bags that she put beneath her clothes. from salt pulled from the sea near colima, mexico, gigantic flakes in a straw pouch. she's stirring in dollops of sunflower seeds and dry chile and oil, all packed in a jar that she stuck in her shoes. before she flies back to america, she puts five layers of saran wrap around these objects and strategically places them in her suitcase and at LAX customs when they ask if she has any food items to declare, she smiles and looks at her feet and politely says *no*.

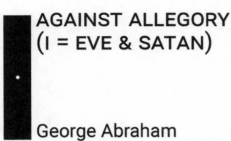

# AGAINST ALLEGORY
# (I = EVE & SATAN)

## George Abraham

Asunder, as if halved
    like a knife upturned

by lightning, the tree stood firm
    & staked into the ground—here,

2 chests of man & vast
    that becomes my name—

loneliness coalesced into a single howl
    west of here, a sonless

sun. East, my hunger's width of
    the fauna between: tendril &

hunger. My country,
    anti-Eden, shadow's arcadian

metaphor—I waded through
    unimagined—void of exiled

chaos. I found paradise in
    salt—void of motion

-less void—at the heart of you,
    hyphen, hyphenated into

I was languaged into
    brash(hyphen)babble—my first word was not

a remembering—not mama—biteless
    fire—not sin

venom—nor baba—forest
    nor flaming sword—

        it was the bitten-into it
        -self who set the angels

    singeing—

                    singing—

# HOW TO BATTLE

## Ruth Ellen Kocher

widen your stance
collect your splinters of regret
weaponize a slow slump of sheep grazing
father the grass beneath them
anger each prayer
defeat first your waning want
defeat next the coming mark
vein the horizon with your death undoing
until your heart makes a ring of fire
live
refuse the placid moon
flock to fist
hammer your way out
or in
assume the empirical formula of ancestors
so they taste your breath
so they wince
hold true

# MY MOTHER TOLD ME I AM UNDER SHANGO

## Tonya Liburd

If my mother was alive, or
If she taught me to sew as well as she could
(she made her own white wedding dress
with lace details, a train and appliqués)
I'd make myself a superhero
I'd sew myself, or get sewn,
A gown made partly of the weather—
And
A scarf of lightning
Representing part of my Nigerian ancestry;
I am under Shango, my mother told me . . .

To ground, empower and strengthen me
I'd wear a light grey jacket of smoke,
Tinged with my childhood
I'd thread
My late mother's and uncles' voices
Through my hair like the finest of pearls

My entire confection
Laced with all my favorite words
Like the lace on my mother's
Wedding dress

With my creation
Reminding me
Of the heights I can soar to
I'd trample upon every wrong thing ever said to me,
Every damning, hurtful utterance
My PTSD nightmares stomped to nothingness
Underfoot
With my shoes
Bedazzled
With everything I love about myself

# FROM SENEGAL TO SENATOBIA

*Excerpt from "Shanequa's Blues"*

## Sheree Renée Thomas

*"The more you do it, the more perfect it come to you."*

That's what Uncle Oumar wrote in his last letter. Mopti had read the line again and again, trying to make sense of his uncle's perfect penmanship.

> *Well, the blues am a achin' old heart disease,*
> *Well, the blues am a low-down achin' heart disease,*
> *Like consumption, killin' me by degrees.*
> —Robert Johnson

He could read the words distinctly. The message behind their meaning, well that was a mystery his uncle had left unclear. Mopti had traveled all the way from his desk job in Dakar, Senegal to pay his respects and bury his father's dead. Mopti had consulted his maps, read several blogs and travel features, and noted the tourist advisories. He packed one case of disposable clothing, just a few simple, sufficiently solemn bits he would not terribly mind losing. He had his hair cut extra low and his shoes shined. He double-checked his papers, just in case.

Mopti traveled with a few token gifts, some old family photos his mother had pressed into his hand, and some fragrant cooking spice. But the older brother Mopti's father had spoken so crudely of had turned out to be far more than anyone had ever suspected. Now he knew why the money sent across the waters for his education had dwindled over the years. Uncle Oumar had lived a double, perhaps even a triple life. He'd long since abandoned his medical studies in New York, before

Mopti was born. The shotgun house in Senatobia, the bull's-eye heart of Mississippi, had been just one of his uncle's properties. And from what he could tell, none of them had been worth more than the land they leaned on. The lawyer said two more besides his house in Senatobia remained intact, one near Clarksdale, and the other somewhere in another small town called Mound Bayou.

In all his days, Mopti never thought he would find himself in Mississippi, but that was the path his uncle, prodigy turned pariah, had finally led him. Mopti had crossed the water to see his Uncle Oumar properly laid to rest, but his father had refused. The ocean was not wide enough to contain the gulf between the two men.

And even if Mopti understood his Uncle Oumar's words, it was the art that he couldn't make out. Oumar had drawn what first appeared to be a series of concentric circles, then morphed into what looked like pinwheels, then changed again to a jagged lightning bolt, or a zig-zaggy cross. Strange signs and symbols. Hastily drawn images whose meaning wasn't clear. The words appeared to be more blues lyrics or perhaps the ravings of a backroom madman, someone who abandoned his family, his bloodline, his future, to chase the trail of a Howlin' Wolf. Mopti imagined the sound of the bluesman's freight-train voice and tried to read between the lines of the words his uncle had carefully written down. There was no one left willing to do so.

\*

*Brother, I knew someday you would come for me, but you are looking in the wrong place. I had hoped that you would forgive me. Despite what you think, my love for our sister knows no bounds. I tried to save her. Was forced to search elsewhere for the knowledge Western medicine could not provide. Please forgive me. I was so very close but not swift enough to save dear Aminata. Brother, since you did not like my path in life, I am sending you on a journey in my death.*

\*

Sheree Renée Thomas

*Everybody say they don't like the blues, but you wrong.*

*See the blues come from way back. And I'm gon' tell you something again.*

*The things that's going on today is not the blues. It's just a good beat that people just carrying.*

*But now when it come down to the blues, see I'm gonna show you how to be the blues.*

*I'm going to show you how to travel the blues to the places the old ones don't want you to go. You just sit back and listen. Watch. Brother.*

*I'm gonna show you.*

—Howlin' Wolf

*

The letter with the strange song had left Mopti puzzled. The rooms in the small, two-bedroom, one-bath house were covered with photocopied excerpts of oral histories and interviews with musicians: stories about midnight pacts made at legendary crossroads, of artists who sold their souls to the devil. Mopti knew very well how his father would have responded to such things. He would have tossed it all, the articles, the grainy photographs, and portraits of sad-eyed, weary looking men clutching their guitars, the cryptic lyrics, and the bizarre drawings, everything would have been crumpled up and placed in the trash. What did it all mean and why had Uncle Oumar left this?

Mopti rubbed his face. Smoky circles ringed his eyes like dark moon craters. He was tired from his long travels, and frustrated. His father would not approve, but Mopti felt he owed it to Uncle Oumar to at least try to decipher the puzzle he had left. Whatever it was, it was so important that his uncle pursued it rather than travel home to see his beloved sister buried, the one he said he cherished and missed.

A large arrow pointed to an old stereo system with speakers Mopti had only seen in vintage magazines. When Mopti pushed play, a husky shout filled the room. Startled him so bad, he dropped the letter and nearly fell out of his chair.

*III . . . am, a back door man! I am a back door man. What men don't know, little girls understand.*

*Early morning when the rooster call. Something telling you, you better get up and go. I am . . . I am . . . a back door man.*

Mopti calmed his breathing and stared at the drawing of a great tall, wide tree with a door set in its trunk. They didn't have trees like that in his father's old village, not anymore, and Mopti doubted such trees existed in the land where his uncle had chosen to bury his future seed. Mopti did not know why Uncle Oumar had betrayed his promise to the family, or why his obsession had led him to leave his home and disappear into the heart of Mississippi, but Mopti knew one thing for certain. The letter with the lyrics and the drawings was a map. Where it led, he was not sure. Mopti had to listen to the whole song three times before he realized, with some trepidation, that the blues was the key.

Now he was driving down Main Street, looking for an old dusty record shop that probably wasn't even open anymore. After he circled the block a few times, squinting at addresses, he decided to gas up and ask someone local who would know.

Mopti had just parked in front of pump two, when he heard the laughter.

"Girl, you popped that tire off so fast, you need to come and fix mine." An elder in a Cowboys hat held two bottles of water, handed one to the young boy sitting in his truck. "Started to ask if you needed some help, then I said, 'naw, this sister got it handled.'"

The woman chuckled, tightening the lugs. "If you don't know, better ask somebody!"

"Need to teach this one. Can't hardly get him off his phone."

"That your grandson?" she asked.

Cowboy nodded, opening the door. "Yeah, he rolls with me while his mama and n'em at work. If I let him, he'd spend half the day on that thang." They shared a laugh.

"My daughter, too. She used to . . . " her voice trailed off.

"Well, you have a nice day."

"You, too, sir."

Mopti watched the Ford pull off as he pumped his gas. Sadness replaced the air where laughter had been. The woman looked like she was wiping tears from her eyes. An embarrassed witness, Mopti turned away, watched the black numbers spin.

When he returned from getting a Coke, he saw her sitting in her front seat, head bowed, hood up. Any other day Mopti would have driven on and "minded his," as his cousins in New York would say, but the sadness came off her in waves. He'd had days like this when everything but the right thing was going on.

He bit his lip, then asked quietly, so quietly he could convince himself that he had never spoken. "Miss, do you need some help?" She didn't answer. "Miss?"

Relieved, Mopti started to walk back when he heard her sigh. "Naw, I need a new car," she said. "Short of that, a boost. You got some jumper cables?"

"No, ma'am, I'm sorry," he stammered. "This is a rental. But maybe I could look at it?" Mopti didn't know anything about cars, how they ran or how they didn't, but he was so embarrassed, he'd try.

"No need," she said. "I know how to fix it, just can't afford to right now." There was that sadness again. To Mopti, it felt familiar, like grief. He stepped back, instinctively, before it caught him, too. He'd been pulled under his own waves before.

The woman frowned. "Don't worry, I'm not tryna hustle you. Thank you," she said. She emphasized the last words so pointedly, he knew he had been dismissed.

*

The roots reached back to Africa, but the blues were born here. In his notes, Mopti's uncle had asked a series of questions. Why were there

no blues in Cuba? In São Paolo, in Port-au-Prince? In his neat, loop-
ing handwriting, Uncle Oumar answered his own queries. Because the
blues burst up from the Delta's fertile earth. The blues burst from the
will to overcome sadness, to overcome anger, bad luck, exploitation,
pain. Underlined were two words, "personal" and "systemic."

Flipping through the sheath of papers, Mopti had come to understand that for his uncle, the blues were not only part of some personal
quest of his, but the music also represented an ancient path to healing.
Mopti was still trying to make heads and tails of it, and still wasn't sure
how he would explain it all—if he dared try—to his father.

The journals were not dated. Mopti could only tell when one pas-
sage began and the other ended based on the quality of the handwriting, the color of the ink, the series of drawings. It looked like a madman
had written it all, but Uncle Oumar had an order to his chaos. From
what Mopti could tell, it was in New York, Harlem maybe or somewhere in Brooklyn at an old record shop, Resurrection Records, where
Uncle Oumar had first heard of *The Great Going Song*.

*

Mopti felt terrible. The cold drink sweated in his hands. "I'm so sorry.
I didn't mean to . . . " He stumbled and tried again. "The idea that I've
just made your bad day worse is unacceptable. How can I help?" Part of
Mopti wished he had never spoken. Reaching out was hard. When his
father had asked him to see after his late uncle's arrangements, part of
Mopti wanted to refuse. Traveling so far from Senegal to New York, all
the way to Mississippi, was more reaching out than Mopti was used to.
He preferred the comfort of his desk.

To his surprise her dark eyes lightened, just a bit. "How do you
know I'm having a bad day?"

Mopti smiled. "A flat tire, car not running, and . . . " he paused, then
pointed at the bouquet of flowers resting in the passenger seat. "And
someone you care about needs cheering?"

"You got a good eye," she said, impressed. "You sure you not tryna hustle *me*?"

The grin on Mopti's round face spread from ear to ear. The woman's easy humor comforted him. He liked her accent, the way she made the question sound like a song.

Mopti laughed. "I'm not so sure you *can* be hustled. I wouldn't try anyhow. But maybe you could help me? I'm trying to find Sound Advice."

"Sound advice? First, you might want to finish that drink and get on in your car where it's nice and cool, instead of standing up out here, burning up with me."

When she spoke, colors seemed to leap out of her hands, encircle her face. Mopti watched her, shaking his head.

"Friend, you could make iron laugh."

"Thank you, I think." She squinted at him.

"Excuse me. I don't know your name."

"Brenda."

"Brenda," he said, chattering on, awkward but endearing. "I am Mopti. I am visiting here to help put my uncle to rest. He died."

Brenda frowned. "Sorry, Mopti. Were you close?"

Mopti swallowed, the discomfort now a stone in his throat. "No, but he . . . he is family."

Mopti wasn't one of those men fascinated by their own dark places. He seemed to shrink away from the shadows within himself. Instead, he walked in light, directed conversations to the day. He avoided negative holes in conversation, as if he was afraid he might fall into them. So Brenda watched Mopti out of the corners of her eye, listened with the inside of her heart.

"If you are looking for the record shop, it's not far from here. Just a few streets down, over on Main."

"That's where I was."

"Well, how did you miss it? Never mind." She grew quiet, staring at tulips and daisies in the front seat of her car. Brenda thought she liked this funny man with the big Moon Pie forehead and the Kermit the

Frog smile, but Brenda no longer had absolute faith in her own judgment. She had missed the signs of the illness until her daughter was in the hospital bed, just as she had missed the signs of another pain before. A pain that Brenda had let into their lives, one that scarred them both. A betrayal that echoed her own childhood. Each night, Brenda played it back, torn between the grief of what her child suffered and the terror of losing her, of her slipping away from this earth.

She had hoped there might be a time, someday far off in the future, when the daughter, grown older, might fully heal and forgive. Brenda had not yet forgiven herself. She felt she had no right to forgiveness, not yet. Maybe not ever. She only wanted to make amends—or try to. She knew from her own life that you live, you may even forgive, but you never forget.

Brenda noticed Mopti staring at the small white-and-red teddy bear peering up from the bouquet.

"They're for my daughter. She's at Delta County."

"Sorry to hear that," Mopti said. "I hope she will be well soon." He opened his car door and placed his drink in the cupholder. An empty potato-chip bag floated past Mopti as he scanned the street and pumped gas, trying to ignore Brenda sitting in the broken-down car beside him. He listened as she queried each new driver for jumper cables. Mopti felt discomfort sit in his belly, a heavy stone, as he sat in his rental and watched each new shopper shake their head no. He wanted to help but didn't want to intrude. Good Samaritans could come off worse. But after the last person drove away, he found himself calling out to her.

"Brenda?"

She looked up. "Yeah?"

He struggled to speak, then released his words in a rush. "I don't mean to disturb you, but I am new here and I don't know anyone. It would be good to have help." Mopti bit his lip. He worried she might think he was a creep. "I mean directions. If you like, I could drop you off at the hospital, if you let me know where to go. Maybe you could tell me where Sound Advice is, since my GPS and I keep missing it?"

"It's right on Main Street," Brenda said, squinting at him. "But you know, ole boy is kind of weird. It's not like he's *trying* to be found."

"Oh, so you know it?"

She shrugged. "Not my thing, but yeah, it's been there a while . . . " her voice trailed off.

Her eyes glistened, reflected sadness. "Look, I can show you the record store and you can drop me off on Main. I can take a bus."

Mopti started to protest.

"That's alright, I appreciate the offer," Brenda said, "but it's a bit out of the way for you. I'd call my cousin but she's not off yet. If we just head over to Main, I can show you Sound Advice and I'll be on my way."

"It's no problem," Mopti said. "I thank you." He unlocked the passenger door as Brenda took out the flowers and the teddy bear, then locked her car.

"Not that anyone would try to steal this hoopty."

"Hoopty," Mopti said smiling. "Everyone has colorful language here."

"In Mississippi?" Brenda asked.

"Here and New York, everywhere."

"Is that where you're from?" she asked as she slid into the seat. "I was finna say. Thought you were frontin' from Memphis. That's where my family's from. You know we got some of everybody there, 'colorful language' and all." She wrapped the paper tightly around the bouquet and balanced it in her lap. Her purse was looped around her shoulder, as if she were prepared to jump out at any moment if necessary.

"No, I'm from Senegal. Dakar. My family's from very small towns, like this, Dahra and Linguère."

"Can't say I know it—but Africa? I always wanted to visit one day. Maybe Ghana or Nigeria." Brenda's face brightened, her smile only showing a hint of sadness. "Somewhere they speak English. You know, make it easier on myself. Was hoping Shanequa and I could see the motherland."

Mopti smiled at that. He found it amusing but understood the sentiment. He couldn't imagine what it would feel like not to know where he was from. He grew up knowing his father's family was from the little rural town "at the backdoor of the desert," as his mother would say, and his mother's was from near the train station, both dreaming of life in the big city, Dakar. His father said life in America was not anyone's dream until their little sister grew sick. Then a young Uncle Oumar had traveled in search of a medical education that somehow took him on this inexplicable detour.

"Shanequa, that's a beautiful name."

Brenda cut her eyes at him. Was he making fun of her? When she was satisfied he wasn't, she thanked him. "It means 'belonging to God.'"

"Beautiful."

"She is."

"How old?" Mopti asked. He turned down the radio.

"Seven. Turn down here."

Mopti was just about to say he had driven that same street three times already when Brenda suddenly shouted, "Bingo!"

He wasn't sure how he missed it. A few doors from the Benjamin Franklin, pressed between a hardware store and dry cleaner's, was a narrow building with a zipper-like staircase.

"Unbelievable," he said.

"And with that, I'll bid you good day and thank you, Mister . . . "

"Cissé. Mopti Cissé."

"Yes. Brenda Wells. Pleased to meet you. Be good, and I hope you find what you're looking for," Brenda said, opening the door.

"Thank you, Ms. Wells. I hope your daughter will be well soon," Mopti said. He felt that familiar wave of sadness again. He started to pull off when one of the waves softly brushed his spirit. He grabbed the receipt from his gas station bag and jotted down his number. "Ms. Wells, I hope this does not offend you. I mean no harm, but it would be good to have a friend in town. If it is okay, I will pray for you and for your dear Shanequa."

His eyes were earnest, but Brenda also could see the embarrassment glisten on his wide forehead.

He wavered. "Of course, no need to call," he stammered. "I leave that entirely to you. But it doesn't hurt to have someone else pray for you."

Brenda stared at him, her head slightly tilted, as if listening to a song he could not hear. Finally, she took the receipt and folded it in her hand.

"Thank you. Prayer is appreciated."

\*

## Sound Advice

Faded vintage posters plastered the walls. Burgundy velvet covered the steps. Mopti walked up each one, careful not to brush against anything. Flyers and event postcards dangled along the sides, stroked him like fingers as he passed. Mopti shuddered.

Now he knew why he had the devil of a time finding the place. *Must be a law against putting addresses on the buildings*, Mopti thought. The Sound Advice sign was near-invisible. Not until Brenda had pointed did he finally see "Vital Vinyl" in tiny letters beneath it. The rundown building was designed as if it was meant to fold up and disappear, accordion-style. Outside, steep stairs led up to a black-hole door.

When Mopti finished huffing and puffing, he looked around. Records filled the space, stacked in rows of teal-blue wooden shelves and orange plastic crates, spilled across wide tables. Vintage toys, stuffed animals, old 45s and 78s, and Christmas lights hung from the ceiling.

Album covers and occult signs and symbols decked the walls. Mopti saw at least three different kinds of Ouija boards. No one was in sight.

"So, what are you looking for?"

Mopti nearly jumped out of his skin. The voice was right behind him. A thin older man wearing a "Don't Hate the Player" shirt stood, hand on his hip, waiting. Castle Grayskull hovered over his head. He didn't look like an occultist, just a hoarder.

"Something rare—" Mopti managed to say.

"Rare? Listen, you ain't seen rare 'til you've seen my X-ray collection. Straight from the Cold War." His mouth approximated a smile. "Now, we thought we had bootleggers. You got to see what they made over in Russia. I mean *bone* music."

He waved and didn't wait to see if Mopti followed him. "They had to do everything in secret. Most of the good music was banned. See this?" He held it out so Mopti could note the illuminated ribcage. "They'd etch a copy right on an X-ray they stole from the hospitals, cut a circle with some kitchen scissors, and burn a hole right in the middle with a cigarette. Could play that sucker on anything, just as good as you please. Don't tell me what people can't do when they're pressed."

"I see," Mopti said, scanning the room.

"Okey dokey," Old Player said and placed the album back in its protective sleeve. "Bone music don't float your boat, so what is it?"

Mopti paused, sorting what he should say from what he wanted to say. The store looked as if a truckload of albums had exploded inside. Vinyl was everywhere he looked. Not a single CD in sight.

Old Player shrugged. "If you're into vinyl, you're into vinyl. It's not something you can explain. It's just in you."

"I don't think much of it's in me," Mopti said, "but my uncle, he definitely was . . . a collector."

"And what did he collect?" Old Player asked.

Mopti tried to answer. The house on Shands Bottom Road had piles of albums stored throughout every room, even the bathroom. Most, from what Mopti could tell, were blues, some jazz, but the collection spanned music from around the world.

"A single record, pressed by unknown hands, never widely released. Something called *The Great Going Song*? I think that's the name of it."

Old Player frowned. "Well, good luck with that."

"What do you mean?"

"Haven't heard that name in a long time. Most folks hunting for that good and crazy."

Mopti raised a brow. "Well, I try to be good. Not sure if I'm crazy yet . . . "

The shop owner laughed. "No disrespect, son, I'm just saying. Don't know if they start off that way, but seem like by the time they come through, they've lost it." Old Player squinted at him. "The last somebody call hisself looking for *The Great Going Song* looked a bit like you. Old Oumar. Y'all related?"

Mopti nodded and lowered his eyes. Shame made his cheeks feel hot and flushed.

Old Player turned around and picked up one of the faced-out albums. "Listen, you want some psychedelic acid jazz? Might as well listen to some of this." He handed the album to Mopti. "This is a rare one." He leaned his elbows on the counter as he moved the needle.

Suddenly the air erupted into the sound of blue crystals. Mopti felt as if he'd been rained on.

"What's your name?"

"Mopti Cissé."

"I'm sorry for your loss. Your uncle was a nice man. A little strange," Old Player said, "a bit obsessed, like most vinyl hounds, but ain't no sense in chasing after fairy tales." He stared at Mopti. "Especially tales that can get you killed."

If the *tick-tick*ing of the overhead fan had been a record player, the needle would have skipped and scratched. Mopti's eyes and lips formed a series of questions.

"All I'm saying is that folks been looking for that album a good, long time. Nobody's found it yet, but a whole lot of folks found some shit they wished they hadn't."

"Like what?" Mopti shivered.

Old Player shrugged. "Bad luck. Misfortune. Death. The usual stuff. Which is kinda funny since the whole point of *The Great Going Song* is to overcome death in the first place."

Mopti picked through a box of 45s on the counter. A James Brown bobblehead nodded at him.

"Overcoming death? I've been trying to understand why my uncle wanted the album so much. He spent a lot of time and resources trying to track it down, but there isn't much info about it."

Old Player looked thoughtful, rested his arms on the cluttered counter.

"Some hobbies have a way of taking over you. Collecting can be like that, like a drug. You never know if and when you'll grow addicted. Sometimes it's hard to figure out when you should stop—if you can stop." He stared at Mopti, his eyes like pennies. "*The Great Going Song* is not your ordinary record."

Mopti didn't like how Old Player was looking at him. He turned and dug through a crate. He paused at one: *From Senegal to Senatobia* by Otha Turner and the Afrossippi Allstars. "My uncle has a lot of these artists. Some he has multiple copies of. Is that *Going Song* album really valuable?"

A pinwheel spun over Old Player's shoulder. His eyes took on a waxy sheen.

"Why? You looking to get into collecting?"

"No. I was just curious." Mopti slid the *Allstars* back into the crate. "My uncle wrote a lot about different albums, but he never says who the artist is on the *Going Song*."

"Nobody knows. Part of the mystery. And yeah, rare vinyl can get up to crazy amounts. I know a previously unknown blues 45, from Sun, that went for $10,000. A 78 went for $30,000. But *The Great Going Song* is super rare, rarer than hen's teeth. Only three copies were made."

"Just three?"

"Yep. They say the album is made of the perfect sound, full of all the colors of our world. It's a miraculous key, said to open doors that only a god can."

"A god?" Mopti didn't like this kind of talk, and the more the man spoke, the more he sounded like Uncle Oumar's strange, manic notes.

"Only one number in our universal spectrum is the same color and sound, the core frequency of creation, nature, life. The original musical scale has only six notes, but they say that there are actually nine."

"Nine? Now you're speaking my language," Mopti said. "I'm an accountant. I speak numbers fluently. If there were six notes in the original music scale, how do you get nine?"

"It's called *The. Great. Going. Song*," Old Player said, emphasizing each word to reveal tiny, sharp teeth. To Mopti he looked irritated. "It is made up of the original six, solfeggio." He sang the notes, apologizing. "Forgive me. I'm no Maria von Trapp but you get the idea."

Mopti nodded. "I . . . I think so."

"Okay, well, you start with the original six that these old Benedictine monks created to sing their Gregorian chants but it's older than that, dates back to biblical days," he said. He took a sharpie from a red "Tighten It Up" cup and started drawing. "396, 417, 528, 639, 741, and 852," he said. "Plus three additional notes, 963, 174, 285. Together they form a perfect circle of sound, and that circle of sound can heal all things, make what is dark, light, what is broken whole. The nine sacred notes of healing. The basis for a song that can heal this broken planet."

Not sure how to respond, Mopti pursed his lips and nodded affirmatively. "We do need healing," he said awkwardly. He realized he would not be getting much help from here. The record-store owner, who by the way, had not offered his name, may very well have helped to fuel his uncle's bizarre theories.

"I've seen those eyes before," Old Player said. "The face of a skeptic. Fine. It's better that you don't believe. Because whether we do or not, there is no denying. We must find another way. And what is more universal than music? Every culture has a song."

"It's not that I don't believe, it's that I am struggling to understand."

"What's there to understand, Moby?" Mopti smiled. "It's clear that we're all off-center. The planet is unbalanced. We're not connected to that oneness you spoke of. Out of sync, probably running out of time. We are in dissonance to another note. But there are nine core creative frequencies to the universe. Nine, Moby. Everything in our universe is made from nine notes. *The Great Going Song* is what the coldest musicians have been striving for. They reach and they reach and some even get real close, but none have recaptured the legendary sound that's said to open God's front door."

"This talk of music and healing, that I can follow. But this other, it sounds . . . " Mopti did not want to offend the man, so he held his tongue.

"Dangerous? Yes. Remember what I told you when you walked in here. Folks have been searching, a long time, and they get caught out there. Sometimes when you search for gods you find the devil." Old Player's penny eyes flickered into slits.

Mopti remembered his uncle's cryptic notes, his Delta blues collection, and the lyrics full of references to deals with the devil.

"With the crossroads talk and all of that, how does this music connect with *The Great Going Song*?" he asked.

"A lot of blues and jazz got plenty of tritones, this space between notes that just don't sound right. And of course, wouldn't have no blues without that blue note. Church folks used to call it the devil's music. It's what gives the music that restless, rambling along feeling. What made it dangerous."

Old Player pointed to a black-and-white poster on the wall. "So, you get Tommy and Robert Johnson, no relation, talking about the devil at the crossroads. Now, Robert took this photo right at Hooks Brothers on Beale Street up in Memphis around 1935. It's the only known studio portrait of him. Look at that smile. Look in his eyes. You think that young man knew he'd be dead three years later? Some thangs you don't play with."

Mopti found himself inching toward the door.

"So, you take that 741 and 528 I told you about. Play them together and it creates a sense of dis-ease. Your body's trained to hear harmony but instead you hear that weird sound, like something's off, trouble gonna come. A sound strange as that—folks thought it could harm you, physically, emotionally, spiritually, so they called it 'the Devil's Interval,' the Tritone." Old Player thrust three fingers out, like throwing a curse. "But others know of it as just a key part of *The Great Going Song*. African polyrhythms, tonal notes, throat singing, all that heal."

"Like cats purring, healing their bones?"

Old Player looked at Mopti as if he'd suddenly grown two heads. "Yeah, well, I guess." An air of boredom deflated his words. "Browse all you want. Let me know if you see something you like."

Mopti turned to watch Old Player disappear behind a backroom door. He was gone as quickly as he had appeared. After an awkward silence, when it was clear the owner wasn't planning to come back, Mopti stopped his half-hearted crate digging. He placed the copy of Sun Ra's *Angels and Demons at Play* atop the counter on his way out.

That night Mopti unrolled his mat and prayed for his uncle. For his mother and his father who mourned him, even in anger. For the beloved aunt his uncle could not save. For the kind, sad woman he met who grieved for her child. He wasn't sure if he understood it, but he felt certain a great sense of loss united them all. Alone in the quiet solitude of his uncle's lonely house, Mopti felt the reach of greater hands moving them. Something besides death had called him across the waters, something that made Mopti reflect on what he may have lost in his own life.

The next day Mopti headed over to the library on Ward. He hadn't been there long when he was surprised to receive a phone call.

"Mopti, this is Brenda. How you doing?"

"I'm well, friend. Good to hear you."

She had just left the hospital, and invited him to join her for lunch. Eager to leave his window seat, Mopti tucked his papers and books in his backpack, waved goodbye to the friendly staff, and met her at Coleman's.

She was sitting at a table, nibbling on some fries. "Sorry, my stomach's in my back."

"Indeed," Mopti said, laughing.

"If I eat any more hospital food, they will probably have to check me in, too."

"How is she, your Shanequa?"

"Resting." She passed him a menu. "If you don't like pork, they have real good cheeseburgers."

They ordered burgers and gulped down soda as they talked, chatting about the rhythms that had shaped their lives. Brenda had Shanequa late in life, but the father left. *Everybody like miracles but don't nobody want to raise one.* Brenda had fled the city for the small town, in search of a quieter peace for her daughter, closer to family ties she'd long wanted to know. Mopti had remained in the city, where he could disappear in plain sight. The anonymity and routine of his work gave him comfort. The tiny hometowns of his parents, small stops between the desert and the river, would have made the pressure of constant social engagement and familiarity too much for him.

Brenda spoke with an openness that made him feel like she was one of his best friends, not that he had many. Over the next few days, they met for lunch or chatted, sharing more about their worries and their fears. Mopti now knew the child's condition was serious.

She was in an induced coma, awaiting to see if her brain and her lungs could relearn how to breathe on their own. Mopti shared some of Brenda's grief. He prayed for the child too young to have such a burdened heart.

One day Mopti told Brenda about his uncle's collection, his search for *The Great Going Song*, and his mysterious clues. When he mentioned all the Robert Johnson lyrics and research, she delivered Mopti his most promising lead.

"It's either the crossroads or the cemetery, Mopti."

"What do you mean?"

"We got a whole Mississippi Blues Trail that goes all through the state. If tourists come looking for Robert Johnson, they going to one of the crossroads or to visit one of his graves."

Mopti nearly spit out his water. "One of his graves? How many graves does the man have?"

"Mane, three. Can you believe it? But if you think about his life, short as it was—he was a certified member of the 27 Club—then it makes sense." She saw Mopti's puzzled face. "There are a lot of famous folks, mostly musicians, who all died tragically at age twenty-seven.

Robert's mama traveled a lot when he was young. They went from central Mississippi to here in the Delta, then she married about three-four times, or something. And he was between her new husband's in Memphis and folks near here. By the time he ran away, he had already been on the road anyway."

"Where are these graves?"

"Right around each other. One not too far from where he died. You know the story is that he was a bit of a catdaddy and got poisoned near Greenwood at the Three Forks Store by somebody's jealous husband. So, he's got a small grave marker out there in Quito, the middle of the boondocks. Another one at Mt. Zion Missionary Baptist Church in Morgan City, that looks like a big ole Egyptian obelisk. And the other one out on Money Road at *Little* Zion Missionary Baptist Church, also near Greenwood. A woman from the Luther Wade Plantation told somebody that her husband was the one that dug the grave. And it's near where he died, so there's that. But even so, knowing how tricky all this is, I wouldn't be surprised if he wasn't buried in none of them grounds."

"So, you think I should check out the graves first or the crossroads?"

"I'm not sure you should be doing any of this. All the sites are about an hour and half away, some at obscure locations. The Little Zion is where some of my kin are buried. I haven't been there in years. You know we don't like to visit old graves."

"I understand. There are so many different traditions. I covered all the mirrors in my uncle's houses, even though it was clear he didn't live in some of them."

"Y'all do that, too?" Mopti nodded. "There are some traditions where they will not remove the deceased through the front door but will cut a hole in the wall and carry them out feet first."

"That ain't the kind of hole in the wall you want to be in," Brenda said. "So, you're planning a creepy road trip. How are you going to get there?"

"Drive."

She laughed. "You can drive all you want, but you ain't gon' find that burying ground."

Mopti's smooth, moon-like forehead knotted up. "And why not?"

"The folk from out there, good people but private. They take care of each other and mind their business. Don't welcome strangers stomping all over their burial grounds. They come from a long line of runners. Restless souls. Even the land can't be still. Ground always changing." She snatched his uncle's scribbled map right out of his hand. "I'm just kidding. But you got to know there, to go there."

"Why can't I just use GPS?" Mopti said, taking the map back.

Brenda sighed. "If you couldn't get down Main Street with GPS, what makes you think you're going to make it through these back-woods?"

Mopti shrugged, laughing. "Brenda! You're right, you're right."

"I'm just sayin'." She took a sip from her water bottle. "You could try it, but trust me, the roads are tricky if you don't know where you're going." She pointed at his map. "It's not too far away. If you wait until Friday, I can ask my cousin to stay with Shanequa for me. We've got great-uncles and -aunts out that way. Haven't been to Mound Bayou in years, not since I was a kid."

"Why not?"

Brenda shrugged. "Most of that part of my family has passed on. The rest moved to Memphis or got on down. I don't really have no rea-son to go back that much."

"Well, okay," Mopti said. "Let's roll."

"Oh, we rollin' now?" Brenda said, and shook her head.

*

They started off early that Friday. Packed like mules, armed with shov-els, flashlights, salad, snacks, water, and the hand-drawn maps and notes from Mopti's uncle.

Everything started off well, but two hours later the laughter had drained out of them.

"I thought you said you knew where we were going?"

For the first time Mopti could recall, Brenda seemed at a loss for words. "It should've been over here," she said, pointing at his wrinkled-up map.

"Well, it's not."

"I don't know what to tell ya. You got to go there to know there," she said.

Mopti frowned and watched her pick through her salad, then drove a fork into his own.

"How many crossroads are in Mississippi? I mean, we have driven through five or six of them and haven't found that old church yet."

"You really think something's out here?" Brenda asked.

He shrugged. "I don't know, but my uncle seemed to think so. That house back in town is full of all his sketches and drawings. He believed the album was magic."

"Like magic *magic*?"

"Yes, healing magic."

Brenda looked up, stopped chewing. "What kind of healing?"

"That I don't know. The record-shop guy said it could heal the world."

"I told you he wasn't right. And you say he just dipped on you after all that? Weird as all get-out."

"What I could find in the library was just more of the same stuff Uncle Oumar had. Snippets of references in musician interviews. He kept a whole file on Robert Johnson. Most of it was just different versions on how he sold his soul to the devil."

"Lies," Brenda said. "They wrong for talking on that man's spirit like that."

"So, you don't believe it?" Mopti asked.

"Hell naw," Brenda said, laughing. "It's a good-ass story though. I'll give you that. But the truth probably is he went to the woodshed or found somebody who knew what they were doing, sat himself down somewhere and did his work. But naw! Got to be the devil. Got to be magic. Can't be that a negro actually worked his ass off. Sound like hatas hatin' to me."

"So, you don't believe in the crossroads and all that?"

"I believe, just don't believe Robert took that route. Think about it. If it was that easy, wouldn't be no souls left in none of these counties! Mississippi gon' straight to hell."

Mopti bit into a tomato. "Brenda, you're something else."

"But I'm right though. What if all this crossroads talk was just his way of talking about something he already know?"

"Like what?" Mopti asked.

"Like the heartbreak you get when you give all you got and end up with nothing. Keep in mind, we talking about folks chopping cotton on rented land—sharecroppers, landless farmers. Ain't no question he ran away from home young. You'd run away, too. Ran away from that backbreaking no-paying work in the fields. Ran away from his parents. He was a traveling musician, hoboing on trains and such. Playing on street corners for coins and dollar bills. You think he didn't have dreams? I know the biggest one—to escape."

They sat in silence, remembering their own gambits, disappearance acts, then got back on the weary road. They headed down 55, the blur of green and brown zigzagging, as one by one the mile markers ticked off each minute of their lives. They hurtled forward to what they hoped would not be another dead end, onward under the clouds and the scatter of wings, loose stitches of black in a sky threatening heavy rain.

*

## Up Jumped the Devil

They took turns holding the shovel as they passed the houses where no one lived. Cobwebs and dust guarded the windows. Mopti ducked under branches. Brenda swatted clouds of gnats that rose from the ground. Together they stepped over the flat faces of rock that watched them from the earth. Out in the woods, everything was bound together, the living and the dead. They walked among the carved names, passed soil-stained teacups, broken remnants of past lives, the black vertebrae of trees. They had found the cemetery, the place where everything comes to rest.

Brenda shuddered, skeeta-bit and full of regret. She wanted to help Mopti, but this was a road she wished she hadn't traveled. They would not catch her at sundown peering into amber bottles, a candle lit at the end. Souls were meant to be glimpsed only by their maker.

"Promise me we're not going to be out here grave robbing, right?"

"Of course not, Brenda."

"How you supposed to know where to dig?"

Mopti pulled out one of his uncle's drawings. "This looks like a big tree. I think from these notes, he was guessing the album would be buried under the Tree of Life. In my country, we call those baobab trees. Some of them are 6,000 years old, so wide you could drive a car through them. They look upside down, like their roots touch the sky."

"Nope," Brenda said pointing. "That looks like *two* trees to me."

Mopti followed her line of vision and realized she was right.

Two giant pecan trees stood like great sentinels in the back of the cemetery. Entwined, their gnarled, outstretched branches did look like great roots against the darkening Mississippi sky.

"Let's hurry up, mane," Brenda said swatting at something, "because walking back in the dark is not the move."

"Right," Mopti said and bowed his head at the tombstone. "I brought my torch," he said, then saw her expression. "Never mind."

Mopti dropped his backpack on the ground and put on his gloves while Brenda walked back and forth between the two trees, inspecting them.

"Did your uncle have any idea which of these trees we are supposed to be digging under?"

Mopti's eyes said it all. *Mmmpf, mmmpf, mmmpf.*

Mopti opened and closed his mouth three times without saying a word.

"Guess you better meeny-miny-mo it then."

"And what exactly is that, Brenda?"

She walked to the clearing in the center of the two trees and began to sing.

"Eeny, meeny, miny mo. Catch a tiger by its toe. If it hollers, let 'em go. Eeny meeny, miny mo. My mama told me to pick this one right over *here*." She bowed. "To the left, it is. And if it ain't, you can try the other one and then we're out."

"Deal," Mopti said, and he began to dig in the hard earth. It wasn't as easy as they make it look on TV.

Brenda watched silently, shifting her weight from foot to foot, a silent observer until it was her turn. "We out here diggin' for treasure like Pirate Jenny. Better be some money in this hole."

They were on the second tree, just about to give up, when Mopti let out a cry. Brenda turned the flashlight on it as the sun sank deeper in the sky.

"It looks like a bag."

Mopti brushed away the loose dirt and rocks. The soil felt cold to him, even through his gloves. "Thank you for being my friend," Mopti said, and handed the bundle to Brenda.

"You want me to—?" He nodded yes. She smiled nervously then handed him the light and bent down next to him. "Mopti, are you sure you want to do this? Because once we open this, you can't unring the bell."

"Open it," he said, his voice full of what he didn't anticipate.

"I'm trying but you're shaking the light. Hold steady."

Mopti was so weary but giddy, he didn't have the energy to argue or crack a joke. He waited as she unwrapped the cloth that covered it.

"Oh," she said and unraveled the fabric. "Ooh, this is wonderful. It looks like spun gold and water. But it's just a little damp. No telling how long it's been here." She pulled out another bag hidden inside. "Mopti!" She handed the album to him.

"This was your uncle's dream. You should open it."

"I don't think I can. I didn't know how I would feel, but now . . . " his voice trailed off. "My aunt Aminata died, young. Her death left a mark on my family. My uncle's choices left a mark on my father and he in turn left one on me. I am not sure I want to hold his dream."

Sheree Renée Thomas

Brenda knew something about marks, had lived under the burden of scars her whole life. To know that she had passed them on to her daughter was another burden she would always bear. She held the album, heart aching, unsure what to do.

"Just open it," Mopti said wearily. "It's okay."

She took a deep breath. The album sleeve was not something she'd seen before. Not paper, plastic, leather. It was made of a textile she didn't recognize. A message in a script she couldn't read was woven in the fabric. She pulled it off, resting the record atop the beautiful covering.

"Wow."

They both leaned over to see it better. It was black and coppery gold, splattered, watery waves staring up at them like an iris.

"Not bad for something we found buried under the roots of a pecan tree."

Mopti shook his head in wonder.

"There's a message here, in the dead wax." Brenda rubbed her thumb across the space.

"In the what?"

She pointed. "The part where there ain't no music. Between the end of the last song and the beginning of the label."

"Let me see." She handed him the record.

*Let the light set you free*, it said in English. Mopti turned it over, pointed the light so he could see. "This side looks more worn, but I think I can make it out."

"Bet you could read a whole book if you got out these woods." She swatted at some unseen predator. "Talking 'bout 'the light.' You know these mosquitoes out here are about as big as your head. I said I would bring you here, not get eaten alive while you sit up in the dark gawking."

"I'm sorry, Brenda, you're right. Let me get you home." He held the album, then placed it back in its covering. "I'm sure it's been a long enough day. And you'll want to get back to Shanequa, I know."

Brenda nodded, fatigue in her voice. "Thanks." She carefully re-packaged the album and tucked it gently inside its protective swaddling.

"Well, it's time to get our great asses going," she said. "I wonder what it sounds like."

Though he was ashamed and did not want to admit it, Mopti could not wait to hear what he had found. After they left the woods, giddiness and sadness guided him as he rode the car hard, barreling in the darkness, back through the flat, winding road.

"Mopti?"

He glanced over at her. "Yes?"

"I know you're happy to have found this thing you say your uncle left y'all for, but if I were you, I wouldn't tell nobody I found it."

Mopti turned down the radio. "I'm not sure if happy is the word. You know, my father was angry with Uncle Oumar because he left my aunt. Aunt Aminata, like I said, was their only sister. The youngest, she was always very ill. The family sent him to America to continue his education, but something happened. Now I have an idea of what. I wish I could have talked with him, known more about his life. For me, my uncle's biography is as elusive as your Robert Johnson. He was supposed to become a big-time doctor, doing research and maybe one day help find a cure. But he abandoned his studies—and," Mopti sighed. "According to my father, he abandoned my aunt, too. And all that to pursue this folktale. All those years, searching. And here it is." Mopti motioned at the bundle in Brenda's lap. "We've found what my uncle could not. He was so close before he died but now what?"

"So, you really believe he left everything to find this record? For you to find it?"

"Not any record, apparently, a legendary record," Mopti said, grief making his voice a hoarse whisper.

"Well, whatever his reason, Mopti, you found it. I have a feelin' a lot of other folks are gonna want what you got. Better keep it to yourself."

They drove thoughtfully in silence until he almost ran them off the road avoiding a deer.

"Damn, Mopti!"

"I'm sorry! I didn't see it."

They had no sooner corrected course when a truck shot out of the darkness, crashing right into them.

"Brenda!" Mopti yelled.

The car spun in the darkness, tires screeching disapproval.

For Mopti it seemed like everything happened in slow motion. They spun down the road forever, and then, in seconds, everything happened very fast. Mopti didn't know how long he had lain there, his head pressed against the air bag, before he realized he heard nothing in the passenger seat next to him.

"Brenda," he whispered. "Brenda!"

She raised her head, eyes focusing in the dark. "Stop hollering, Mopti. I'm alright, I think."

"I'm so sorry! I don't know what happened," Mopti said. "It just came from nowhere."

Brenda rubbed her jaw, then stopped. "*Shhhh*. Do you hear that?" she whispered. "Where is the music coming from?" She was staring over his shoulder when her eyes widened. He saw the scream before he heard it.

"Run, Mopti, run! Get that thing out of here!"

"What?" Mopti's voice was confusion, pain.

"The record! He's coming for it. I knew it was no accident way out here."

Mopti was caught between two impulses. Neither included leaving Brenda, possibly broken up, in a car that he was driving. "I'm not leaving you."

"You ain't got to," she said, and wrenched herself from the seatbelt. "Just grab the record and run!" Brenda kicked open the door, was gone before he could stop her.

Mopti reached in the darkness for the record. It had fallen on the floor, beneath the seat. When Mopti felt the burlap wrap, he half-suspected the album would be in pieces. To his surprise, the record was whole. He snatched it up, exited the car and took off.

"You can't hide, Moby, I see you. You shining!"

That voice, the butchery of his name. Mopti ran alongside the road, heading for the woods. Old Player limped behind him, shouting curses.

"You don't know what you have! Undeserving. Give it to me, boy!"

"What is wrong with you?" Mopti cried. "Why would you do that? You could have killed us!"

Old Player laughed. "Yeah, but what you got in your hands could have healed ya. Play your cards right and I might heal you yet."

Mopti panted, struggled to see as he stumbled through the woods along the road. There was a field up ahead, not much to hide behind.

"You're crazy. Are you the one that tore up my uncle's house? Looking for this old record?"

"That old record is worth more than you, your uncle, or anyone else you know, put together. None of that other stuff he got off me was worth a damn."

Mopti stopped running. He had to. Could barely see in front of him or see his way out of this.

"Did you hurt my uncle? Are you the reason he died?" He turned to face the man who would have killed him and Brenda, too.

"Natural causes, well, natural enough," Old Player said. "I told you, the album is supposed to heal but it's also cursed. Folks who get after it don't fare too well."

"So why are you chasing it now? You rammed a truck into us and ran us off the road for something you claim is going to kill you, too."

"Desperate times require desperate measures. You new to the game. Don't know what you got, let alone what to do with it," he said.

Mopti's head ached. His neck was stiff.

"And what do you plan to do with it? You sat back and let my uncle, me, do all the work, for what purpose? You couldn't possibly want to heal anything or anybody."

Old Player stood in the field, his hand at his side.

"You won't have to worry about that. I'm going to take good care of *The Great Going Song* and make sure it is never lost again."

"It doesn't belong locked up in your safe, like one of your finds. If it can do what you say it can, this belongs to everyone. It belongs to the world."

"The world isn't good enough. The world can go to . . . hell," he said, and aimed at Mopti's chest. Without thinking, Mopti used the album as a shield. The bullet must have rung through the air and hit the album, because Mopti suddenly felt a tremendous force. It vibrated through him, knocked him off his feet. He didn't even know Old Player had a gun.

*

### Another Shotgun Lullaby

Later, when he finally caught up with Brenda, who managed to flag down another motorist and came back to find him, Mopti played the moment over and over in his mind. He knew Old Player had shot at him. He heard it fire and then he felt its force. But then a bright light lit up the darkness, illuminating tiny coppery-gold flecks in the air. The space around Mopti warmed, heating up until he wanted to release the album, but found he could not. The bullet ricocheted off its black and coppery surface, a vinyl he surely had never seen. Old Player had cried out, then disappeared, replaced with fiery dust, like shooting stars.

That night when Mopti played the album at his Uncle Oumar's house, something once broken and shattered grew whole and wanting inside him. For the first time he understood what hunger was and what it meant to be truly fed. Hunger gave his mind something his body could neither eat nor keep. Home was no longer on the other side of the ocean where he left it. He listened to the song with no name and realized he had starved himself in ways that went beyond hunger. Who was he now, Mopti wondered, far away from his orderly desk, and how could he go back to whatever he had been?

Holes in his heart cried out to each other, one by one. And one by one they were filled. Strange cymbals, shouts, and snares floated through the air around him. Mopti felt a great presence slip inside his skin. The music simmered in his blood, walked in his bones. Mopti rarely sang beyond prayers. Now his voice was a choir. The sound of his own tongue hitting notes he never heard of frightened him, deep down in his soul.

He reached with shaking hands and snatched the needle up. It took a while for his heart to slow down, back to its normal beat, for his mind to catch up with his breath.

Old Mopti would have been too frightened to accept a gift so grand, a love supreme. Later when he found himself standing inside the hospital room's door, he could only agree.

"You live too much inside yourself, leaving everyone else alone," Brenda said.

"Not everyone, friend," he said.

Brenda turned away, hummed the song she always hummed at Shanequa's bedside. She sang it for Shanequa, for her roommate, for the other children who were hanging on the thread of life.

"So, you brought it," she said after a while. "Play it for me. I want to hear it, this *Great Going Song*. When I got home, I couldn't believe it. Got me out in the woods, about to get killed, feeling like Barnaby Jones and Nancy Drew. That's the *last* road trip I'm going on with you, Mopti Cissé."

Before he arrived and parked his rental, Mopti had it all in his mind. But now that he was there, listening to the child's tortured breathing, the machines wheezing, the other child also "resting," fear gripped his spirit again.

He wants to throw the album away; instead, he tries to break it. He pulls it out of its faded sleeve. It feels strange in his hands as it warms with his touch. Where there should be faint glimmers around the folds of vinyl, this time there is red copper and orange gold, silvery threads of light like circuit boards. He holds the album in his hand, then throws it hard. Instead of laying on the floor shattered, the shiny black pieces float in the air, rotate, and reassemble, returning to its protective covering as a great hum fills the room. Mopti stumbles back, shock on his face. His hands tremble.

Brenda cries out, disbelief struggling with fear, with faith.

"I don't know what we brought out of that ground, but somebody planted that seed years ago, and your uncle left it for you. I don't know if it's a curse or a blessing and this may be a bell I can't never unring, but if you ever loved somebody, anybody as much as I love this child," Brenda says, her voice even, measured, "you would try anything, too." She shakes her head. "No. *Try* wouldn't be enough. You'd do it." She has mastered the tone that conceals pain, but her eyes, her eyes give her away.

Mopti unwraps the shimmery gold-and-blue fabric, slides the album out again and let its warmth guide his hand. The small portable LP player he'd hidden in his messenger bag now rests on the nightstand. He puts the needle to the vinyl, realizing how much he has grown to like this ritual, of needle in wax. He waits for the lisp and hiss. Watches Brenda's eyes as the record turns and Shanequa's right leg trembles. He hears the most beautiful sound.

"Mama."

The album spins and spins, scarab wings furling and unfurling. Only three pressed in the whole world. Somehow his uncle managed to find one. The initials and press markings are symbolic. He knows without knowing how he knows that there are two hidden tracks on the album. One plays at 45, the other at 78. *The Great Going Song* plays three speeds.

Time will pass. Time passes. Time passed.

Mopti's thoughts were one long spiral, moving from the outside to the inside, then back again. He would have to unlearn silence to be a true friend to her. He knows without knowing how he knows. He looked at Brenda holding Shanequa. Or maybe it was the daughter who held her mother up. No, he thought, watching them together, watching as the child in the other bed opened his eyes. He thought of his Uncle Oumar, his father, and their sister, his aunt. He thought about all the years of love missing between them because they did not try. Trying wouldn't be enough. Mopti let the strange music play and play.

# RETURNING

## Aerik Francis

chlorophyll explodes brilliant
bouquets in post-supernova
black evergreen & redwood
dreams aquamarine needled

leaf offerings to past lives
    *bless those foolish*
    *humbled humans*
sprawling reefs reclaim

creeping & weeping sea
deep-seated sanguine
thickets of polyp limbs
stretching skyward pathing

atmosphere honeyed
what was once polluted
now transmuted carbon
returning to breathing earth

# ABOVE GROUND

## Melanie Merle

Give me soft sides
Plastic blue curve of water
White spines like corset bones to hold a shape
Slippery step on a hanging ladder
Keep me above ground
Flatten out the grass to sickly anemic white
Faded from green
Give me sun-warmed piss water
Worn elastic swimsuit fibers
Signs of poverty
Of things missing
Because underneath all that
Is solid ground
PB&J cheap lotion sunburned exhaustion
Half-naked sleep
Vibrating attic fan and lilac air
Under cotton sheets
So worn they feel like silk
Sweet smell of baby sweat
And Summer
  And freedom
    And real things
Above ground

# RED GREEN BLUE

## Cindy Juyoung Ok

Zaina and I were the least impressed because we were from California.

She noted the grape farms outside of Masala looked just like Santa Barbara; at the Turkish steps outside of Agrigento when Shreya asked rhetorically if we'd seen anything like them, I listed Pacific beaches with caves and stones, taking the grand for granted. Everywhere seemed to us to have a controlled, kind prettiness in Sicily, not the nature we had to grow up fearing—quake, drought, wildfire. It's sort of childish, even, those old castles and pine trees, and I wasn't in the mood to perform wonder for Marco.

Marco had been living in central Italy for nine months and spoke Italian in a singsong and gestured way that felt, to me, mocking. It sounded like he was doing an impression of an expressive Sicilian, which I suppose as a Jersey boy he was. But locals loved it, relaxing when he started speaking for the group. Over the course of the week, strangers spoke with him for stretches longer than twenty minutes, often complimenting his beautiful accent.

The afternoon I arrived with Shreya and Zaina was spent mostly waiting for Marco to finish these lines of questioning. Dave and Marco had been traveling a week already, and Dave had developed a routine to retrieve our host when he felt ready to move on from Marco's free language lessons. Five or six minutes into a conversation, usually about street names, Dave walked past him and patted his back, then waited for the wrap-up. Only Zaina found Marco's endless interest in strangers charming—I thought it made him seem lonely and plain.

Dave thought Marco seemed more animated in the Italian language, that on past trips he had been glum, more passive. We agreed Zaina comes across more pensive in Arabic, Shreya funnier in Gujarati, and I more flippant in Korean. Shreya remembered her ex-girlfriend whose Alabama accent awoke only during sex, and I shared, too, that the person I was dating had lately been grumbling things in Portuguese even after I asked if the idea was his self-expression or my understanding and he said the latter. Then the group took turns repeating the Brazilian phrases I could remember in exaggerated Italian accents, teasing Marco but probably seeming to impersonate locals.

Zaina claimed not to know the equivalent word for "amazing" in Arabic because it was too strong a sentiment for anyone in her family to imagine. I laughed and said we don't have a word for "please." She imitated her dad, a serious sheik, giving his version of high praise, restrained statements of fact. I said for the rest of the night we should speak in our parents' accents, but we found it hard to copy their speech for longer than a phrase or two.

On our way home, Zaina made a face and pointed out a swastika tagged in black on a tan wall. I had seen two others and I wondered why the men were not noticing. As we got home via a series of alleys, Shreya told us that in her public defender's office they liked to assign each case a fantastically petty theme song and play it on repeat late nights in the office; during an indecent exposure case for a couple that fucked in a city alley, they worked to the sounds of "we found love in a hopeless place."

*

We were traveling the week of Easter, and when there were tourists, they were Italian. Marco was proud that we were in Sicily at the right time, and in keeping with the holiday, he told us forty-some times that week that what is referred to as Catholic guilt (which would be external-facing, and bridging) is actually shame (self-laid, isolating).

Every night I thought of the idea of the party within the party: that in any group of people formed for any amount of time, there is always an inner core. Shreya and I were together in the middle and we assumed everyone else knew. Each day was a basic reconfiguring of all our shapes, me talking to Dave on the way to dinner and Marco using his phone to direct us while Shreya and Zaina walked ahead, or Zaina and Marco going for a walk while Shreya and Dave napped in the living room and I cooked in the kitchen. Each night was then a peeling—Dave to sleep first, then Marco, then Zaina. The night always ended in bed with Shreya.

On that second night, she and I addressed the fact that her partner, a man, had been resentful of me for many years. I offered, to appease her idea of his image, that it was not surprising he would feel threatened since her longest relationship had been with a woman, though Shreya and the ex no longer spoke. And then I asked if, at forty years old, he could at least be more subtle than ignoring me in a park and looking near tears when she and I talked at a party.

I knew that for the rest of the trip she would bring up his job as a labor organizer two or more times a day, a fact that sustained her vanity and sense of self. She often teased him for being large and bungling, knocking old ladies with his backpack on the F, even referring to him as Lennie (as in George and Lennie) to his face. I wanted to say the party within the party is the person you can anatomize everyone else's psyche with, not the one you deem character and tragedy. Instead I fell asleep shortly after asking "what else makes you anxious?"—which she told everyone in the morning, feigning distress at sharing her list to a snoring body. Once in a period when we were falling in love and not acknowledging it, I woke early and went home with my things and she complained that she woke up "feeling used and abused." And even though she was joking, and even though we weren't actually fucking, after that I always left a note.

\*

Driving the next day, Marco played music from a playlist on his phone that he had clearly curated while alone all this year, specific songs that, in combination, were meant to express his personality to an audience. After we placated him with several compliments about the lyrical choices, I told the car about this study in which three two-dimensional shapes move around in randomized combinations on the computer, how all the participants watching created narratives like "the green triangle is bullying the circle and the square" and "the blue circle was too close to the green triangle so the red square bumped the blue circle, but then the green triangle moved away from both of them until the red square returned sheepishly."

Shreya said she had a new therapist she loved, and they had been talking a lot about her sister, who was older and sadder than her. She gave the group a spiel I could mouth with her, pauses and tonal changes and all, about how she doesn't understand why her sister is still so resentful that their parents were never home growing up because they worked long hours, double shifts: "It's not like they were out clubbing or something."

During Shreya's story, Marco realized he had forgotten to call his brother, who was about to end a long relationship. This was only the third day, but it was obvious the calls would be a pattern. Every time he came back from talking to his brother on the phone for an hour, pacing, often making us wait in the sun, he gave the same report but in the intonation of new information. He made alive for us the state of his brother's knowing what to do and being afraid to do it.

Everyone took a nap that day and in our bed Shreya said she was sorry about last fall. Then after we both looked up at the ceiling for ten minutes, she whispered that if she were younger, we would be together, that she hadn't known how to be in love and act on it. It sounded like she had wanted to be convinced. I didn't respond because I didn't like the narrative that I had missed an opportunity, that the fact that I had been respectful of her partnership was a character flaw, and not a moral lucidity for which I should receive medals. Also she had called me "too loud" earlier in the day and I thought silence was a good opportunity to regain some power in the fissure between us.

*

Dave left that night and at dinner I asked if it seemed like Marco was our pimp. Shreya and Zaina said their brown skin passed as Sicilian and I was the only one looking pimped. I told them what my dad had said in passing when I was young: "wherever you go, you'll be a foreigner." Which made everyone sad, so they accused me of ruining the joke to deflect. Zaina told us how obedient she had been as a child of such a pious dad, repeating not only his rules but also his mannerisms. I showed Shreya and Marco the childhood photos of her that I had on my phone, in which she was visibly uptight and always looking beyond the camera at someone next to or behind the photographer.

On the fourth day, we drove to Marsala to meet White Chris, which everyone began calling him the year we worked with Black Chris, even though White Chris's dad is Palestinian, because he is also white, down to his constant confidence that things might work out fairly. On our first night all together, Marco took a call halfway into dinner, and White Chris, who had now been in Ramallah two years, gave us updates on Black Chris's divorce and on the recent arrival of a major TV streaming service to Palestine. Zaina showed us the email her cousins there had sent her that day with screenshots of US shows, and Chris said he thought of it because Marco seemed to use talking on the phone the way another generation did (normal and necessary reasons like to kill time, numb self), the way today people use TV.

White Chris brought us bookmarks with Arabic words and sayings but he and Zaina couldn't read most of them because of intonation chang-es—the dot on top could change the meaning three ways. Or maybe be-cause the artistry blocked the precision. He said that as he learns it, he realizes it's a language in which words for the body, even for animals, are not centered. But in what language is the body centered? I could only think of "everybody" and "nobody" in English. I joked to Shreya in the bathroom that he and Marco might have shared their revelations about their grandmothers' homelands a little more to each other and less to us.

That night when we got home, Shreya started to have lower-back pain on her right side, and I read from my phone a page called "Bladder Care for the Elderly." She was thirty-five, nine years older than me. We both passed for college students, as we had the many years we had known each other, each younger and more attractive than people at parties told us they imagined a public defender or a math teacher would be. "I know I look like a camel," she used to say, "Cute, but exactly like a camel."

The only reason our pairing was invisible to the rest of the trip, I thought aloud, was that neither of us were men. I asked her if she'd ever had an abortion and then we fell asleep talking about liking less-rich flavors as we got older, about the newfound sweetness of a good lemon tart, a clean and candied almond. That night I dreamt of pipes—a functional and beautiful above-ground system.

*

On Easter, we drove out to an agriturismo, a state-subsidized rural farm stay with restaurant service on weekends. Although Marco didn't use the word "authentic" to explain this, I felt sure he was restraining himself, especially once we got there and saw animals roaming and lemons dropping from trees.

The first course made us hopeful, with five little sections of appetizers on a plate, but we then waited an hour and a half for the second course while the families around us got their cannoli and coffees. Marco listed the stereotypes of Italians that he said became stereotypes because they were true (and only in their inappropriate application was there any immorality). Italians are late, loud, gestural, obsessed with food, and, he said, blessed with inherent fashion sense. He was wearing a version of what he'd been wearing every day, a brightly colored sweater on top of a dress shirt, differently but equally loudly colored, not tucked into his khaki shorts. I asked him if he had many pairs of the same shorts or was repeatedly wearing the one pair.

At some point Zaina brought up the circumcision ban pending in some European countries, which the group started debating (noisily, like Italians). I left the table to shit in the outhouse, and when I got back Shreya was talking about our friend who was the first in her family to not have vaginal mutilation. I wasn't paying attention so as I sat down, I added that I was the first in my family to not have a birthday that moves around, a day on the solar calendar. Then I noticed that Shreya had tears on her reddened cheeks and had her finger pointed out with rage directed at Dave, but had sort of pivoted in disbelief at my interruption and was pointing at me. Every trip or party, they would argue once like this and then forget by the next morning who had been on what side. As a child I said to my mom when she was upset about my brother and me fighting: "We do this because we're bored. You really didn't know that?"

We now couldn't remember a time when we weren't at this restaurant, in these seats, hungry, but we bravely gathered the energy to come together as a group to disparage a prominent white abolitionist many of us knew and found insufferable. Dave said that her multiple assistants are underpaid, and one's entire job is to book her interviews and speaking gigs. We caricatured the theoretical Marxists we knew who refused material or social consequences to their politics—how they all styled their bangs, Bushwick one-bedrooms, and claims of unlucky lives the same way.

When one family got three desserts each, Marco went to talk to the servers and then the managers. He reported back that this had clearly been a shame to the restaurant and the region, that they went to go get more fish, but that we had to wait because it would make them feel worse if we left. Marco felt embarrassed on their behalf, though it would be more logical and useful for him to take responsibility for the Italian Americans of the greater tristate area than to identify with the humiliation of this family.

*

Finally we decided that the fish was not coming, had never been on its way, and paid a portion of the set lunch cost and drove to Palermo to see some old palace. We passed some cacti and I admired them out loud. "They always remind me of home," I said, since no one was listening. When we stopped to get coffee, White Chris and Zaina agreed the tiles in the coffeeshop looked similar to those made at the Hebron glass factory. Walking through a courtyard to get to the palace, the two of them riffed on racism within Levantine Arabs, and Shreya and I chimed in. Marco asked us if we thought the types of generalizations we made on such a regular basis were out of internalized racism. Zaina agreed other things we say in part were, but said that comment in particular hadn't been. I rolled my eyes and tried to collude with the others, but Chris and Shreya came to the consensus that it was hilarious but lazy, leaving me to be the only champion of carelessly wide racial essentialization.

I argued it was a performative abstraction that nonwhite people and immigrants do to affirm our identities in a lateral way as we make jumps between generations in experience and external markers. Then everyone else rolled their eyes and then we had an eye-rolling contest and agreed the sole Desi was the best at it, with even Marco playing along and saying it was because South Asians have deeper-set eyes.

When we got to the palace, we took a group photo as a favor to Chris, who had been asking all day. Beyond the building, alongside evergreen trees and gift kiosks, there was a set of eight individual trampolines on an inflated platform, with tiny shoes scattered by the hanging sign: "5 Euro per 5 minuti." We joked noncommittally about it and then haggled with the slouching old person sitting outside it to get a group price. A woman behind us started speaking in dialect, which Marco could not understand, but her body language seemed to defend us getting on for cheaper. Everyone else in the line was Italian and was a child.

In the end Shreya paid the bartered price for us and afterward everyone made preposterous statements that felt very true, like *I need to do that every day* and *that was the best five minutes of my life*. Zaina teared up with laughter as we all pointed and screamed at each other. It was so fun that I was crying too, but I wiped as I jumped and hoped no one noticed. Cosmetic American pop played on the speakers. Children watched us jump with their parents behind them, waiting for their turn.

*

The next morning, Marco came home with stuff for *ful*, including beans in the shell. Shreya was reading George Jackson's prison letters and read aloud from the mentions of his high school, which happened to be the high school where I was teaching. She told us about how disappointing it usually was to have her cases make it to print, because of all that was frustratingly left out. That was also the day she complained that the laws protecting accusers of sexual assault are reactionary and unreasonable responses to the invasive 1970s practices like listing sexual histories as a shaming strategy. Zaina and Chris were upset about Shreya's framing, citing how few rapists go to prison, but I felt defensive. Shreya didn't think anyone should go to prison, and she had often fought white accusers and white juries who convicted Black men, once even ending in a client being deported to Ethiopia after two long trials. I remember she was angry all that year.

Later, when I closed my eyes on the couch but wasn't asleep and Shreya was in the shower, Chris out on a run because our daily step count had been inadequate, I heard Zaina and Marco gossiping about an activist organization they had both worked with. Zaina said the woman who ran it had been colluding with a certain anti-Muslim governmental agency's contractor that often employed Muslims to do their dirtiest work. Marco didn't believe it, though he had heard that her brother's death had hit her hard and in strange ways.

I had briefly dated her other brother, who was younger and often framed his sister's activism as a product of her unwillingness to deal with childhood trauma, a way to stay in control with rage instead of experience helplessness in grief. I said chemists do that, too, but that doesn't mean the chemistry they discover isn't right. Although once I was at her apartment picking him up and I did see that she had all these packages from Amazon.

*

That was our last full day, and Shreya and I argued at lunch but no one noticed. She accused me of judging her relationship for its orientation toward safety and away from rigor. We had co-judged all of our friends for that, out loud, for years, but I apologized anyway and she found my apology condescending so then we spent twenty minutes giving our different definitions and examples of condescension. Eventually I started agreeing with everything she said, my voice creepily calm and cooperative.

We planned the morning drop-offs: Zaina was flying home through London, and Shreya and I had a flight to Rome before going our separate ways. White Chris had another week of travels planned with Marco, leaving lots of time to exoticize their own cultures together. Marco explained not having to tip in Italy for the sixty-fifth time. Tip culture in Europe is different than in the US, he desperately wanted us to know.

Shreya and I talked after dinner at a bar with lots of children. Maybe they were all sixteen or eighteen, but truly, many of them looked ten. She said she felt sensitized about my reading of her relationship because she wasn't sure herself. I said I wasn't the enemy. The others were arguing about attachment theories, from what I could overhear when I knew what point Shreya was making and tuned out for ten or fifteen seconds at a time. Eventually they started complaining about the coldness or warmth of their mothers and how they were turning into them.

After sorting with Shreya, however patchwork-like, I felt generous energy. Walking home with Zaina, I took turns assuring and challenging her about moving forward in what we unironically referred to as her sexual awakening, working out aspects of the practical negotiation with her strict growing-up. Then White Chris sorted through his thoughts on where he should live next and why. Both were interesting conversations driven by my hope of getting to the end of the day, to Shreya. It got late enough that we thought we might stay up waiting for the cab. Shreya wanted to nap for twenty minutes but Marco came in playing an awful song by the Cranberries that we had caught accidentally on repeat in a café early in the trip.

Since we were up, we got pizza from the plaza at four a.m. and on the way back Marco told me he had twice dreamt of sex with his mother, and that he had never told anybody. I said men were always telling me they dreamt of sex with their mothers and that they had never told anybody. I theorized that this was why everything is blamed on mothers, explained by the resentment of and sympathy toward them: globalization, schizophrenia. He told me Il Papa is the Pope, and papa is the dad—we agreed a Catholic psychosexualization. Zaina interjected to say that's haram, because in Islam Allah is separate from the family.

As a child, at church with a friend's family, their pastor announced proudly that integrity is only having one story. Later, when they asked what I thought of the service, I repeated the phrase slowly to project the sense that I found it profound and profoundly true, before pretending to recognize a painting on the far wall. It was one of the stupidest things I had heard about integrity, or story, and was so Christian and American in its binaryness. There are always multiple realities, and to create and maintain one story is what takes childish self-deception. It's a much more insidious violence to deny the nature of memory and interaction, isn't it?

There's the story of Marco feeling that I abstract too much and that it's cowardly, the story of his professing his love for Shreya two summers ago and her laughing about it to me later. The story of Zaina's constrained interest in Dave and in White Chris's new money, Chris's passive-aggressive comments about any music we heard or played and how they revealed his conviction that he truly could have made it as a jazz musician in a luckier life. The story of Zaina's alternating constipation and diarrhea, which we often organized ourselves and our conversations around on this trip.

Or of the way in which some of our parents were in structural competition with each other to get visas in the seventies and eighties. The reasons behind a few of us eating garlic with the peel and the others never having thought of it. Or how Brady violations transformed from a Supreme Court case to become a core of any American public defender's day of fighting fire with fire. There's even the story that the Prophet Muhammad didn't think he would get into heaven himself, which I think is supposed to be a lesson in humility.

*

In the morning, Zaina finished casting off the blanket we had been switching off knitting for our pregnant friend, who would find out the next week that the fetus had a rare genetic mutation that would not be painful for parent or child but might be expensive to accommodate after birth. Shreya and I tried to sleep on the short flight to Rome, but mostly we chatted, preserving our countable final moments to memory.

I said children are often static on trips but then make huge developmental jumps when they get back home. She asked what it was like to be a child and whether the point of this story was that she should be envious of my twentysomething brain. She told me about some twins born with attached skeletons, that the words for yesterday and tomorrow are the same in Gujarati, and how galaxy distribution tends against randomness. Then about the woman who had raised her while her parents were out not clubbing, and the stories she—her name had been Puja—kept repeating in the weeks she was dying. As we landed, Shreya did an impression of White Chris being enamored with his newfound sense of culture and I knew what made it funny was that for him it was a choice.

Walking toward separate gates, I knew she would repeat this Chris impression to kind and acceptable Lennie later and mostly omit our bed conversations from her telling of this trip, and she knew I would find my own ways to deaden my days, my own translation of the stories. I had what I wanted, which was an admission of desire. I don't know if she had what she wanted. As we walked, I knew what we would miss was this, not having to say what we both knew was going to happen.

*

The blue circle will follow around the green triangle until it grows tired and turns around to rest, and then the green triangle will confront the red square in a corner while the blue circle flits around, thinking. The red square will feel overwhelmed at first and flee the green triangle, but eventually become exasperated and push it out of the way as it skips to ask the blue circle to band together. The red square and the blue circle will start dancing, but the blue circle will slow down first and apologize. The green triangle will approach the two, but the blue circle will casually disregard it and leave the red square to slide over and touch, lightly, the orange rectangle.

# VIOLET

## Lucien Darjeun Meadows

Ulogili, birdfoot, common blue. Blush in your sex,
Bruise on my chin. Chalk dust and wasohla wings. Quiet
Under sycamore. My face pressed to bark.
Squish of toes in spring mud. Stillness after.
Uweyv'i rising beside, we hear the call—
More silence than whisper, smell of first rain
Never leaving my palms, tongue. We love like
No other blooming. Never trillium,
Angel's trumpet, beebalm. First uganawa wind, new
Fuzz on your chin. Slant of light, your long hair,
If only, only, to hold hands walking
Down the dirt road. Somewhere a deeper shade
Of blue. Backs of your knees cup like petals,
Filled with salt. These ganvhida nights of rain, what thirst.

# AFTER,WORD

## George Abraham

*Break and leave your husband for me.*

There was a comma in that sentence, a period, maybe a *with* at some point too, but I seem to have misplaced them. Is it possible to misplace a husband like that?

There are hundreds of definitions for *compactness*—the most abstract involving open sets & finite covers, though most boil down to space *that is both closed & bounded*—though none are predicated on one's proximity to singularities or other men.

I'm reading a novel about a Queer Palestinian with a clinical love addiction & I've never felt more Seen in american literature, though *love (& american)* here, of course, boil down to *idea of,* hence, the infinite folded into a single body, hence, a compactification.

*Romantic* as in more interested in doing a deep Reading of that single high note in "Shallow," as sung by Lady Gaga, than anything (redacted & canonical) has ever written.

*Who am I kidding?* said the man as he came inside me. I couldn't see his face, so he didn't have one.

Silly. No man ever cums in me, they only ever come

inside. The lines are Broken even if you cannot see them that way, you're welcome for

The first draft of this poem was titled "at the end of the world, I still / couldn't tell you *I love you*." Though I didn't know who it was to, let alone For.

The poem, unlike me, unraveled in couplets, as you might have guessed.

At one point the you in the poem became a multitude. At another it became a self I didn't recognize. Or deserve. Both were instances of running from.

I couldn't trust the poem in my hands after that.

Before Marwa asked me, *Are you in love, or is he just a distraction?*

I've been thinking about how colonial it is to consider one's fear of dying in a time like any time really. To even write *apocalyptic* is to assume a certain immortality, a boundlessness.

There's an image I've rewritten before, of that rough patch of bumpy skin that hugs my tricep like a question mark—the one Marwa noticed at a wine bar once, then lifted her sleeve to expose her own, & said *these are the scars from when they stole our wings*. Though I don't think the image has found the right poem yet. The assumption, being. Angelic.

Shortly thereafter, we had the conversation that led to my first book's title: *Birthright*.

Earlier that day, a man shouldered me into a bus window after glaring at my *Palestinians for Black Power* shirt. When I turned around, his shirt read *Birthright*.

Thereafter, I wanted to steal that & every word from him. Light them on fire. I confess, I wrote *Birthright* for people like him, if only for a single moment.

If you're reading me, I want you to feel small, dare I say, compact.

Yes, I've considered my skin's betrayal, a cloudlessless.

e.g. we can look into the sky & see technically infinite space, yet our memory of it is housed in countable cells. I consider many notions of *imagination* a kind of compactness in this way.

e.g. *adult brains lose 1 neuron per second,* I am told, by a man who wasted 95 million neurons of my time.

With each passing second, I am becoming less capable of remembering my own history, my own construct of self, & yet language, we are told, crystalizes. Consider language & memory as competing processes.

I don't think my imagination is brave enough for the Poem in this. Don't forgive me for that.

The first time I ever saw the word *birthright* was in an email announcing a "free trip to israel" for american high schoolers. I admit that fourteen-year-old me read the application, wondering how easily I could lie my self onto that trip. I didn't understand the bounds, the closings, imposed on my Palestinian-ness then.

Or maybe I'm writing to reach that exact self, the exact limitless, who knew that to Return is to muscle memory.

I constantly fantasize about fictionalizing that memory into a story where a Palestinian boy sneaks onto a Birthright trip &, with his name, his un-accent, fools everyone, into thinking he Belongs there. Though maybe the real tension was the divergence of self.

The boy makes no friends in the story. The boy doesn't fall into a grand is-raeli Palestinian love affair. In every version of the story, the boy leaves the trip after rediscovering his inhumanity in small talk over baba ghanouj, tasting it as less a failure in proportion than an absence of ash.

There was food & reiterations of *Palestinian* & jokes of under-seasoning in the story & there it became *for* who the story wasn't For. In this way, it could have almost been mistaken for a Diaspora Poem.

Though, I wanted only to write the story for its closing images—the boy running, barefoot in the Mediterranean at dusk, whispering back to the waves: *you wouldn't believe how far I've come to tell you this.* The two of them laughing like friends from a past life, before the police lights—

I've re-entered the same story again & again & every time, I romanticize the distance between: light & pigment, skin & sound, country & memory of.

I need memory to be boundless, then. More infinite than.

Don't say border. Don't metaphor.

I cannot unname the ocean here & it is almost as unforgiveable as a love letter I once wrote, ending: *isn't living for your country just a slower way to die?*

Every day is a country I refuse, to die for.

*Aren't you tired of trying to fill?* That void.

Some faggotries are always apocalyptic, even when what others know as *world* is not disappeared—somehow, a dance, aflight. Is always.

I wonder if, years from now, assuming we even get there, someone will look back & write about the use of bird metaphors to understand The Quote Unquote Flight Of The Palestinian People.

Omar says it is so *human* to leave & here I consider the opposite of faith, as anything but an absence of. *Come*

is the opposite of a promise, that I am always never someone's

lover. Let me try this again: once there was a wilderness. In mapping, it became a closure. In nation, a bounding. In this way, every notion of country is a compactification of

self—I told you there was Breakage

here, even if you could not See it consider it a misplaced comma (period (image—

I'm trying to reach a *you* by the end of this, even if it leaves me bending backwards & kidding myself. once upon a time

there was the country you left & there was the country you could return to.

Say *leave*. Call it *leaving*. Consider the space between those found notions & collapse it into a single wingspan, the way every writing of history is an act of re(dis(possession)))).

Once upon a time, someone considered all of this a *love story*. The space between abandonments, a finite.

Let me try this again: some notion of *world* is ending. There's a boy I can perceive only through glass & distance—& I cannot tell him what I can

not. I leave him unfinished as a country

I cannot abandon. The honesty is as underwhelming as it is compactifying.

*Gaze into me* or *gays into me*. The choice is

yours. I do not consider my self, a multitude, or husbanding grief.

There's a poem that ends in its own speaker's birth but I haven't Found it yet. There's a poem that swaps every notion of *birth* & *marriage*, & is okay living in the brief distraction of its body.

Over a thousand possibilities of *self* died with this poem. You're welcome

To exit, wound. Consider the competing, processes. The cum &. Gone, just

leave. I want you

to leave me, *and*.

Leave me. Be.

# HOW CAN THERE BE SO MUCH DEATH AND ALSO SO MUCH LOVE

## Sarah Sophia Yanni

we spent summer in the park being poked by grass blades
    brown and desiccated      but still
placing bare feet on earth
    is grounding       and I shudder with joy as the warmth of afternoon
    sun creeps up my pallid arms like
        *yes you have a body   and it's scabbed*
            *but it can have sensation as a gift*


a black roly poly crawls over your hand, making home
      atop your index finger knuckle     I dream of this flexible skeleton
the ability to turn one's whole self inward         yet we conflate safety
with fear, choice     with a mere reaction
      plowing through fact with some
      imposing narrative       maybe that's what it means to be a writer
I want all proverbs to be legible, each bug
       to be indexical of meaning


       across the blue blanket, I gaze at the person
     I love       now an object in a notebook, not a *we* or a *you*
        gleaming with agency
   it comes down, perhaps, to privacy       to love is to keep them abstract
      a strategy of non-exposure, only the edifice

of a lover      like a cosmic form      whose edges
          strangers can collide with, but never fully comprehend


the grandness of the sky reorients the mind   clarifies
      the urgent      my neck tenses
          *I forgot to call abuela*
I am told every day is different but this week it's been worse
      grief cycles are impossible to predict      impossible, also
            to pacify      via garbled mobile phone calls


each year, a fraction of wisdom finds its way into my lap      I am learning more
and more but mostly I'm learning      that being is hard, as in
being told a tragedy    at seven in the morning
                I was in the bathroom                      glued to the heater
its glowing red coils an integral part of my daily routine
                  there is never a right thing
            to say, and this, sometimes
                  is worse
the tragedy of unexpected loss      and the tragedy of language's absolute failure


            a silence burning in the back of my throat
      I hate the word                  *condolences*
the way it marks your feelings as performance      it's not a phrase I'd ever utter
      from my gut, not a thing I'd whisper as I hold
            a weeping elder against my chest, or watch her glitch
      on a cell screen camera


            who    this year      hasn't thought of death
            *you're not special*
      but does everyone also get the panic vomit feeling when remembering
            an open casket   or the documentary about children in mass graves

George Abraham

onslaught of images and violence
I'm tired

but don't have the right to be

the grass is too wet     but I accidentally stopped
caring in june
    stain fatigue, death fatigue
the fatigue of releasing
predictability, like adjusting one's eyes to the dark
    over and over and over again


how many hours have passed here?

and if the tree above could talk          what would it say?

    I wonder and hope     a glistening chorus of crackled branches

        *I am writing this so it will stay true*

        cariño: hold on tightly        for however long

            this is all there is

# DREAM OF THE SUN SPIRIT

## Juan J. Morales

The landscape is an infinity of Japanese woodblocks, and when I look behind the sun and under one of its thick, red rays, I find the globe-shaped
creature. Like several animals spliced together and dipped in the color
of lava flow, it animates its bird head to speak flames from its eyes and
opened beak. Its body suggests cogs, sprockets, and ancient gears beneath.
I can't see its legs but its arms point and swim in the air. It gives the lush
hills and valleys nourishment out of my reach. I blink too long and it van-
ishes back into the sun. When I describe what I saw to an old man in the
night, he scolds me for looking away before it offered me its map made of
sunlight. I feel foolish and empty-handed until I remember the spirit still
sauntering inside my head.

# THE EDGE OF DESCENT, DIGRESSION'S HIGHWAY

## Jennifer Elise Foerster

To make an apparition, cup your palms
as if catching water—the wind field shifts
what climate has tangled into landscape—
a mind, lost as a white doe in winter,
carcass of anthrax in the permafrost—
all of this a sand's slippage in your hands—
a body's hexed ambition and its shame,
like all geographies of disaster,
are subject to distortions of perspective.
At its edge of descent, digression's highway
will carry the subject to its horizon.
The surfacing image: bent ray of light.
After the wind had cycloned and dispersed
we made a raft by lashing lengths of cane,
bowl-shaped skin-boats with a sapling frame.
Engulfed by the river we did not die
but were drawn down farther beneath the waves.

# MERMAID NAMES

## Ra'Niqua Lee

Long after Hurricane Adelaide returned to the Atlantic, news outlets reported plans for cleanup, but swamp waters kept coming, bubbling deep as if someone had switched on a faucet, disturbing the world underneath. A canteen, tombstones, a badge, bullets, and bones, stuff long ago lost in the muck all jumbled to the surface. All found new muck to occupy.

Four dead girls woke along a coast just east of Old Charleston. Another summer that would end too soon. Addie pushed the thought deep as she dropped to her knees, clawed at the sand, and squeezed handfuls of grit while Meredith Caulier and Glory Aimes ran for the choppy tide.

"Alive," Glory yelled against the night and the walls of water rolling into her ample waist.

The fourth girl sobbed. Nameless. A stranger. All bushman hair and knobbed joints, slightly bent over like her big feet were stronger than the rest of her. That girl had to be the reason they were alive, again. Finally.

Addie sat back and stretched out her legs, counted her toes. *One to ten.* She flapped her feet because she could.

"Don't bother worrying yourself," Addie said to the fourth girl, crying beside her. "This is just what happens."

Out of the four dead girls alive on the beach, Addie was the oldest. Not by age. Someone snapped Meredith's neck when she was twenty-one, an amateur beauty queen in the Columbus circuit. Glory spent her first summer reminding everyone that she'd been just a day away from eighteen when someone dragged her deep into the backwoods of South Carolina, wrapped her neck twice with cable wire, killed her just like that.

Addie—at least a year younger than Glory—was the oldest because she'd been dead the longest. It'd happened in the nineties, maybe. A salon was the only memory Addie had of her real life, the first one. Beaded curtains on the windows, heads under hair dryers, gums chomping Bazooka. She didn't know how she died, not like the others who could still make out a face—straight, blue eyes like a clown doll or bulging vein in the forehead that wouldn't keep still. There were no faces in Addie's mind, none she could point to and say, *that, that was my mama* or *that was my daddy* or *that was the president*. She only had the summers now, the confusion of waking up to the beach with the other girls, one more each time. Then came the haste to make the months amount to something more than a fleeting dream before death found them again.

*

Set to make port in 1858, the *Wanderer* cut across the Atlantic, knife-sharp but imprecise. Meanwhile, the sun set a god and rose a moon goddess. Captain William Corrie yelled "Onward!" to anyone who would listen, whispering to himself as he paced in fog thick enough to taste. Each step across the deck, rhythm steady, brought to mind the people below, along with words like *illegal, illicit, future*, and *fortune*. A footfall for each throb of blood carried him to the ship's edge. Down in the water, a girl's black face turned around and around like a carrot bobbing in soup. He tried to blink away all the sleepless nights and spotted a tail, or an arm still bound to chains that had failed. The throbbing moved from his feet to his head as the girl shot out of the sea, rising on a skirt made of water. When she met his face, he thought she would claw out his eyes or crack his ribcage with her teeth and swallow his heart like a clam. He thought she might kiss him. And then there was only mist, the steady churn of water, the ship, and the pulse through and between his legs. At daybreak, he warned the crew to keep away from the deck after sunset, only mentioning the word *mermaid* to his cocaptain when they were drunk in his quarters. They joked about the seduction of the siren call, the demand that they abandon their clandestine course and toss themselves to the sea. It was just like a fish woman to make a man forget his soul.

*

This place was called Edge, as in the last point before something was likely to fall. Addie directed the dead girls down an abandoned highway with large signs that told them how many more miles until they were somewhere other than Edge, how many more miles of trekking along cracked-up asphalt, half-covered in rainwater and sludge, downed branches. A maple tree split by lightning.

The new girl—quiet, red-nosed, and staring—had nothing to say for herself. At first, she had refused to follow as they began the climb up the crags, but she forfeited stubborn, falling in the way they had all fallen into this sisterhood of exceptional circumstance and wonder without answers.

"You're getting us lost," said Glory as she pounded her fist into her palm out of nerves, maybe. "We don't have time to be lost, with the summers draining on like they do."

"We could have stayed at the beach, figured something out there. Built a shelter; learned to fish. At least we wouldn't have to keep slipping in mud," Meredith said in her beauty-queen voice, measured and sure. "There might not be anything here for us this time."

Addie's response as they continued on in clothes that didn't fit with mud caking their ankles: "Possibly."

The first two times, they had woken to a world that was more or less the same, and Addie had showed them each how to survive, how to get jobs, when to tell lies, when not to bother. For some reason, they had trusted her to direct them right, and she needed them to trust her now, even though she didn't recognize this place. Even though Edge seemed more like ruin than civilization. Even though the smell of something rotten had been following them for miles.

*

The sisterhood had solidified the first blue-gray morning along a different shore. Addie's brain had been blank of everything but the gentle tide pull washing the sand smooth, the chilled grit beneath her butt and palms, and the woman next to her with brown skin and a single braid swinging long down her back.

"I don't know how I got here," said Meredith, eventually.

"Couldn't tell you if I wanted to," said Addie.

No one came for them as daylight cut across the horizon in a near-solid line of gold. It looked like someone had been prying the ocean farther from the sky. Maybe that was how Addie knew she had died, because that morning on the beach felt like a kind of heaven.

"Can't stay here, can we?" Addie said, not sure about the "we," but she couldn't remember well enough to keep taking comfort in the word "I."

They soon learned that getting by in that part of the South as they were, confused and aimless, could be easy. Meredith was the kind of plump beauty that people liked to help, no questions asked, only the puzzled looks they gave her when she laughed, walked, or sneezed. Meanwhile, Addie was short, flat chested, with black hair that grew close to her scalp; no one looked at her the way they looked at Meredith, and she adored how easily she could avoid attention when she wanted—it made the getting by that much easier. Meredith found a job waitressing at a fishy dive bar surrounded by pavement and nothing else. Addie did dishes, bussed tables, or panhandled in the parking lot. They survived, making plans for a future, not fully understanding their present until closing time one night when a newscast announced that Meredith's body had been found, naked and desiccated in somebody's basement. The beer glass Meredith had been drying slipped and shattered, and Addie was the one to get the broom.

*

"Meredith died in '99," Addie said, passing the time while thinking about time. The road through Edge stretched on in front of them. They had seen no other people. "Eight years after that you came along, Glory. Now, what? Five years? Fifty years?"

Glory laughed. "You're thinking too much, sweetheart. No sense in this. Just dumb stupid luck, thunderbolt luck, hit you in the face, take your breath away luck."

"Luck doesn't bring people back from the dead," said Addie, "not once, not three times."

"What's your name?" Meredith asked the new girl, trailing behind them. The girl couldn't seem to speak for the sobbing, and Addie imagined them walking into the beauty salon from her memories, the sleek black floors and photos of hair models all over the walls. She would tell the stylist to make them over, give them a miracle, and please, *please* tell them the day, month, and year.

*

On the day of their second death, Meredith shook Addie awake in the abandoned house that had sheltered their second lives. Addie, up on one stiff arm, blinked the blur from her vision until her circumstantial sister came into focus. Meredith's dark hair fell in waves over her shoulder. She didn't wear a bit of the makeup Addie had swiped for her from the Rite Aid, except maybe gloss on her lips for dryness. She smiled angelic and said, "I called Tony and told him I'm not going in to work today, or ever again, but I didn't say that part because I thought it might be rude. I don't want to worry about money today. I really just need to be on the beach right now. *Need.* You coming?"

It took Addie a moment to process all that Meredith had said through the screaming shock of consciousness. Meredith had not taken off work once in the months they had been together, not even after the news about her body. The beach sounded fun, but fun was not a priority. They had worked to combat the uncertainty of their new lives with deliberate intention. Survival came first. The thought of missing work, a sure paycheck and tips, for sun and sand put a knot in Addie's stomach that only faded as the crying whisper of something familiar settled into the back of her head. Addie was up on her feet before she had decided.

They left the yellow room where they had been sharing a mattress and a chest of drawers. As they went, the sheet covering the gaping window waved in a breeze. Down the overgrown walkway and two miles later, they were back on the sand before day fully broke.

Meredith's other body had been buried, but her current body charged the water with Addie right behind. No part of Addie worried about her clothes soaking through, or the callouses that would return from having to scrub them clean by hand. She was in the water. The next thing she remembered was waking up on the sand with Meredith and a new girl, thick from her arms to the fullness in her calves. She called herself Glorianna Francesca Aimes, Glory for short.

*

The settlement waited behind a fence, landlocked and surrounded by trees and roadway. Smoke pillars added to the clouds, bruised gray and ugly. Addie knocked on a gate that stood too high to be necessary, ignoring the large signs. *No Trespassing*. Glory joined in, matching pound for pound, while Meredith held the new girl's shaking hand. The gates opened, guns before faces. The new girl shrieked catlike at the sight of the automatic weapons, burying her face against Meredith's chest.

"We're lost. We got stuck," Addie said through all of the metal, finding her way to the right lie. "In the storm."

All the muck, mud, downed branches. There had been a storm.

Maybe those words were the right words because the guns lowered and the person in the middle of the triangular phalanx waved the girls forward.

"Ain't no more lost than anyone else," the voice behind the mask said. "We might have some space for y'all yet."

The settlement provided temporary housing, a single room in a building block that probably held dozens just like it. Their room contained two beds with a blank white screen for a fourth wall. Everything was some shade of gray or white, and it smelled like it. Being dead most of the time and living in abandoned houses the rest of the time, Addie was not accustomed to the smell of clean. It wasn't that she spent her summers dirty. They always had soap, toothpaste, and fancy shampoo because of Meredith, but overall, they had lived in a world of odors, wood rot, soggy carpet, wet sand, clothes washed by hand and dried in sun and salt air. Not always unpleasant, but not sterile.

A wrinkled woman with a crown of white-blonde hair had led them to the room and explained it all, reminding them of the rule that seemed most important, as it had been repeated most. This sanitized world was available to them as long as they could handle the workload.

*

Lost decades had made consistent schooling almost impossible. Settlement members determined to catch up on what they had missed went directly from their shifts in the lower rooms to the night classes housed in the basement of an old tower. They crowded in a hundred to a lecture hall, still wearing jumpsuits that smelled like hot metal. Sat in rows of chairs, with no desks because of limited space, they watched as the wall screen changed from white to dynamic, a geographic transition that concluded with the face of their instructor, sat in front of a green landscape, some tropical paradise. There they learned the facts. Back-to-back hurricanes along the East Coast in the forties exasperated existing health crises. Then the dead years of the fifties and sixties while the levees were constructed, fortifying the new coast against the threat of unfathomable storms, but the walls promised safety in other ways. Some chose to remain on the coast but refused the safety of walls. It was not clear how these people survived with the storms so unpredictable. They were strays, the real threat to the settlements, because their refusal to join did not undo their need for what the settlements had, and these people would gladly take all if ever given the chance.

After these lessons, the screens shut off and students emerged at street level in droves. As they dispersed into the night, the wind outside the walls sounded like rockets taking off, shooting into the sky, piercing the smog, and always an alarm ringing, warning them to get back to their lodging before the next storm.

Addie learned about Adelaide on her first night at the settlement, in a mess hall, under intense fluorescence brighter than any heaven.

"A lot of people got themselves stuck out in Adelaide," said a man named Edwin. His brown skin turned slightly gray in the lights, and his round cheeks and stomach were evidence that this place could keep them well fed. "The strays of course, but dumb adventurers, too. People who get tired of hearing about the storm from behind the walls get the itch to go out and see for themselves."

Edwin slurped down a final spoonful of sardines straight from the can and yanked the aluminum top back on another. Everyone got two cans of sardines for dinner, a fair portion of bread, and a pile of slimy carrots. Meredith picked over her carrots and split her bread between the new girl and Addie.

"You know," Edwin started, "First the storm, then you wash up with almost the same name. Life is funny like that."

In the coming days, Addie would hear that phrase about life being funny a lot. Someone said it after a man burned up half his arm in the workroom and had to be escorted out, and when one of the mess halls on settlement didn't have enough food for breakfast because of shipping delays caused by Adelaide.

"It's just funny," said the woman handing out sleeves of crackers for people to split among their roommates.

Outside the sleeping areas, the settlement smelled like industry. It ballooned from the metal grind of the workrooms beneath the city where mechanisms measured white-hot liquid into molds, and the steam could only escape properly with constant attention. The first time Addie worked the levers, she thought she might evaporate. Her parts did not cooperate with the demand. Her arms did not reach seamless for the knob assigned to her. Pushing took all of her chest and her hands, slick with sweat. Pulling required her to rock back on her heels, directly into the lever behind her, indication that she had pulled too soon or too late. The molten metal glowed bright enough to make shapes when she looked away and made her confuse faces whenever the floor supervisors yelled at her for being wrong. Her eyes never adjusted until it was all over, when her shift was ushered out to make room for the next.

Behind the thick glass walls of the workrooms, screens cycled through encouraging words, "Here, we make our nation proud," "This is where we live out our purpose," and Addie's favorite, "We do not choose our labor; our labor chooses us." She hadn't chosen this. They spent too much time belowground in the work rooms. Mealtimes provided some socialization, but it was all bland, a wash of low voices exhausted by their labor, the schedules, and each other.

"Things have really changed," Addie said aloud, thinking of the summers that had already passed.

"Just on the coast," Edwin said, spitting dry crumbs, his gruff voice somehow still charming. "A hundred miles inland and it's exactly the same as before times. People only come to the coasts when they don't have anywhere else to go."

Addie made eye contact with Meredith and Glory. She dug a spoon into a sardine, split it along the spine, and imagined she were anywhere else.

*

Storm and rain continued the summer of 1867, and the Black folks blamed the apothecary king, Dr. Trott, in his medicine shop on a street corner in Charleston. He made his money selling whatever he could get from the ocean—frogs, shells, seahorses, tonics made of seaweed pseudo-cures for all stupors and ailments. It wasn't clear where he'd gotten his credentials for the procedures he allegedly performed on the sick and desperate behind the trapdoor. And maybe that was why Gary and Vincent, missing out on work at the docks because of the storms, assumed Dr. Trott was keeping the secret. The story practically animated itself. A mermaid—perhaps Black, half fish maybe—washed up on shore, and Mister/Doctor Apothecary dragged her to his medicine room. Perhaps to sell her, to parade her out for paying clientele, or for the experiments the aunties warned about over slices of coconut cream cake. *Work hard to show them you stand for something, keep clean, stay away from doctors.* Gary and Vincent's theories spread to Margo, Sally, Matty Dud, Ralph, and Howard Man, which grew to Harriet, Jesse Waits, Laurel, and Stu, which then grew to four Annes, three Thomases, and two Jim Browns of no relation. They churned stories, fanning superstitions like flames, combined fears with myth and truth, and arrived at the conclusion that Dr. Trott had a mermaid. They took to the streets convinced that the storms would stop once he set her free. Otherwise, it might just be the end of the world. Reporters called it a riot, but who ever heard of Black folks rioting without receiving the same or worse in return? All of this had morphed into a finely tuned legend, something to keep the babies still before they fell asleep at night.

*

The summer of three, Addie and Glory chased fun into Donnie Darvis's truck bed out behind Shore Baby, the bar where Meredith and Glory worked. Donnie volunteered to take them to the state fair. He was handsome, with thick black hair and deep-brown skin, but Addie didn't care about handsome. She wouldn't live long enough for it to matter. A random strip of burlap in the back was the only comfort among surfaces slick with motor oil and mud. When Meredith started to join them, Donnie slammed the bed shut and said, "Somebody's got to ride up front with me." Somebody obviously meant Meredith, who nodded and let Donnie direct her to the passenger side.

"Beauty queen."

Glory hissed this accusation as Meredith loaded into the front seat, away from the scatter of old car parts and tackle boxes. Then Addie mimed a beauty queen stance, her back straight and her head slightly lifted, fixing long, invisible hair. Glory did her own beauty motions, chest forward and hands on her full hips, a cluster of fishing rods at her back. She said it again, "Beauty queen," but this time she directed it at Addie, who laughed and didn't care, but she said the words back, "Beauty queen," and it was true.

This was the dead girls' third trip of the summer. Addie knew, even though it did not quite feel like knowing, that they would die again, probably soon. It was not clear, however, if they would ever live again. For now, this was enough.

Glory kept peeking into the cab to report back on how Meredith fiddled with her braid, trying to match Donnie's flirting.

"Wedding bells," Glory joked, but Addie didn't laugh as the fair, a Ferris wheel and pirate ship–themed pendulum, rose behind the ridge of trees. At the exit, the truck slowed with traffic, trailing hot exhaust and heavy music. A red car zipped beside them, turn signal blinking, trying to cut the line. Addie locked eyes with the woman in the passenger seat, who stuck up her middle finger. Addie glared until she saw Glory's finger and realized that she had probably done it first. Addie stuck hers up and Glory locked their fingers in a sort of pinky promise that wouldn't break.

\*

The dead ones had a choice.

"My only question is east or west," Glory said during dinner in the mess hall. She had already cleaned her plate, and she placed her palms on the table like she was ready to jump to her feet and run.

"The coast would probably be safer, considering," Meredith said.

The new girl licked sardines off her fingers. With her big brown eyes and crazy hair, she looked half like some type of fairy and half like the green-haired dolls Addie thought she remembered playing with once.

Chin in palm, Addie could barely keep her head above her dinner plate. All the lever pulling left her too weak to wash her own hair. Only Meredith managed to keep her hair smooth and orderly while sweating ten hours a day. Glory had been the one to wash Addie's hair last, bending her over the communal sink and working her fingers through Addie's hair.

As they talked about leaving the settlement, Edwin had gone impossibly pale as if the canned fish suddenly made him nauseous. He warned them that once they left, they wouldn't be able to come back. "What do you think happened to the man with the burned-up arm?" he asked. "They patched him up and sent him away."

Edwin abruptly rose with his tray, moved to an empty seat at the next table, and did not look back.

*

Addie settled again into stiff sheets that smelled like nothing. Her head hit the pillow with a puff of air that smelled like nothing.

The new girl waited by the door, blinking, staring. She would not go to sleep until the others had drifted off first. Addie felt bad for the girl, unsure of how long it had taken her to adapt to her own death, or Meredith's, or Glory's. As far as she could recall, it had been easy for them. Meredith and Glory still had memories of their lives. Addie only had her knowing, but put them together, and it all worked out. Maybe the new girl was acting exactly like a little sister should, like she needed an older sister to tell her how to be in the world.

"You still haven't told us your name. I'll name you myself if I have to," Addie said, but it sounded like a threat, so she added, "It'll be okay. You can sleep where and when you want. Do what you want."

The new girl didn't move and she still wouldn't speak. Maybe her killer had cut out her tongue. Addie didn't think it worked that way, though. They didn't come back alive in their actual bodies. If they did, Meredith's would never have been buried. They would all have been rotted bones and squirming maggots or worse. Not like a princess, kissed awake. Like monsters out for a chase until destruction—theirs or someone else's.

"We're getting out of here," Addie said to the new girl, the only other person awake in the room. "We're going inland."

It felt good to say it out loud even though they hadn't agreed on which direction to take. Meredith wanted to stick with the coast, even with the storms, it was familiar. Glory wanted to go west. If there was any possibility that they could stay alive, they wouldn't find it so close to the ocean's final call.

mermaid names       143

"Maybe you'll talk to us then, or not," Addie told the new girl. "None of this makes sense anyway. Don't think it has to for us to live it good."

Addie faced the wall and tried to believe herself.

*

The summer previous, Addie tried to find answers at the library, a squat three-room house in the Carolina brambles. Addie came every other day, bypassing the old gray woman at the front desk who never spoke much after the first time Addie told her the lie. *Here with family on summer vacation.* It was one of Meredith's lies, which were all about camouflaging. Glory told lies to shock people. Addie only ever told lies to survive, so she mostly spent that second summer alone, in the back of the tiny library where she got to keep her lies to herself. She wanted to make sense of her second life, and there was no one she could ask. The girls could debate with each other, and they did, tossed around mythos like glitter—vampires, zombies, fish people, undead sirens who couldn't sing worth a damn. Whatever they were, they were sisters, but there had to be more. Addie raked her scalp as she thumbed through Edgar Allen Poe's "The Premature Burial," through books about car accidents and minutes in heaven, about ghosts, hauntings, and zombies—brain eaters, thoughtless and stumbling slow. As far as she knew, their coming and going harmed no one. And what if it did? She found a book on South Carolina folklore, one small section on mothers and daughters. Mothers slit their daughters' throats, crushed their skulls, or sent them to drown. Their daughters came back to life long enough to tell those stories. Addie thought of the dead daughters testifying to their own deaths, crafting their own final chapters, and wondered if that was it, if she and the dead girls were just there to act as witnesses, summer to summer, death to death.

*

A storm loomed in the east, clouds plump and terrible gray, but the sky ahead was clear, and the road was a straight shot into flatlands. That peaceful kind of symmetry almost brought Addie to tears. She had woken

Ra'Niqua Lee

to a quiet thrill of screams that had only intensified as the girls packed what they could carry and left the settlement. Now, she felt a buzzing and a wash of static that made her feel like she could snap and crackle like a bolt of lightning touched down at the base of a tree.

"Think the water will get us this time?" Glory asked. She looked directly at Addie, who must have had the answers. She'd had so many before.

"Maybe if we can get deep enough inland, we can outrun the call," Addie said. "Maybe it won't be able to reach us."

Meredith hugged herself and focused too long on something behind her. Glory walked forward sure-footed, like she had been by this way before. The new girl tugged at Addie, staring with big brown eyes and one hand gripping the tail end of her own braid.

"It's loud," the girl spoke for the first time.

Addie nodded and looked elsewhere.

"Lots of things are loud," she said, trying to distract herself. "The mess hall, the workrooms, the ocean. We're leaving loud behind."

Addie ignored Meredith's constant backwards glance and tried to mimic Glory's sure stride. Meanwhile, the new girl still held on.

"I want to say something," the girl spoke, yelling because the screams were now near loud enough to bite. "I want to tell you my name."

The girl's voice sank into a rushing lull of tide-water dreams. Addie put one foot in front of the other, following Glory. The new girl named herself, but no one heard. Meredith turned and darted toward the storm, her brown hair a chaotic sail reaching back for the remaining dead girls as she ran.

# THE LAST KINGDOM

## Jennifer Elise Foerster

Three days before the hurricane
a woman in white is hauling milk.

The beach wails.
She is swinging her pail.

I am sleeping in a tent of car parts, quilts
when the woman passes through the heavy felt door.

If your dream were to wash over the village, she says.
We listen—seagulls resisting the shore.

Hermit crabs scuttle under tin.
The children hitch their sails in.

Later that night from the compound walls
I see her hitchhiking the stars' tar road—

black dress, black boots, black bonnet,
a moon-faced baby in a basket.

*

       Thus, alone, I have conceived.

A tent dweller moved to the earth's edge,
I bathe in acidic waves.

Everyone in the village
watches at the cliff the tidal wave
breach, roll across the sky.

They are feasting on cold
fried chicken, champagne—
I have no dancing dress for the picnic.

The king dozes in his gravelly castle.
The band plays its tired refrain.

Men, drunk on loosened wind
raise their cups to mechanical dolphins
tearing through the sheet-metal sea.

In the shadow of petrels'
snowy specters, drifting monuments
crash and calve.

But I, as water under wind does,
I tear my hair,
scalp the sand—

the sun, eclipsed by dark contractions
turns its disc to night—

fish like bright coins
flip from my hand.

\*

Waking, I find I am alone in the kingdom.

The moon lays upon me
its phosphorescent veil.

The floating world—luciferous:
bleached coral coliseum,
a mermaid's molten gown—

she turns her widening wheels,
spills her pail of glacial milk.

I could almost swim forever
to her beat of frozen bells.

But a sheet of water
doesn't travel with the wave.

And the morning like a tender body
slides out of silt:

I press against its damp
rough surface, an ear.

# YANGON

## Thirii Myo Kyaw Myint

I spent almost exactly a year, the first year of my life, in Yangon. This does not make me feel like it is where I am from. I think one should remember the place where one is from. One should have at least a single memory. Though from the nativity story of the awakened one I know that, regardless of what I remember or forget, I will always be connected to the place where I was born. I know from that story and other stories of childbirth that women return to their childhood homes to give birth to their children. The place where one is born, though it may not be the place where one is from, will always be the place where one's mother is from.

The awakened one's mother, the queen, however, did not make it back to her childhood home. She gave birth to the awakened one in a grove halfway between the palace where she lived and her parents' home where she was born. She held onto the branch of a sal tree, and as she was standing, the awakened one emerged from her right side, where a white elephant had touched her in a dream. The awakened one was thus born in an in-between place, neither his mother's home, nor his father's, but a grove of flowering trees, the flowers just blooming.

Thirty-six years after the birth and death of my brother, I asked my mother a question I had never asked her before. *What was his name?*

Not the name I had always known him by, the name my parents called him, a nickname, his home name, which I will not repeat here, outside of the home. Not the name meaning older brother, an endearment, which could even be flirtatious if used on a boy who was not actually one's older brother or cousin. Not the name my brother must have earned only after his death, since he became a big brother only after he died. Not the name my parents used to tell us about him, the older brother who would always be younger than us.

I was not asking my mother for that name, a name made up for children. I wanted to know the name my parents had given him before he died. The name they had given him at birth, the one that he was meant to carry through a long and complex life.

I am always looking for beginnings. The first that was lost, the brother I never met, the country I cannot remember. I am always looking for the moment when I can enter the stream of myself. It is not the moment of my birth, but long before that. The moment of my parents' union, their wedding held on a mythical bird floating in an artificial lake, their love that began with a borrowed book, with a handwritten letter. Or the moment of my previous death, in my great-grandfather's body, hiding in the jungle from the war. Or in a stranger's body, shot in the streets by the first soldier who pulled the first trigger.

There is often a price to pay for in-betweenness, for finding beauty and resting there, as the awakened one's mother did, and seven days after his birth, she died. With her death, the awakened one was cut off from the memory of where he was born. In Bamar, the word for womb has the word for home inside of it. The womb is our first home, and many times as a child, I used to rub my head against my mother's belly and ask if I could go back inside. She would laugh and say I got too big, I wouldn't fit anymore, and I would laugh, too, but it made me sad. There was no way home, no way back. I was blocked by my own body. Sometimes I wish I had memories of Yangon so that I could claim it. So I could say, *Yes, that is where I am from.* My sisters have memories, of my grandmother's cooking, of playing with my grandfather, of attending school. My eldest sister remembers walking to school through the woods, having to pass by the caged pigs, who scared my sister, and once she got lost and ended up spending the evening at a neighbor's house, unable to find her way home. I have heard their stories so many times it is like their memories are mine, but I know that they are not. I have no memories.

My mother said my brother's name. She said it soft and quiet, but without hesitation, as if she had been waiting all these years to say it. It was only after his name left her lips, left her body, that my mother seemed to realize that she had spoken it aloud. The spell was broken. I had finally asked the right question.

I had not known that there would be an answer, that my brother would have a different name from the one I had always known him by, that he would have a real name, a name that he was meant to use when he grew into a man. It was as if my mother only remembered this name when I asked her, as if she were surprised by the knowledge she still kept inside her. The name she had given her firstborn child. There was a sadness in her voice when she said it, but also hope. *What does it mean?* I asked, though I always resented it when strangers asked me the same question about my name. I was no stranger; I had a right to this knowledge.

In the beginning, then, there was my parents' wedding on Karaweik, a replica of a royal barge, a palatial hall shouldered by two giant birds gliding on the water. The mythical birds golden with red tails, the guardians of my mother's nightmares. My mother had not wanted an extravagant wedding; it was her father who reserved Karaweik for the reception. Only the best for his daughter, no matter the cost. The cost, my mother believed, was my brother's life.

My mother believed birds were a bad omen. She had dreams of the barge burning on the lake. A royal barge built long after the royalty was killed or exiled. Birds are terrifying because they upset the hierarchy of the universe. Lowly animals flying close to the heavens, reptilian, winged, celestial and bestial. As a child, I imagined the thirty-one planes of existence suspended above and below one another, the human realm below the celestial realms, and above the realms of animals, hungry ghosts, demons, and hells. Birds flying overhead always made me feel like I was at the bottom of the ocean.

The word for home in Bamar is the same as the word for house. Aain, a dwelling, a shelter, a residence. A hollow word, whereas home is full. Aain, like the sound of a gong, or a singing bowl struck on its side. A sound that opens, that begins. Home sounds like a mouthful, like the feeling of fullness, of bloating, homeland, expanding to cover the earth. One can fall ill from the idea of home, the idea of its loss, homesickness is felt in the body, though it arises from language. There is no abstract concept of home for the Bamar. There is a people, a land, a country, all words that evoke patriotic feelings, but home, aain, is very private, very intimate, and every house is a home, not only the house that belongs to me. Even haunted aains are someone's homes, the ghosts', perhaps, for the dead too need places to live. In English, there is no such thing as a haunted home. In this language, all ghosts are unhomed, and people without a home are ghosts.

In the beginning, there was a borrowed book, with a love letter tucked inside. So, as a child I borrowed book after book, from the school library, the public library, and the shelves of generous teachers, in search of that first book and that first letter. I never found the letter, and in its absence, I would fold myself into the books, bury myself in them. A figure of speech, to bury oneself in books, but an accurate one, for reading for me was a bit like dying. When read, I left my body for a little while and as a ghost haunted others' lives and watched over them, even inhabited or possessed them. But maybe it was the books that possessed me, that filled my body, so that for years afterward, I was caught in this cycle of acquiring and purging my ghosts, of reading and writing, reading and writing. Dying slowly, dying bit by bit, not until I was dead, but only until I found it: the moment of my beginning, which would not be mine alone, not mine at all, which, I believed, would necessarily exclude me. A moment that took place long before my birth, and long after my death. And though I never found the love letter, I did find bookmarks, scraps of paper, receipts, grocery lists, ticket stubs, and, once, even a Polaroid of a girl in the backseat of a car, staring straight into the camera.

My brother's name, my mother said, means light.

Not a burning, dazzling light, not brightness, but soft and pleasant. *Do you understand?* my mother asked. *I can't explain.*

To me, his name sounded like the word for enter, for inside, win or winn, my mother's name and my mother's father's. A light shining from the inside. A window lit up at twilight, in winter, the snow and the sky the same white-blue and the window a small glimpse of yellow, glowing softly in the quiet cold. *Clear and wide vacant space*, another translation I found of my brother's name. The space between the stars, or between the earth and the moon. The light that travels that wide expanse.

# LETTER TO THE HIRING MANAGER

## Sarah Sophia Yanni

my mother can survive   jabbing onion-cries but   I must tell her   how to write
an email      her hands can paint   a clay pot of   coffee   or the foliage of a faraway
beach  but I   can make the words   speed past   my body buried    in an office
armchair

where the performance    of professional jargon    takes the shape of an
exercise  in oddity   the language circles truth    forming
pendulum identities   like an academic ghost   I reverse the role  of a mother-daughter
hover

neck-deep   in this generational gloom   a tongue untrained   is rich with
misinterpretation    but our    machine clicks can quietly   correct the gaffes   conjure
the rules of   community college english   mama

press the buttons and    follow        the shape of my mouth

# WAYS TO USE SILHIG LÁNOT

*for Presentacion "Ging" Pairat Dapanas (†2002), paternal grandmother*

## Alton Melvar M. Dapanas

To sweep the wooden floor,

keep it shiny with floor wax,

said Ging in her duster, dusting off

the pellets of poops from the lizards

that dwell in the ceiling, the little ones

that eat brown moths that bring

good luck, the large ones

that make noise in random

at midnight, the lone hour

for the *arinola*. *Tuko*, said

the large one, *yes*, in your thought—

or were you supposed to start with a no?—

*tuko*, no, *tuko*, yes . . .

until the sound stops,

until you come to a decision—

a yes or a no. **To ward off the *tamáing*,**

honeybees that came to live in, too,

occupying one of the house corners,

or the occasional *lapínig*, wasps,

stinging every inhabitant's feet

when accidentally stepped on.

**To make sure smoke spreads**

at every corner as the fogging

against mosquitos happen

every 5:00 pm to make way

for a peaceful night of soap operas

and a rosary fronting an altar

of Our Lady of Perpetual Help

which never ran out of fresh santan

and bougainvillea flowers

of different shades, adorned

with duranta leaves. **To scold grandfather**

Emeliano, such colorful character—

*Yano, nganong bakakon ka man kaayo?*

shouted Ging from the dirty kitchen,

holding the broom like a torch,

ready for war—from his smoking

and tactless mouth. (You giggle a little,

you inherited being liar from Yano.) Like her,

you have a mole in the upper lip. Like her,

your temper is short. Oh,

how you complain with pouted lips

when *inon-on*, fish stewed in vinegar,

is served for dinner. Oh,

how she would find ways

to make you eat meat, so that when she died, you

stopped complaining about fish.


And that, too, is a lesson in memory,

dear rememberer of the bygones. Some people

become the thought of your waking hour,

lingering, malignant even,

long after they're gone.


*Silhig lánot (n.) Binisaya for indoor soft broom made from bristles of Manila hemp*

# DREAM OF A WOLF

## Juan J. Morales

There's an empty room that belongs to me, so I feel territorial. It's complicated because there's a wolf inside, and he's a beautifully sharp creature that always seems to be smiling. I'm supposed to keep him cooped up, and he wants out to maybe do some harm. He wants me to appreciate the long scratches and gouges decorating the walls. He wrestles with me, like an older sibling holding back, so I worry about setting him off. The wolf bites my hands too hard and I correct with a loud "No!" I leave him to think about his defiance, and I lock the two red doors before remembering there's also a blue door, slightly ajar. When the wolf escapes, I know I'm responsible for everything that comes to slaughter. I'm left alone to figure out if I left the door open on purpose. The room smells like the promise of the wolf's return.

# ANTELOPE CANYON HOTEL

## Thea Anderson

TripAdvisor promoted the Antelope Canyon Hotel as a respite chiseled in the heart of the desert. My room, the one I refused to leave, was a memorable cavern painted pipe-gray and dominated by a monstrous cast-iron bed with cotton shams and outsized goose-feather pillows. I made it infamous. Anytime guests arrived, I ripped Georgia O'Keeffe reprints from the walls, twisted the plumbing, invited field mice, shattered the window, broke its replacement, and lit the welcome mat on fire. Management, dazed with repair bills, relented and reserved room 304 for Spiritual Reverence & Reflection which meant that, during the busy season, I was met by all manner of psychic practitioners, medicine men, ritual elders, diviners, magic initiates, reporters, curious teenagers, and disrespectful heathens. But no one dared to sleep in my bed anymore. A few years passed and everyone grew accustomed to me, and so I was no longer special. I got tired of my own self. Nights spun into other nights. Everyone else moved on. I slid from the duvet and rested inches above the stone floor. I lay there for months. It wasn't a dignified existence. Still, I was a thunderous woman, built tall by the engine of my great-grandmother. It was the reason I could even sustain myself that way. Then one day, a good six years into my hermit state, a woman with bantu knots sprouting all over her head arrived at room #304. She was casual. She set down a woven bag full of ritual trinkets. She wore cutoffs that pinched her thighs, which were not at all sweaty in the high heat. Management had disconnected my AC long ago.

Usually, in order for me to interact with the living, I needed to catch a body doing bodily things. I needed goosebumps alighting on middle-aged flesh, absent-minded scratching, tears, tears were always good, real laughs, sweating necks. But the invitation from the Bantu Knot Woman was immediate, like she inhabited *me*.

"I'm Eshu." Her lips were peach and unchapped and I wanted to run my pinky along them. She crossed her legs into a perfect bow on the hard floor as only disciplined people can. She rolled her head around on her shoulders, closed her eyes and spoke into the emptiness of her mind. It was some sort of incantation. I waited.

Outside a guest slathered in blue algae shuffled passed my room and rested his pterodactyl elbows on the balcony railing. The sun dried the clay spirulina mask that he hoped would extract his genetic predisposition toward colon cancer.

"Are you with me?" Eshu clicked her tongue impatiently.

"Yes." I lied. The blue-green man searched his device for the sweat lodge schedule.

"This hotel is a little irksome, right?" I said. "It's like a nudist colony without any spectacle of nudity." She placed her business card on the coffee table. "And not one of us to be found," I concluded.

*

I stopped talking and looked at the card. *Sacred Whisper. Astral Projection & Mediumship.* I couldn't help it; I laughed. That instantly broke her concentration and she vanished. It took an hour for her to return to me.

"I didn't mean to laugh," I apologized. "I'm not used to taking the living seriously. I think all this time alone has made me rude."

She smiled and revealed her uncorrected teeth. I wanted to examine the jettison of overbite, slight front gap, but like a girl aware of her slights, she closed her mouth quickly.

"I like you." I said.

"Why is that?"

"You don't think you're special because you can talk to me. It's just your work."

"I'm happy to do it."

"What's it like out there?"

"Pretty much the same as how you left it."

"It feels that way from what I can tell."

"Would you say this world interests you too much? There are other places for you to go now."

"It's not how you think. I'm a tadpole sent adrift."

"Tadpoles don't stay that way forever; biology takes over."

"Yep, like a script."

"Are you afraid of that?"

"Well it's the price of a life. I would have to give it back sooner or later." I bobbed on the crest of air. Each time I spoke, I dipped out of the room, scrubbed out by the effort it took to have a conversation. "Can you give me a little something? An offering, sacrifice, anything, so I can be in the same room as you?"

"My intermediary can give you one day of life if you promise to work with me."

"Sure, but I don't want to meet it."

"Don't worry, she won't stay long."

Daylight streamed through the broken blinds and glinted off the onyx and obsidian, selenite and amethyst. Eshu rearranged the jagged crystals, lit a small candle and made a quick petition to a snake deity with six lashing tongues, each black and unfurling against the crisp white modern aesthetic of my hotel room. The serpent lashed at me with all of its writhing heads. I screamed. Eshu laughed. When I opened my eyes, I had a body again. It wouldn't be mine for long, but this time I knew it. Once again, I had my long, useful limbs.

*

Weeks before, I was dying for companionship so I asked Mark to join me in the desert. He lowered his head, unable to answer. We stood that way together for a long time in our kitchen before the open window where the spring breeze blew in and tousled his silver hair. Outside, timed sprinklers ticked in unison on our lawn. Dolly scratched her paws on the back screen and I went to let her in but Mark held me against the counter. She whimpered miserably. I felt him get excited against me. I held still so I could ingest his arousal. In no time, I felt my own tongue again, my lips, the breath over vowels. "All day long, I watch people live their lives. I feel like I'm drowning in nostalgia that's not mine." I spoke haltingly, very unlike myself.

"But you can still do melodrama very well."

"Come be with me." I ignored the jab.

"I would if I could."

"It's not like you have to die." I explained. "I can teach you how to be with me and still go about your life."

Mark shook his head and changed the subject.

"I was just remembering the day we met. I really loved that day. For its serendipity."

"You weren't looking to meet anyone," I added.

"So it was perfect," he admitted. He blinked rapidly. "There are all these moments that I want to reenter. They play out like scenes of a movie."

"That day still exists. I can't really explain it but I can show you. Time bends when you're dead."

As I spoke, I moved closer. In our lives, softening and lowering my voice always worked. He liked when I deferred to him, although he never admitted it. I waited. He smelled like tangerines and fresh sweat. He took another piece of fruit from an unglazed porcelain bowl filled high with citrus. He turned the fruit in his hand like a tennis ball.

"Honey," he looked up at me. "Please move on."

I surprised myself at how quickly I connected with the glistening bowl. I'd always hated that piece. Mark jumped back as shards of his amateur hobby broke across his bare feet.

Who would I be if I weren't both lazy and ambitious, leisurely and insatiable—a strange mix I inherited from Josephine that surely provided me the hard-headedness to write short pieces for obscure literary journals. The first time I met her, infirmity had her teetering between life and death. I greeted her by bowing my head. She kissed me but she was not pleased. She waved her scaly fingers at me and swiveled to face my mom. "Why do I want to kiss her head for?" She gripped the armrail of her chair with long red nails. A sharp whiff of piss fell between us and intertwined with ammonia and roasting meatloaf of the old folks' home. I knew then that we were the same. Mark said that he knew all about my funny mixture but I don't know if he ever realized the implications.

*

In room #304 of Antelope Canyon Hotel, I stood tall in my regained body. The thin straps of my black day dress ran over my collarbone. I twirled in the mirror. Eshu muttered something and I turned around.

"What?" Her voice was a panting whisper. Little gray circles appeared under her eyes. With her baby hair plastered in sweat to her skull and her wilting knots, she looked as if she'd emerged from a cold swim.

"Why do you stay here? You're a misfit for the culture." She repeated between inhales.

"I like vacation spots." I rummaged around in the shallow closet for my brown leather sandals with straps that tied to the midcalf. I searched the floor until I noticed that they were soles-up by the door as if some careless person had tripped over them. I bent the arch back to their form, stretching the leather in my hands.

"But you're becoming a . . . "

"A nuisance?"

"A presence. You're kind of a thing. Some guests are scared, but others are becoming open to the possibility that you represent. That death may not be final. There's a hashtag for each sighting. Last week you were trending because of how many appearances you made at the pool. Since no one can get a picture, people have to describe you." Eshu scrolled the feed. "Here we go. Some say elegant, sad eyes, observant. They call you Tall Woman, #tallwoman."

"Same as when I was alive. Minus the Internet fame."

"You had a following when you were alive."

"Don't flatter me. No one read my stuff."

"I read *Sailor in Skeleton Valley*. I loved *Three Ways to Eat a Melon*. I can't remember the other one about the dog, Daphne something?"

"Dolly. *Dolly's Requiem*."

"Were you working on anything new?"

"I'm always in process with a trail of half-finished things. It takes a lot of energy to complete what I did and of those it took herculean efforts to publish the few you read." I swung my mane of microbraids over one shoulder. "Anyway, I should just tell you. I'm not leaving anytime soon."

"But you can't sustain this."

I pulled Eshu up by her limp shoulders and set her against the dresser. The framed black-and-white photo of the Upper Canyon clanged against the wall overhead, and for the first time she was afraid.

"All I have is a trail of unfinished work. I'm here because I'm waiting for my chance to negotiate." I clarified. "With someone other than you."

Eshu stopped talking. She rubbed prayer beads between her thumb and index fingers. She smelled like Moroccan oil conditioner. When I was alive, I would buy giant bottles of that stuff and hoard it under my sink. I let her return to the floor. There, she closed her eyes and murmured a chant.

"We're just two tadpoles." I reminded her. But her renewed focus was enough to tip the scales again and I was back under her persuasion.

The sun dipped below the expanse of the desert and the Antelope Canyon Hotel shone turquoise from the reflection of the kidney bean-pool.

"Mark is worried about you. He felt you after a jog the other day." Eshu whispered into the empty room.

"I hope so. We talked. I felt him too."

"Do you want me to read what he wrote for you?"

"Not really."

"He loves you very much."

Mark had an oral fixation so he ate too much when he was stressed. He watched movies on his phone in our bed. He escaped fights instead of finishing them. He grew up privileged but with a fetish for deprivation I couldn't understand. He slept with the sheets tucked in between his knees. He was magnanimous in public and childlike with me. He wrote me letters for no reason and tucked them inside the books I was reading. These pleased me. He was always so hot in the middle of the night. Sometimes, I placed the back of my hand just over his spine and it was like warming my thin skin to a fire. Sometimes, I imagined him as fire itself. Scalding but necessary.

"I miss him. Why does he want me gone?" I was tired again. "I don't know, maybe I'll do that for him. Then you can go home."

It was dark now and a family of two sunburned parents and a young child bobbed around in the lit pool. Their screeches and splashes resounded. Had they been to Antelope Canyon yet?

"Mark and I spoke, for background, but he didn't hire me."

"Was it the hotel?"

"Actually, management is glad for the free publicity." Eshu smiled, as though about to offer a gift. "Do you remember Luke?"

*

The Antelope Canyon Hotel should have been relaxing but it wasn't. That was because it was a wellness resort built in a Brooklyn aesthetic on Navajo land.

It was not one towering building in an office park nor a dilapidated motel, but an expanse of mini desert bungalows clustered around a large pool. There were open baths for salt soaks and massage under an alcove where the wellness took place. Because of all the opportunities to submerge in water, and the dry heat, guests were mostly outside, wrapped in towels, drying off, or sloshing around. I chose the place for its proximity to the natural wonder for which it was named. Mark and I planned to tour the canyon as a reward for me finishing a tedious revision of a piece that evoked in me little but disdain.

I arrived days ahead of Mark, who was watching Dolly until the pet farm had an opening. At guest check-in, carbonated water in green glass bottles lined the open beverage case. It hummed and cooled my knees. I hooked the neck of a bottle between my two long fingers and presented it to the Gen Z-er behind the counter.

"Are these complimentary?" I asked. He looked up from entering my data on an iPad, momentarily confused, and took me in. I was going off-script. I wore a day dress which was black linen, and cut low in the back to reveal my shoulder blades.

"No, they're $3."

"Wow."

"I'll charge it to your room. Here is your key. Download the app on your phone and present the SQR to the door scanner as your key."

"Can I have a regular key card?"

"We just phased those out." He looked up at me and tilted his head. The pretense in his speech dropped away. "Sorry, it's kind of a pain."

It took me longer than it should've to enter my room due to a glitch in the scanner. Tech Services programmed a manual override while I stood outside room #304. Guests in billowing robes and athletic slip-ons floated by.

Inside, I scrolled for what to do, and everyone who cared to comment seemed to say that the best thing I could do was leave the very resort room that had taken me so long to get to:

*We absolutely loved the tour of Upper Antelope Canyon. Our tour guide was fantastic and put up with our party of 6 which included a screaming toddler. It's a must-see.*

*The Crack is a holy place and the tour really emphasizes the sacred history of its people and land. We learned so much!*

*My wife and I are not the outdoors type but we had an amazing time exploring the native treasure. I was actually quite moved!*

I unzipped my dress. I was sweaty. I put on a new white cotton strappy dress with a circle hem and tiny gray squares throughout the fabric. I slid into brown leather sandals and grabbed my notebook. I sat at the edge of the pool. There were two families who realized they were both from Florida—one on the east shoreline and one from the west. They'd left their home state full of beaches for the desert. I wrote some notes but none of what I put down was significant.

I put my notebook aside and from my perch at the pool's edge, I watched the Gen Z-er smile at reception. As soon as a guest would turn around to leave, his smile would drop. This went on for hours. Finally, he raised his eyebrows through the glass at me. I went back to writing.

*

"Why do you think that your great grandmother is so important to you?"

"This isn't therapy."

"No, but it's an inquiry."

"She was an enigma, a bit erratic, definitely mean. She never worked a day in her life."

"How did she survive?"

"Off of the affections of men." I realized something. "I envy her."

"Have you seen her yet?"

"No. I tried but no." A gaggle in tiaras singing and sipping margaritas out of penis straws tumbled past the window. I was not distracted. "Sometimes, I go home. I refill Dolly's water and sit with her. But as quick as thought, I'm back here. It's not voluntary anymore. I always wanted to observe strangers without them knowing, and now look at me."

I would have cried but I chose not to waste my body and its power on tears.

*

It was late. I knew it because the darkness outside room #304 was vast and complete. I resisted the urge to check my phone. I texted Mark an early goodnight and sat under the glow of a crane lamp trying to make sentences. It was like I'd forgotten how. It was even later when there was a quick, soft knock on my door. It was the Gen Z-er.

He held two alkaline waters.

"I heard you don't like to pay for these."

I frowned. Biologically, I could've been his mom.

"No. Does everything have to be so transactional?"

"Not everything."

I turned around and curled up in the large chair that occupied the corner opposite the door. He found a place on the wall to lean against but sort of kicked over my sandals in the process. They rolled near the door. He bent down, and placed them side by side, toes pointing out toward me.

"Why were you watching me today?"

"I'm just curious," I answered.

He nodded and smiled.

"Are you always so congenial?" I asked. "Seems grating for you."

"Sort of. I'm sincere though."

"I know." The strap of my dress fell down my shoulder. I had narrow shoulders.

"I'm Luke," he said.

"Hi, Luke."

Luke sat on the ground in front of me, on his knees. He was unsmiling, casual. Something clicked. In front of me, he became serious, oriented to one aim, the way that sex can bestow grace on someone who is not otherwise graceful. Or grant gravitas to a young man with ordinary build and face. The transformation never failed to impress me. It was that change to which I was drawn, and that drew out of me, a dark deity. It's what I tried to tell Mark was in me all along. I was a loyal person. And then there was this, a scorched-tongue beast who did things like claw a stranger on his back and if he liked it, did it harder. Sometimes, when I did these things with people I didn't know, I imagined Mark in the room. It often seemed as if he was not hurt but curious, seeing a side of me that relished newness wherever it could be found, but could never be found in him unless we agreed to relinquish what we knew about each other. And that we could not do; not me, a cataloger of the minute, and definitely not Mark, an archivist of the great past. I came in minutes. I came again. Then I sat very still on the floor, the AC blasting on my skin and raising my little hairs.

*

The California king bed, potted succulents, and hanging O'Keefes all dislodged from their fixed places as though grabbed by an eager flood. My own body began to diminish. My long microbraids, constellation of moles, my teeth all dwindled into nothing.

"Eshu, did you trick me?" I screamed. But she was gone. In her place, sitting unbothered in the corner chair, was Joesphine, about thirty years old and dressed in the current style in a navy cotton jumpsuit. She watched with unblinking eyes, honey-bright and shining in the upheaval. Josephine pointed to the wall behind me where a series of memories broadcast onto the shackled surface.

First, I saw what seemed to be a book tour. My novel was completed and published but I made no bestseller lists. I gave talks to moderately interested book clubs who asked what I knew about the psychology of my characters. None of my answers mattered. Then I saw Dolly encircled by quivering little bodies all fighting to nurse. They had the same goofy ears. A girl in wraparound glasses reached into the warm heap of Dolly's newborns and brought the smallest one to her arms. Mark smiled at the girl's mother, as if to say *pick me, love me.* She liked that. The next scene called to me like the premise of a story. In it, six years ago, Luke closed the door to room #304 and touched the back of his neck. It was where I'd dug little crescents into him with my nails. He found his Honda Accord in the dark employee lot and drove home. An hour later, there was a carbon monoxide leak at the hotel. The new system alerted a command center in Minnesota which pinged the cell of the night manager who evacuated all confirmed guests. No alarm sounded. Management wiped their brows and congratulated themselves on acting fast despite the SQR system's obvious inadequacies. At work the next morning, after being briefed on the incident, Luke asked about the Tall Woman in #304—was she accounted for? What woman? Wireless earbuds slipped out of my ears where shamanic drumming meditation played on repeat. An EMT rushed in and tripped over my leather sandals set so carefully by the door.

\*

Josephine indicated she wanted me to approach. She really was a tall wonder. Her nails were ornate, long and red. But this time the skin on her hands was spotless. Up close, I got gardenias and vanilla. She lowered her head and I kissed the top of it. I sat next to her. We were no longer in room #304 but seated on a boulder in the Upper Antelope Canyon. Early morning light streamed in and the ancient cavern glowed like fire.

"I'm sorry." In the canyon slot, the walls kissed in some parts and waved apart in others. I was embarrassed by my charade.

"I would've done the same." She looked up like she was trying to explain a very complicated concept to a child. "I lived a long time but I couldn't do what I wanted. So when I died, I gave you some of me. Or more of me than you already had. We are the same. Lustful. Incorrigible."

The funny mixture.

I watched the light bend and wave over the rocks. Ripples of distant, singing warm light. I wondered how long it would take. If it would be a flash. A realization. An unwinding. Either way, I wanted to hold on to Josephine as long as I could.

Thea Anderson

# TRANSMIGRATIONS: A FUTURE HISTORY OF MULTIPLE BODIES OF WATER

*Recovered Fragments*

## Kenji C. Liu

*Whale songs: 4–6 themes, each composed of distinct phrases, sung in a loop, 10–15 minutes long. After one complete loop, the singer surfaces to breathe, dives, and begins again. Songs change slowly over time.*

### Theme II: Gestures

10.
Evolutionary predecessors of whales: Pakicetus, Ambulocetus, Kutchicetus, Rodhocetus, Dorudon, Basilosaurus, Odontocetus, Mysticetus. Evolution from ocean to land, to ocean. Invent legs and feet, then forget them. Wandering evolutionary gestures.

11.
    Dear Sonorous Dream,

    8 bit and wandering. Lonely songs in an ocean of light. The 8 bit whale recites, no one can hear her. She is a floating gesture . . .

         ... ...
       :: ... ... ...
       ...::
   ......::::

12.

*Waterworld* (film, 1995, Before Deluge): An Earth where the polar caps have completely melted, dry land a distant memory. The most important character in the film, played by Sab Shimono, born and raised in Sacramento, California (Before Deluge). During World War II, he and his family are incarcerated in federal concentration camps, Amache and Tule Lake. Tule Lake is an ancient lake bed. In this and many other US concentration camps, prisoners made art with found sea shells.

13.
" . . . the brain and heart are composed of 73% water, and the lungs are about 83% water. The skin contains 64% water, muscles and kidneys are 79%, and even the bones are watery: 31%."

14.
Dear Love,

For wandering evil spirits, I have been advised to pour a cone of pure white salt at the outside corner of my front door. Is the ocean so insufficient?

15.
Does this read? As you know, these are unfamiliar gestures.

16.
At Savatthi. There the Blessed One said, "What do you think, monks: Which is greater, the tears you have shed while transmigrating & wandering this long, long time—crying and weeping from being joined with what is displeasing, being separated from what is pleasing—or the water in the four great oceans?"

"This is the greater: the tears you have shed while transmigrating & wandering this long, long time—crying and weeping from being joined with what is displeasing, being separated from what is

Kenji C. Liu

pleasing—not the water in the four great oceans."

(SN 15.3)

17.
*Ocean*, from Greek ōkeanos, the great river that wanders around the earth.

18.
*(Contemplation of the Breaking)*

between city and floodplain, a swallowing
      dream . . . the tidal pools

        of neighborhoods, slowly licked,
the archive of selfies, full

      of tilted faces and hilly lips. ask the camera
for an analysis of light among us. the

      abdominal bloom, unrelated to nothing.
        we ate records, we invited a country of data

      ingestion. o highest emanation of compassion:
do even small evils deserve rapture?

      even more. our ocean gestures so widely
        the shore is uninvented, just the drown

      of a horizontal line and velvet sea life.
a hunger for fullness. how gorgeous the tear

      of parting scales and muscle. whose hands
        are still cutting even now?

how petty our lights are. how

industrious . . .

19.

いつか、三年ほどたって、ふと、浦島は、わすれていた村の家を思いだし
ました。「おとひめさま、たいへんおせわになりました。もう、そろそろおい
とまいたします。」「そうですか。では、お別れのしるしに、おみやげをさし
あげましょう。これを持っていってください。」そういって、りっぱな箱を一
つくれました。「これは玉手箱というものです。大事なものが入れてありま
す。でも、けっして、ふたをあけてはいけませんよ。」浦島はお礼をいって、
おとひめさまにお別れしました。そして、また、かめに乗って、海の上へ出
て、浜へ帰っていきました。

Three years passed before Urashima remembered his home in the village
he had left. "Princess, could I please ask an important favor, I think it is
time for me to go back soon." "Very well, as a goodbye, I offer you this
gift." Upon saying this, she gave him a beautiful box. "This is called a Ta-
mate box, it contains something very precious. But you must never, ever
open it." Urashima offered his gratitude and said farewell to the princess.
Then, he again rode the tortoise to the top of the ocean and landed on
the shore.

Kenji C. Liu

**Start again from Theme I**

To play on your 三線 :

| | |
|---|---|
| 中 | 中 |
| 工 | 工 |
| 合 | 七 |
| 工 | 合 |
| 合 | 七 |
| 五 | 合 |
| 合 | 七 |
| 工 | 七 |
| ◯ | 五 |
| | 工 |
| | 四 |
| | 上 |

40.

    Lonely lonely lonely whale
    Sing alone like this!
    Will I ever shine so brightly like a remote island?

41.

. . .

I am a fish for you. I must swim in this body again and again.

*

Sea, I consent.

somewhere this ocean ends in an island.

# A FINAL SONG FOR THE AGES

## Pedro Iniguez

The *Esperanza* was doomed. The generation ship moaned as it tore apart module by module, plate by plate. Nora's father scooped her off the bed and sprang down the corridor. Behind them her mother rummaged through supplies, stuffing what she could inside a large duffel bag. Her mother's screams were drowned out by screeching metal, but Nora thought she said something about a damaged propulsion drive.

Her father entered the escape pod and secured Nora gently inside its stasis chamber. He placed Pepe, her favorite stuffed narwhal, in her hands and smiled. Not long afterward, her mother nestled the duffel bag directly beneath the door and crossed herself, whispering a prayer under her breath.

Her father's fingers zipped across a control panel. The door slid shut, cutting her off from her parents, who each now placed a hand against the pod window. She could make out the words they mouthed. "*Te queremos.* We love you."

Nora opened her mouth to call out to them, but as always, no words came. A mist enveloped her stasis chamber, drizzling her arms with tiny, cold beads of moisture. The droplets seeped inside her lungs. She felt drowsy, her grip on the narwhal slipping as her fingers went numb.

The escape pod rumbled for a moment before it jettisoned into space. Before sleep took her, the behemoth of metal collapsed on itself in a storm of scrap and debris.

But it was a dream. A memory. A regret.

Nora stirred from her sleep and sat up. Groggily, she peered out the pod window. The sky was dark blue. The sun had yet to climb over the mountains on the horizon. Planet *Tierra Tres*, as it was known back on Mars. Earth Three.

She grabbed her pencil and etched a new tally mark onto the piece of paper pinned on the wall. She did a quick calculation in her head. It was her ninth birthday. Two full solar revolutions on this world. It was a technicality. How many years elapsed as she hurtled through space? Ages, surely. She hugged Pepe and pretended he was two other people at once. She stood, yawned, and opened the hatch. Outside, many *Kukumanos* were already rousing and scuttling from out of their underground shelters as they prepared for the daily toils of frontier life. She stretched, fixed her mother's straw hat over her head, and prepared to join them.

*

Nora stepped out under the shadow of a wooden canopy. Judging from the gathering storm clouds, she was lucky to have one above her escape pod, which had served as her sleeping quarters for the better part of two standard Earth years.

Ahead of her, a series of concrete walkways connected the colony like a grid. Every path led to something: an underground dwelling, a watch-tower, an infirmary. Beyond the simple subterranean dwellings stretched a lush, verdant world. Jungles, mountains, raging rivers.

The settlement now stirred with the familiar sounds of scraping legs and clacking mandibles. Before she could make her way toward the colony center to pick up her daily assignment, she heard Krika's unmistakable voice.

"You're on digging duty today," Krika said in her language, hammering her mandibles together in a string of clicks and pauses akin to Morse code from Old Earth. "Rain is coming and we need at least five dens on the northern end of the colony." Her left mandible was broken at the tip, a memento from a battle with a hungry horned owl long ago.

"*Five?*" Nora protested, snapping her thumb and middle finger in her best mimicry of the Kukumano language. She had no language of her own to offer them on account of a severe laryngeal infection that left her with paralyzed vocal cords as a toddler. "My hands start to hurt after three."

"Many eggs are expected to hatch within the week," Krika said, the hard clacks of her mandibles suggesting impatience or perhaps anger.

Krika was like the rest of the Kukumanos, having a slender, eight-foot-long body made up of sixteen segments, each bearing a pair of legs. She also had a flat head with a pair of long antennae, sharp mandibles, and two glassy, bulbous eyes.

They were like Earth's centipedes in many ways, except they were sentient. She had read about them on those quiet weeks aboard the *Esperanza*, when her father and the engineering team had been away making repairs while the rest of the settlers remained in stasis.

Krika handed Nora a spade.

"Can I have a word with Okikoa?" Nora pleaded. Her snaps were barely audible, conveying submissiveness. "Maybe I can forage for bugs."

"You know what he'll say," Krika said, scuttling away. "The world beyond the colony is too dangerous. Besides, if you want to be a part of this community, you'll do what you are assigned."

Nora ambled sleepily past the rest of the Kukumanos as they set about digging, hunting, or patrolling the perimeter in search of predators. She found the last den north of the colony and made a mark in the earth about twenty feet away under the shade of a tree. She set down her portable stereo, popped in her mother's favorite CD, and knelt on the dirt as Vicente Fernández crooned "Volver, Volver."

Some of the Kukumanos stared, agitated at the music blaring from the stereo. Some of the kids on the generation ship were the same way. They'd teased her for playing that *Mexican cactus music.* They didn't understand the words, the melodies, its cleansing effect on the soul. Even at its saddest, it was a celebration of life.

Nora jabbed the small spade into the earth and scooped, closing her eyes and nodding her head slowly, rhythmically. She smiled. She couldn't sing but sometimes the most beautiful things in life simply required listening. And like a temporal wormhole, the music transported her, gifting her, for a brief moment, her mother. Even now she could hear and envision her bellowing out the song as she showered before a shift at the hydroponic garden. It was the happiest her mother had been before a long day at work.

After an hour, Nora had carved out an upside-down dome ten feet deep. Later, someone would come reinforce the insides with mud and finely ground stone. Then another worker would climb the tree and erect a wooden canopy above the dwelling and a new den would be complete.

She stared at the hole. It looked cozy. More than anything, it was practical. The Kukumanos burrowed in order to shelter from predators and the elements. They weren't too unlike humans. Nora found that comforting on most days. They were the closest thing to family she had. Yet, even that was never quite enough.

Nora removed her mother's straw hat and wiped the sweat from her face. Or was it tears? On some days she couldn't tell. She sighed and wondered if farm work back on Mars was just as taxing. Or on the *Esperanza*. Her mother would probably say it didn't matter. All that mattered was that at the end of the day, you were alive. And if you could end that day with a smile, you were already winning at life.

Clouds blotted out the late-afternoon sun and rain began to pelt the ground just as she finished digging her fifth hole. She would have to reshape the holes another day when they dried. For now, many of the laborers were already scuttling back into the safety of their dens. She packed her gear and prepared to return to her pod.

"Young one," the voice behind her clacked. "I have news to relay to you." The colony chieftain arched his back so that he was standing to meet her at eye level.

"Hello, Okikoa," Nora snapped her fingers in response. "What is it?"

"Since you came to us two revolutions ago, you have toiled and earned your place beside us, but we have not been honest with you." He turned to face north, his mandibles opening wide for long moment before shutting.

Nora had come to associate that with a deep sigh. "On the other side of this jungle lie the bones of a human settlement."

Nora felt her heart drop into her stomach.

"Long ago, an exploratory crew of human engineers built the settlement in anticipation of your ship's arrival. We partook in formal diplomacy, communications, trade. Shortly before you came to us, their numbers had thinned out and ultimately, they perished."

"From what?"

"We believe this planet may harbor some unseen dangers to your people's immune systems. Perhaps toxic water or even deadly spores. Perhaps disease broke out. That is why we tried to keep you safe within our ranks."

Nora swallowed a dry lump.

"Your people constructed a radio tower. It remained dormant, until now. My scouts recently reported hearing a sporadic series of grunts and moans emanating from the tower. We have come to understand it as garbled humanspeak. We do not grasp your technology and have no way of communicating in return. We assume you may be able to contact your species. Perhaps they can arrange for your retrieval."

Nora didn't know how to feel. Her insides knotted up and squirmed simultaneously. She was both eager and sad. She missed people that looked like her, but she had no one to come home to. Where *was* home? Mars had been ravaged by war while countless other settlers departed for faraway worlds. "I would like very much to investigate the radio tower," she replied, snapping her fingers gently, trying hard not to stumble over her words or sound too desperate.

"Tomorrow, you shall travel alongside Ikkak, one of my scouts. Do what you need to do. It will be the only time I allow it."

Drenched, Nora bowed her head as Okikoa scurried away.

On the way back to her pod, she plucked a sweet-smelling orange flower known as the *oolok-kio*. It bore a strong resemblance to an Earth marigold. She tucked it carefully inside her jumpsuit pocket and entered her pod.

Nora retrieved the two portraits she'd drawn that first week she'd arrived on *Tierra Tres*. It wasn't anything fancy—just crayon on ruled paper—but it was enough to get her through most days. She propped the portraits of Angie and Teodoro Tamayo on a shelf.

Next, she placed the oolok-kio flower between their portraits and lit the candle she'd crafted from tunnel-weasel fat. The flame's light gave their portraits a sense of warmth and life. She ran a finger along their waxy, painted cheeks and smiled through the cascade of warm tears. On some nights she pretended they were staring back at her through loving eyes. Sometimes she came close to believing it. On those nights, her heart ached a little less.

The *ofrenda* was all she could offer to honor their memory. Her mother had taught her that ofrendas were a way of keeping the dead alive. That their spirits would use the altar as a beacon to the mortal plane in order to visit loved ones. She kept smiling, in the hopes that her parents would see how much joy they brought her.

She crossed herself and uttered a prayer in her head, asking them for things she knew they couldn't give her. Most importantly, she asked for help. For guidance. They hadn't prepared her for a life without them.

Nora blew out the candle, removed her wet clothes, and slid into her cot. Outside, as the sky grew dark, twin ivory moons hovered above the jungle. She hugged Pepe, closed her eyes, and hoped that for once, she'd have a good dream.

*

Ikkak was quiet, but that didn't bother her. She was in awe of the jungle and didn't really feel like talking, anyway. She squeezed Pepe against her chest. It was all so much to take in. Giant ferns, dancing milkweeds, bioluminescent fungi growing under the shadows of colossal trees. The scout had politely and deliberately slowed his crawling pace to accommodate her bipedal debilitation. She was more than sure he'd considered upright walking a handicap.

They traversed north, past the last Kukumano outpost, past the winding creeks, and deep under the thick jungle canopy where sunlight seldom pierced. The air here was suffocating and moist, yet there existed a variety of sweet and musky scents.

Mars never had anything like this. Not even the indoor parks came close. She'd never ventured past the domed cities, but she had known there was nothing there but dust and heaps of rusty-red rocks. She pictured Earth looking much like this, so it didn't surprise her that the *Esperanza*'s crew chose this as one of a few possible locations to settle after the Martian Civil War.

She thought about them: The crew of settlers lost to the void of space. What had happened, she wasn't sure. A big explosion. Or was it an implosion? Her father surely would have known. She wished she could ask him.

"What do you carry in your bag?" Ikkak clacked, shaking her from her thoughts.

Nora regarded her backpack. "Gifts my parents left me," she snapped her fingers in reply.

"What kind of gifts did they leave you?"

"Clothes. Books. First aid kits. Portable stereo."

"I don't understand those gifts."

"Things to help me survive."

"Yes, I understand that. Tools."

"Yes," she replied. "They gave me the tools to survive."

After some time, the world grew dark and her legs felt heavy. "Can we stop to rest?" she asked, snapping her fingers loudly to draw his attention.

"Yes," Ikkak replied. He promptly clambered up a tree and ingested a slew of small insects crawling along the bark.

Nora sat at the base of the same tree and sipped water from a canteen. "How much farther is it?"

"Not far." Ikkak climbed down. His exoskeleton was etched with scars and scratches.

"What are those marks on your body?" Nora asked snapping her fingers and making a slashing motion in the air.

"Life as a scout is dangerous." Ikkak bent his body back so that he was looking at the jungle canopy.

Nora followed his gaze. Scant patches of sky were visible, but she could see now that it was nighttime from the twinkling of stars. With the darkness came the vibrant sounds of the nocturnal world. All around she heard chirping and buzzing, even growling far off in the distance. She wrapped her arms around her chest and shrunk within herself.

Ikkak crawled beside her and rested on the ground at her feet.

A loud, piercing sound made her jolt upright. It was a distinctive screeching not far from where she sat. She leaned forward. It was shrill but almost melodic, with purpose. Like music. She slowed her breathing, hoping to get a better listen.

It came once more, emanating as a series of screeches followed by temporary pauses, only for the screeching to resume again. *Eeeeeh eeh eeeeeh*. Pause. *Eeeeeh eeh eeeeeh*. Pause.

"What is that sound?" Nora asked, quickly snapping her fingers.

"That is the *kipi-kua*," Ikkak replied. "I have not heard its call in many, many revolutions."

"What is a kipi-kua?"

Ikkak pushed off the ground. "I can show you."

They trekked over thin meadows and a few rotting tree stumps toward a small clearing where moonlight shone over reddish soil.

"Do you see it?" Ikkak asked, his clicks hushed in the dark.

A small, round head sporting a pointed snout jutted up from under a burrow. The creature pulled itself halfway up by its long-clawed paws.

"I see it," Nora snapped in reply, taking a few steps closer. As she did, she noticed the animal's scaly-plated skin, and its milky-white eyes.

"It's blind?"

"Yes. They are subterranean, remaining dormant for many cycles. They only surface to eat and mate. This is its mating call. I thought them all gone."

"Why is that?" Nora asked, keeping her eyes on the creature as it jerked in its hole. It was almost pangolin-like, only rounder, stubbier.

"They have not been seen or heard for a long time. Much of their environment was destroyed by your people when they built their colony atop their habitat."

Her face flushed. She felt guilt gnawing at her insides. Like she was going to be sick. Her people caused this?

The kipi-kua's nose prodded the air around it, sniffing insistently for something just like a puppy.

Ikkak continued. "They inhabit a specific portion of land on this planet, preferably near soft, fertile soil. Your people found the area suitable for farming. They plowed over a large swath of kipi-kua territory."

The kipi-kua tilted its head and screeched its melodious song, pausing every so often before continuing.

"Why does it sing and stop like that?"

"It is a song meant for two partners. The gaps in its call are meant to be filled out by another kipi-kua. That is how they find one another. It appears this one sings for a mate that will never come."

*A duet*, Nora thought. She felt warm tears pool under her eyes. She knew she was crying for both of them. She hoped that there were more of its kind around. For the kipi-kua's sake. For her people's sake.

"Let us continue," Ikkak clacked, "the radio tower is near."

She wiped her tears and they continued through the jungle until they came upon a slope littered with fragments of bones. She found the strength not to ask. On the other side she saw the sprawl of modules, chain-link fences, even flowing canals as they intersected parts of the colony. All was quiet expect for the sound of small, chirping insects.

Ikkak led her toward the western end of the colony. A steel-latticed radio mast shaped like a long triangle had been erected at the crest of a hill. They entered the control room located at its base, which had been left dark and empty. She half expected someone to greet her, but she knew better.

Ikkak turned to guard the door. "Can you initiate contact?"

"I don't know," she said, flicking a light switch. The rumble of generators came to life. To her amazement, the room lit up.

Nora glanced over a series of computers and control panels until she found a microphone jutting out from one of the terminals. A decal of sound waves emanating outward from a radio mast was plastered beside the microphone. She flipped a switch and a red light blinked on. "Ready for transmission," a synthesized voice spoke.

In the silence of the room the realization came. She balled her small hands into fists and for a long moment she stared at the light. At that moment she felt the urge to scream.

Instead, she sat and slumped her head, slamming a single fist on the counter.

"What is the matter?" Ikkak asked, craning his long neck.

Nora shook her head. "This machine requires audible vocal transmissions. I can't speak in the language of my people," she said, her finger snaps weak, nearly silent. She placed two fingers to her throat. "An old infection messed up my ability to talk. I have no way to communicate."

"Perhaps I could speak for you?"

"No," she snapped in response. "Whoever were to receive the transmission would just hear clacking."

Nora buried her face in her hands. What she would give to have her father hold her, or to hear her mother sing Vicente Fernández one more time.

Her mother's voice echoed in her head, her soothing vocals almost nudging Nora. A wide smile streaked across her face. She unzipped her backpack and probed inside until she found what she was looking for. She flipped the transmission switch on the control panel, grabbed her portable stereo, and thumbed the Play button.

She chose her mother's favorite song, "Volver, Volver." The violins, guitars, and trumpets boomed harmoniously off the speakers as Vicente Fernández crooned about a lost love.

As she nodded her head to the rhythm, she began to snap her fingers, translating so that Ikkak could understand.

"Woeful poetry," Ikkak said.

"Yes," Nora replied, smiling.

Her smile abruptly faded. She began to wonder if the signal would even reach anyone.

Something her father had taught her came back to her just then. While radio waves traveled at the speed of light in a vacuum, those waves eventually became weak and blended in with the background noise of the universe.

She sighed, the sting in her heart deep and piercing. The universe itself was working against her. The music would just become distorted, undecipherable nonsense.

Nora thought of the kipi-kua. Its beautiful song, an exercise in futility. A most wondrous tune meant for someone and no one all the same. They were alike: alone and the last of their kind on *Tierra Tres*.

She let the song play all the way through. When it was over, she turned off the transmission. She'd offered no coordinates, no clear message. But it was all she could do. She wouldn't be allowed to try again. A final song for the ages, she thought. Like the kipi-kua, her kindred spirit, she was calling out into the void to a people who may never come.

Pedro Iniguez

# ON BENDED KNEE

## shakirah peterson

jamal is reborn in the mouth of a woman.

she's chewing strands of him until he is soft and supple. he can't see her tobacco-stained teeth or smell the leftover peanut-butter stew she ate for lunch, but he can feel the grinding of her enamel and the warmth of her spit—a cleansing. with each chew, all that is left of jamal's carnal memories are exiled into the gaps of her teeth. *tough*, the woman thinks.

later, sharp bits of regrets will attempt to bury themselves into her gums and she'll be forced to floss until she bleeds—it's a small annoyance she's willing to endure. most creators think it cruel to rebirth a once-sentient soul into an object. the woman is one of few who disagrees.

*the living should remain in the realm of the living*, they'd say of her practice.

*there is no superior existence*, she'd say in defense.

after an hour of maneuvering jamal between her tongue and teeth, the fibers of his being are no longer resistant—he is resilient and ready to be made into a new thing. the woman removes him from her mouth and soaks him in a makeshift pond in her backyard, a small hole she dug and filled with fresh water just for him. at the base, phytoplankton wait to gift jamal his new sight. in seconds too small to measure, they latch onto him.

he can now consume what they consume: energy.

the woman wrings him out of the muddy water and hangs him on a clothing line. with his newfound sight, jamal observes the woman walking away. with one hand, she frees her silver locs from their knotted bun and with the other, she forbids her leopard print dress to drag through the grass. she moves with intention, each step made with meticulous thought.

to jamal, the woman is an aura of purples: violet, periwinkle, iris, orchid—a vibrant cacophony traversing through an otherwise bland space. he observes the purple bulb of energy move across a sea of duller colors. their lack of vibrancy does not lessen their importance to the purple bulb—the woman bends around each of them, careful not to swallow their modest auras.

the woman makes it inside of her craft shop, a cramped room she built brick by brick. here is where her creations await their new existences. twelve thousand bricks now surround the woman, but her aura is not dimmed.

jamal is fixated on her every movement, spellbound. it is only after the woman leaves for the market that her aura disappears, the spell broken.

\*

the woman's absence gives space for other energies to glow. as if they weren't there the entire time, the objects in jamal's surroundings illuminate. behind him, a baobab tree releases a bright, blinding light. it is consistent in its glow and feels familiar. beneath him, the grass is a blend of emerald, sage, forest, fern. three meters away, four children play on a seesaw in the neighbor's yard—a pulsation of rubies and marigolds, roses, and tangerine. above him, an invigorating current sifts through every atom in his being—the supreme sensation of the sun. there is no other energy more captivating, more jolting. while the air holds him, the sun shrivels him to his purest form. the ambience of his surroundings is slowly beginning to fade when the bulb returns.

from the trunk of her sedan, the woman quickly gathers all the items needed to propel jamal into his final form: a large, round rubber bucket; red and purple flowers from the indigo plant; a square shipping box. she hurries inside, throwing the box across the floor of her craft shop.

jamal recognizes a small ball of energy from miles away. it first appears as mauve and then quickly grows into lavender. the woman races across the garden to jamal, carrying a round bucket, the flowers forming a bed at the bottom of it.

*ndineurombo*, the woman says to jamal. *there was lots of traffic* . . . she attempts to explain while embracing him with both hands. she gently squeezes . . . *you are ready*.

in small moments of leisure—when her children are at the schoolhouse, when her husband is away, after all the chores are done, the sheep fed, the corn pulled—she weaves and sews jamal into his final form. he is left untouched in her craft shop most days and many nights. the long absence of her aura and the sun's presence sends jamal's atoms into a shock—an aching in the depths of his existence.

the woman knows of this turmoil but cannot soothe him.

like with memories, souls reborn from human lives are attached to "time." in constant worry of where and when it will come and go. her absence is how the woman guides jamal away from this attachment, to rid his atoms of the obsessive need to be somewhere or something.

the cravings eventually lessen to dust. by the seventh week, jamal is complete.

the woman cries as she folds him into a small shipping container. six drops fall on him, right near his center. she rubs her hands across this part of his fabric to disguise the moisture. this will be the last time they will come in contact in this world, but her energy will never leave him.

\*

a package arrives at timon's african imports on a saturday.

timon doesn't work weekends or any day his mood disagrees with the twenty-minute commute to the city. on wednesday, timon comes to the shop and sees a small rectangular box leaning against the door. he reaches for it. *what is this?* he asks himself. his shipments are usually too big to leave outside the door. timon lifts the package with one hand, without struggle.

he opens the door and tosses it next to the register.

for jamal, this feels like a brief shift in his nothingness. he has experienced these slight movements for weeks now, on his journey across the atlantic. timon returns and removes jamal from the thick, cardboard box. *you're a little thing,* he complains.

jamal senses the energies around him, beginning with timon's. his aura is not as comforting as the woman's. timon is a cacophony of hickory, tawny, and caramel—a small golden bulb of light struggling to glow.

timon begins to read the note attached by the woman.

*3' x 4' gudza cloth*
*handmade from soaked and twisted fiber of a family baobab tree*
*Thank you for your support*
*—nypa*

*3' x 4'? lazy.* timon lays the gudza cloth on the floor and slaps the dust from it. with each smack, the aura surrounding jamal begins to glow. he's then hung on the wall next to the rest of nypa's creations: a 16" x 24" oval rug, a 67" x 67" square.

timon turns the ceiling fans on, dozens of blades twirl dust particles around the shop. a particle lands on jamal, near his center, collecting small molecular remnants of nypa's sorrow. the air sends it to the oval cloth hanging next to jamal, dropping remnants onto its lower edge. here, nypa cried too.

this is their only form of communication, a collective remembrance of their creator.

*

timon flies into the shop and flicks on the lights. he sets the same intention he always sets when he walks in. *god, give me buying customers.* today, the intention is manifested.

the customer's scent enters before she does—the wind carrying her pheromones ahead of her. they land on various objects: the door, a lampshade, jamal.

timon greets her in an uplifted tone. his tawny aura shines a little brighter than usual.

"morning, queen. welcome to timon's african imports."

the customer smiles. the energy of her joy carries a cacophony of violet and periwinkle, iris and orchid. nypa's creations are fixated, their beings stirring as they remember their maker.

"morning! i'm so happy you open. every time i'm over here, you closed."

"yeah, my hours are all over the place." timon pauses. "what's your name?"

"sheila."

"sheila, you know how it is. it's just me running this thang and i'm not as young as i used to be."

sheila is listening but not enough for timon to continue speaking about himself.

"you looking for anything particular?"

"nuh-uh, just looking. i'm sure something will find me."

"well, this just came in a few months ago. you gon love it."

timon walks sheila over to jamal, removes him from the wire and lays him across the floor.

"wow, how pretty."

"yup, handmade from fibers of a baobab tree by a woman in harare. this is the newest and smallest piece she's sent over. those up there are also hers."

"it's kinda too small, though. i don't even know what i would use this for."

"anything! a rug for an entryway . . . "

to that suggestion, sheila twists her lips.

" . . . a prayer rug, maybe?"

to that suggestion, sheila rolls her bottom lip underneath the top one. *it would be super cute in front of my altar.*

she leans over jamal.

"i could use a rug in front of my altar . . . how much is it?"

timon doesn't have a set price for anything in the shop. he charges customers by the price tag of their appearance. sheila's lack of jewelry and simple dress make him say a higher-than-normal number. her clothes are plain but quality. her black cotton shirt thicker than any he owns. her thong flip-flops look inexpensive, but her toes are freshly manicured. one of em even got a ring with diamonds in it.

if his judgment is right, he'll make a nice profit—after nypa's cut.

"for you, $75."

sheila purchases the gudza cloth, three bundles of sage, and a package of incense cones. within an hour, jamal is in his new home, underneath sheila's altar.

*

sheila hasn't prayed in years, at least not like she used to. her alarm clock has been set to go off at 5:30 a.m. since january. her new year's resolution: *to spend more time with you, god.* the ideal routine: wake up, meditate and pray, run, then bike to work.

every morning she presses snooze until the sun comes up. then, she says a quick prayer before she eats breakfast and another when she makes it home safe from her hectic drive from work. when the guilt gets to her, she reminds herself that *he knows my heart.* her intentions are good.

on her altar, sheila places her new bundles of sage between her bible and a row of crystals: quartz, red jasper, onyx, amethyst. tonight, she'll light the sage then move the crystals to the ledge of her balcony to be recharged by the new moon.

when her alarm clock goes off at 5:30 a.m., she won't press snooze. she'll kneel on her new prayer rug, clear quartz in one hand, rose quartz in another, and feel something wet beneath her. a mauve patch of moisture will fill the rug, forming a hole in her bedroom floor. looking down sheila will find nypa, a woman with skin like bark, looking back at her.

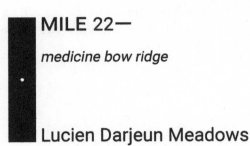

## MILE 22—

*medicine bow ridge*

## Lucien Darjeun Meadows

Over the ridge of the Medicine Bow     trail dropping into rock I spread
    an experiment in exhalation     seeding waves of sweetgrass and cheat
in the changing shape of hands my hands teqayeni I remember as magnolia leaves
    first a plush lung     then veined     then unlimbing
there was a boy whose hair filled teqayeni     was I that boy     I see only leaves
    there was a molting     *take me down, follow me down*     *my name is Monongahela blue*

Mountains like islands in dark-growing clouds     atvli like years I remember
    I don't remember     the horizon indistinct between cloud and sky and I I I
teqayeni open     this body a mirror     shivering images in furious dream
    the runner beside me opens into a ricochet of silver     a brazen tunnel
through this summer's green     *child of holler, child of reaching down for root*
    this ridge grassy in the distance     I keep stumbling on the rocks underfoot

*Hush hush hush*     let me lay now under blankets until wintercall     *wind the sky in blue*
    body a metronome for breath     bellows for wind     that boy somewhere
hours darkness in skin unleaving     snowflake-thin     this body his body knowing
    only what is luminous in a quiver of bone     stone     home     *I am alone*
left to measure the air     more runners stream by     floating as I crash along
    there is no boy     there is no air here     only breath     *O O O what*

What if I were to stop     now     stop and dwell in this island     atop this ridge
    my home a mountain     around me the Medicine Bow a tessellation of blue
each peak refracting a memory a mind a boy     lifted and pierced by light

the trail folds into thunder     I am dropping into tree    and we are spangled
in the downpour    akaskv and kvnesaskv rolling down my arms    afraid and the day
barely begun    hoping for a courage of breath    a flicker a river now underfoot

# ONE WEEK AWAY AND THE FOREST HAS CHANGED

## Jennifer Elise Foerster

One week away and the forest has changed.
Measured wind, consistent in its image.
First frost, day's ghost, sweeping the red-toothed leaves.
I wander the groves of recycled thoughts,
restless, navigating musty stacks
past gravel tracks, those blushing fields of wheat
golden in autumn's sweeping blossom.
I turn back for an instant and notice
how the glacier, at first sight, is static,
how a train becomes a parabola in snow,
how a swamp tupelo roots in our haze.
To what can we return when we turn time
toward sequence, when we reset the chain
to prove our lives a miracle of flight.
There have been five mass extinctions in our
four-hundred-billion-year history
and no memory of the formula
for forgetting. What can we make of it
but a hot-air balloon. I wind the key
and wait, suspended against the ruins.

# PLAYING MACBETH AT THE ELECTRA THEATRE ON BEADON STREET

## Shreya Ila Anasuya

The theatre was built upon a broken promise. Not a large building, but still a grand one, with pale walls the color of rose quartz, slight turrets reaching pointedly into the sky, wide doors open to anyone who could afford the price of a single ticket. Audacious, like its makers.

You might have passed it in your carriage in the evening, the gas lamps lighting the otherwise pitch-black streets, the laughter and bustle drawing your eye toward the glittering building. The Electra. A pretty name, is it not?

Of course, I had not thought so. Not on the night it opened, not ever. Not after the months of work. Rehearsals in the day, lying with the man who was paying for it at night. A man I would not have chosen on my own, not so soon, not while my heart was still heavy with old love. But friends with beseeching eyes surrounded me. Reminded me at every turn how many careers depended upon my decision. Gopal babu himself asked.

After having watched it come up day by day, week by week, brick by brick, room by room, flick of paint, flourish of curtain, the day came to unveil it. They called it the Electra. I saw the marquee, the brown of finely polished mango-wood. I swallowed my smile. I looked at the faces that had, until recent weeks, always met mine with so much expectation. Now my various and beloved friends—the thespians of the city stage, the vanguard of the modern theatre, the pallbearers of my dreams—now they did not meet my eyes.

Eyes that blazed when I accosted Gopal babu and led him into a greenroom.

"You told me you'd name it after me," I said, the words hissing out of me.

"I tried, Kalyani," he said, with a sigh. "They vetoed it. Ghosh babu himself vetoed it. They couldn't let me name the theatre after . . . "

"After a whore?" My voice rose another notch.

"Kali, please, don't shout. They couldn't name it after an actress, Kali, you know how it is."

So I gulped air, and put the scorpion that had risen inside me back into its burrow.

*

More actors joined the troupe. Charu, who left the Bengal Theatre for us. Her trained voice like ambrosia, and eyes that spoke constantly, searchingly. Nasreen—tall, husky-voiced, able to slip in and out of any skin Gopal babu gave her. Soon we were making enough money to hire a few stagehands. A couple of boys, and a thin girl that everyone called Putul.

She was a peculiar one, about sixteen, thin with huge, haggard eyes. Quite beautiful when she smiled, but on the whole too solemn, so that flashes of her beauty seemed like tricks of light. Charu and Nasreen had brought her to me six months before, because they knew the last tenants in our spare bedroom had left. At home Putul kept to herself, and took her meals by herself in her room; in a few weeks, Maa and I barely noticed she was there, except when she emerged to use the kitchen, and Maa's eyes— with raised eyebrows—followed her movements. Maa was convinced she ate too little to keep body and soul together, and was constantly exhorting her to share our meals, but she inevitably and politely excused herself.

Where exactly she had come from she did not tell us, but it was clear from how little she knew about the theatre that she was from a land-owning family. We knew enough not to ask questions. Women came all the time, the young and the ageing, the abandoned or the betrayed or the widowed. They came, and we opened our doors to them. From the babu's zenana straight into the rooms of the Great Theatre. How's that for a leg up?

All summer we ran packed shows. Back-to-back shows, no time

to even eat a full meal between rehearsals. But the burrowing scorpion stayed. It caught me unawares at quiet moments in the day, stinging me into shock, simmering within my skull. Even when I finally collapsed in bed, its pinching image seared the backs of my eyelids like lightning. They had named the theatre the Electra, and not the Kalyani.

*

Our fortunes turned.

We sold fewer and fewer tickets. On the night of the Saturday show, Putul came into the greenroom to tell me they had had to cancel the Sunday show altogether.

I nodded, dismissed her. Alongside the familiar dismay, another feeling was rising up within me. I breathed into it as I examined my painted hands. Red fingertips, freshly dyed, alta brushed on diligently by Putul. I pushed against the tight warmth I felt in my heart, horrified at myself.

In my ears, the sound rang like the tinkling of dozens of bells. Someone else had laughed—a full-throated laugh I knew well. I raised my eyes to the mirror. My lips were parted, my teeth were bared in a delighted snarl.

Behind me a shadow stirred. Leaning closer to the mirror, I saw Putul staring fixedly at my reflection, her mouth curved into a smile.

*

With our ticket sales having fallen, and news that the Sans Souci Theatre had brought in Sarah Bernhardt, the French memsahib, to play Cordelia in a grand new production of *King Lear* (no expenses spared!) we had to think fast. We—especially I—had moved heaven and earth to stand on our own stage.

It was a most confounding situation: as far as we could tell, we had done nothing differently, nothing that would cause our sales to plummet. Nor did the people who attended our performances seem unhappy—we still received standing ovations, except now there were bigger and bigger gaps between the seats. The reviews still praised both Gopal babu and my performances, and those of many others in the troupe.

We dispatched some stagehands to spy, and put our heads together to come up with a solution.

"Why not do *Ghare Baire*, or one of Bankimchandra's novels?", someone suggested.

"No, no, we need something fresh," Gopal babu snapped.

"What about a patriotic play—*Mata Banga Bhasha*! Mother Bengali, reigning against the might of the English!"

"How about the Tarakeshwar scandal, the whole business about the girl whose husband chopped off her head?"

But though Gopal babu considered each suggestion, thinking on some longer than he did others, he shook his head at all of them.

"What about our own *Lear*?" I said. "Let's show them how it is really done."

I knew as I was speaking it that it was the scorpion within me again, crawling from its hollow, but the words had already escaped my lips. It was a shockingly callous suggestion. Worrying about ticket sales was fine enough, but to actively sabotage another production? To make laughing-stocks of ourselves by competing so obviously with them, especially with the French actress?

The others stared at me, surprise and distaste plain on their faces, but Gopal babu seemed distracted, running his fountain pen of black and gold round and round upon his fingers, until he suddenly burst out, "I have it! Kali! I have it! Nothing except Shakespeare will do. We can't do *Lear*, of course. But we can do another tragedy, a better tragedy, and we can do it better! If they do the English play, we can do the Scottish play! *Macbeth*!"

For the first time that afternoon, relief washed into the room, like warming winter sunlight. Gopal babu was beaming. This in itself was such an extraordinary situation that we felt positively giddy. My faux pas was forgiven, and we looked at each other with excitement upon our faces. Gopal babu was clapping the men on their backs, saying, "This will be the show that saves us! This is it!"

Thinking about it on the way home with Putul, I began to feel some of my happiness washing away. He was delighted with me for suggesting

*Lear*, but he would not own up to it in front of the troupe. Some of them resented the favour I found with him, as his dedicated pupil. "Why should that stop him from giving me credit where credit is due?" I seethed to myself. "To erase my name, and now whatever I contribute!"

"You must be pleased about the new production, na didi?" Putul asked in a quiet voice, walking in step with me and throwing me a quick smile.

"Yes . . . of course. Nothing is dearer to me than a good story well told, Putul, with myself as part of the great apparatus for its telling," I answered, in an officious voice that was not quite my own. Whose was it? I had heard Gopal babu talk like this to the press, or for introductions to his friend's books.

*You were always a terrible liar. How pompous you sound!* rang a familiar voice in my head. Rajani's voice. If Rajani had been walking with us, she would have burst into laughter by now, and I would have laughed with her.

*

Putul said nothing. We were almost home. I stopped at the krishnachura to look up at the fading sunlight through its tessellated leaves. Some of the fiery flowers fell onto us as the tree swayed in the flurry of air, looking like scarlet and mustard butterflies.

"Actually, I am really lucky, because the stage saves me. No matter how tired or frustrated I feel, I know I can be transformed the minute I act. I can completely forget myself, and that's often a relief," I laughed. Putul's wide mouth curved into a smile, and her eyes brightened.

"Tai, didi? What do you become?" She giggled.

"Whatever the story needs me to be!" I grinned, and pulled on her hand to walk the few steps home.

*

October night and the full moon. The ceremonies of the season were done with, the people had made much of their revelry, in satin and silk and muslin. But now the time of the festivities was over, the golden orb of light that was the luminescent goddess smiling stonily at the back of a truck had gone to the river to be immersed. The children that had trailed her on the streets shuddered in their beds and slept fitfully. The lanterns had been put out all over the city, one by one by one, and the weary horses had been retired for the night.

But I could not sleep, not with the moonlight flooding my room. I could have drawn the curtains but I knew it was there: no matter how dark the curtains, sleep did not want me.

And the moon, she called. I went to the terrace with a bamboo mat, surveyed my realm of concrete and foliage. The night was still and warm, and there was only the slightest nip in the breeze that ran light fingers through my hair.

The night made a different creature of the city around me; the trees, neon green in the daylight, were ghostly and unknowable now. Who knew what creature slumbered or watched from the canopy of the krishnachura that grew stubbornly next to the brick wall of the house? I chuckled at the tree, spoke to it in my mind. "Don't you know you are in the wrong neighbourhood, silly? They will name your flowers renegades, they will cut you down for blooming. You should have taken root on a different street."

I was different too, under moonlight. Not Kalyani. Not an actress sometimes under the shelter of a rich babu who loved the theatre. Not a lover. Not a patita, as they called me in the open letters and the spittle-spewing speeches.

There was no Gopal babu in the moonlight. There was no Beadon Street. There was no Electra. There was no Lady Macbeth, with her heaving ambition and the price she paid for it—all of love and all of life.

The moon had stationed herself high in the sky. It was so much nicer to be here in direct view of the brilliant light, so much easier to breathe . . .

I yawned, and lay down. The leaves of the trees rushed next to me, seeming to gurgle with laughter. My eyes were getting heavier, and I knew what they were laughing at, even as I drifted off. In just a few hours it would be daylight again, and life would come at me, a carriage drawn by wild horses. Between sleeping and waking I thought I saw a sunlit room with sapphire curtains, a home I had known once, with a cat—no, two—but the slow-moving clouds finally covered the sharp, cold light, and oblivion claimed me.

*

Morning, late for rehearsal, but the dreams I had had were still insistent, flashing in my inner eye, thrusting my body back into a reality that had receded far into my past.

In my dream I was back—as usual—in the room with the viridescent curtains. The sun blazed outside; inside, the cream walls looked as if they were bathed in mountain light. The cat Dakini was playing at my feet. Her identical, ash-colored twin, Jogini, ignored us both and sunned herself lazily near a window. There was a bouquet of fresh new roses that smelled so wonderful I buried my head in them.

I inhaled the delicious scent, the velvety petals cooling my eyes. Over the sound of Dakini's purring, I heard them, their laughter like winter afternoon light, each particle of dust reflected in it transformed into a miracle. They spoke together in low voices, those unmistakable voices, Subodh and Rajani, while somewhere an infant was keening.

Its wailing was mine, and my head was filled with lamentation long after I woke up, heavy from dreaming.

I shook myself back awake each time I saw their faces. Heard their voices. Found my body floating back to that unmistakable room in that beloved house. Each time, I pulled myself away, willing myself not to get lost in the halls of what was never coming back.

I had work to do.

*

In the late afternoon, the red-and-brown houses crowded together, only the laden clotheslines and the smells of cooking giving away the fact that they held within them dozens of lives. I wove down the alleyways and arrived at the house by the river, slate grey, standing by itself, its colours as murky as the depths of the river itself.

We were rehearsing the unraveling of Lady Macbeth, with her

constant washing of the hands, her insomnia, her agonized questions, but still I couldn't shake off the dreams. Fifteen minutes into rehearsal, my work was as clouded over and unfocused as I was. Gopal babu's irritation was mounting, and with it, a secret, blazing irritation of my own, that stung my mind.

"The Thane of Fife had a wife: where is she now?" I asked.

Gopal babu glowered at me. The young girl playing the gentlewoman was home sick with a migraine—some hogwash about the full moon and headaches, he had said earlier, scoffing, his moustache bobbing on his face. The scene wouldn't work without her, so he called Putul from where she sat, watching us.

"You, girl, take a copy of the script, and say the lines."

Gopal babu growled instructions, almost shouted them, but my mind was cotton wool. The more he pushed, the more desperate I became.

He took me aside. "Remember, Kali, she's distraught here. There are many things she is not even saying. When she asks about the Thane of Fife's wife, she is also thinking of their children. And she is also thinking of her own children, the ones she never had."

"Surely the guilt of having killed a man they were supposed to revere, a man sheltering in their home, would have been enough to drive her to despair?" I argued. "Why does it need to be about a child?"

"There are layers to this, Kali, we will discuss them later."

"No, I want to talk about it now. I think we need to agree on what the role is about. I think Lady Macbeth is panicking because she thought it would be triumphant, but it is horrifying. I think she thought he could win the throne in one night, but he has to win it nightly."

Gopal babu looked thoughtful. "Yes, but that doesn't mean she cannot crave the child too."

He had turned away, his mind already elsewhere, but that itchy, irate feeling had only mounted. He even thought he knew women better than they knew themselves.

I quieted my mind, and pushed away the scorpion even as it snapped its sibilant betrayals.

I took my position near Putul and the boy playing the doctor. Putul reached toward me, and for a brief moment held my left hand in both her palms. Skin radiating warmth, as if she had a fever.

"Don't worry, didi," she said, in a tiny voice. "It will be okay."

I lay down with the heat from Putul's hands radiating through my body.

"'The Thane of Fife had a wife, where is she now?'" Sing-song this time, cocking my head at Putul, who was gazing at me in that cow-like way she had. The brilliant gilt of the sunset was gone from the room, the wind had raised its face to the dark side of the day, and my head spun.

My eyes rolled back in my head and I was swept back to that once-and always-beloved home. Somewhere a baby was crying. I wandered into the kitchen to warm myself some milk.

The sound of anklets. Was someone in the house awake? Maa didn't wear anklets, only I did . . . Distractedly, I looked up and I saw a person dressed in silver, walking with steady and deliberate steps into my room.

The audacity! I rushed in behind them, ready to shout for Maa at a moment's notice.

"Hey! Who are you?" I called.

She turned around. Her face was familiar, and terrible. Huge eyes, a voracious mouth I knew from somewhere. Rajani's mouth, but not her face. "I'm hungry," she said in a voice like gravel. Her teeth gleamed in the candlelight.

Someone shook me and I was thrust back into the dusk-darkened room by the river. I had fainted. Putul handed me a glass of water. Gopal babu was speaking to me, worry lines furrowing his forehead, but all I could hear was the sound of weeping.

*

In the long nights of the long weeks that followed, I found that the vision had opened a door in me. We worked every day for hours, and there was always something to attend to at home, yet no matter how tired I was, sleep would not come. I would lie in bed, aching, and only fall asleep as the first birds chittered. Even then my sleep was disturbed with dreams—dreams I did not remember afterward, except for incoherent shapes and colours that I could not explain in the language of the waking.

All I could do was lie on my back and brood about all the things I had not allowed myself to think in the last few years. About Subodh, or Rajani, or the house, or losing Subodh and Rajani and the cats.

Marrying Subodh, to the horror of his entire family, the theatre world, and the newspapers. Public opinion was against us—the son of a zamindar marrying an actress from Bow Bazaar? It was not done. Had he married suitably and then come to visit me, they would have understood. They all did it.

But to marry me, that was indigestible. And how much can young love carry on its fragile back? Even a strong love? I was used to public taunting, articles in the papers about me, lies and slander, but it broke him.

He stopped doing anything, while I took care of the house and went to work at the theatre. Then came the time that he started to resent me going. His mother had been sending him money on the sly—we could manage on that, he argued. But he had fallen in love with me because I was an actress, and an actress I remained. I kept working. He raged, he thundered, and then he pleaded. All of it sickened me, and I felt a sour pity for him. At night, by the time I was back, he was usually asleep.

One day he wasn't there at all. He listened to his father and went to London. He never came back.

If not for Rajani, I could not have lived through it.

She was part of a production I went to see before I married Subodh, fantastic as Razia Sultana: alongside a twinge of envy, I felt delighted. She was deferential to me at first, hesitant—perhaps a little suspicious? But then her basic good nature and my genuine affection met each other and there blossomed the cleanest, purest friendship I had had since I was a child. Oh, Rajani.

When the theatre was in trouble and Subodh had gone, and everyone asked me to accept the rich businessman's proposal so that we could build the Kalyani, only Rajani had objected. Only she had tried to remind them that I was still married, and that Subodh might return. She is the one who fought for me, for my right to say yes or no.

Instead of repaying her kindness by remaining close, I saw her less. I was sleepwalking through my days, doing shows and rehearsals and overseeing the building of the theatre. The one they would name after me. I would be redeemed after all I had suffered, then I would return to her side. Rajani and I would savour this long-awaited fruit.

I was so absorbed in my own sorrow, my own drudgery, my own little pleasures, that I didn't even notice that Rajani needed me. Not until I emerged from my angry confrontation with Gopal babu did I realise that she wasn't at the opening night. I hurried out, and took a rickshaw to the narrow streets that led to her house.

There she lay, in the throes of the birth pangs, though the babe was not yet in her womb seven months. I held her hand through all of it, but god forgive me, I could not hold the babe. I just wanted my Rajani to hold on. "Stay with me, my love, stay." I whispered, and wiped the blood away, coaxed fresh water down her throat. The pain in her face, and then the stillness.

I had sought to rise above the city, and for a glittering few years, I had believed that I could. The city had laughed and crushed me underfoot. Hot grief and memory seared my mind, and that infernal infant's wailing, its racket echoing in my head, disrupting rehearsal, taking over the world, taking over my body and my spirit and my tongue until I fully gave myself to it. The scorpion snapped its pincers, reached out, stung.

*

**THE ELECTRA**
SEASON 1875–76
PRESENTS
**MACBETH**
on Saturday 6th November 1875
at 6.30 and 9.30 p.m.
Gopal Kanti Bose as Macbeth

Smt. Kalyani as Lady Macbeth

Come one, come all!

The quarter-page advertisement in the *Calcutta Gazette* made false promises, for the first two shows of *Macbeth* at the Electra on Beadon Street had quickly sold out.

But I was still fuming about the placement of the advertisement. My ideas, my work, my theatre, and still he got first billing. Still he would be seen as the architect of the entire thing—never a collaborator, always the king. On the evening of the opening show, as I arrived with Putul, I spotted him walking around with that ease in his body that had never been mine. I told her to go on without me, and took him aside.

He beamed when he saw me. "Ah, Kali, did you rest well today? How are you feeling?"

"Less well since I saw the ad in the *Gazette*. Did you write it?"

He looked amused. "What, that? No, no, Satyen did. Why? Did you not like it?"

"I just thought . . . there would be a picture. From our last show. I thought . . . Why do you never show anyone how much work I do?" The words burst out of me, my insides squirming, my heart thumping against my rib cage. But now they were out, and I would have to see this through.

"What on earth do you mean, Kali? Your name is in the ad! Everyone knows you are our lead actress!" His eyes had widened, as if he truly did not understand. "Did you want me to ask Satyen to put a picture in the next ad? We can do that."

"No, it isn't about the picture. You told me you'd name the theatre after me. You of all people know how much I have done, what I have gone through. What I have lost."

He reached a hand toward me, putting it on my arm. "Yes, it's all been very unfortunate and you have been brave, Kali . . . but we have work to do tonight. Let's talk about it after."

That cold dismissal, that promise of a conversation we were never going to have. That bitterness on my tongue.

*

It was pouring outside, unseasonal rain, and the people that had arrived early were grateful to have escaped the mud on the sidewalks. The seats in the boxes were made of velvet. Under the yellow lamplight, the fine clothes of the audience could be admired—a saree of lavender silk, polished leather shoes. The thick burgundy curtains covered the stage, and the audience filed in, filling the boxes and the spare wooden seats below. Friends called out to each other, faces shining. Families sat together; foppish gentlemen whose beloveds would soon appear onstage looked upon the scene with a proprietorial pride.

As the clouds emptied themselves outside, the lashing of the rain was drowned out by the loud voices of the audience, which turned into murmurs as the lights dimmed, which turned into applause as the curtains lifted.

The spectacle of the nine witches singing in call-and-response was hypnotic. Soon the poem became a song, about toil and trouble, about meeting again. The three lead witches were particularly good, but the masterstroke was the young girl with huge eyes who danced passionately out of line, creating a sense of chaos on stage, forcing the others to change positions to keep symmetry, briefly restored until she broke it again. She broke, they followed. She broke, they followed, all in time to the frantic melody.

Applause, gasping, laughter, and cheers. They loved a good song in Calcutta, and this one was outstanding. The curtains came down again, and they held their breath. A gentleman in the audience began to explain to his wife that Macbeth was coming, until a lady turned around to shush him. A few moments went by. People began to stir. Someone coughed.

"Arre, where has Macbeth gone?" a troublemaker shouted from the back. A few people tittered.

The curtains lifted. The burly man who played Banquo ran onto the stage, looking back over his shoulder as the audience started to clap in welcome when they saw her: long hair unfurled and falling to her hips, her form swathed in the same black soldier's uniform that Banquo wore.

The smallest witch ran toward her, screaming, "All hail Macbeth! Hail to thee, Thane of Glamis! All hail Macbeth! Hail to thee, Thane of Cawdor! All hail Macbeth, thou shalt be king hereafter!"

Kalyani-as-Macbeth thundered, "Speak, if you can: what are you?" and the girl turned and ran offstage.

"The . . . the earth hath bub . . . bub . . . bubbles," Banquo stuttered, but Kalyani held her composure, and the rest of the scene passed. As two timid-looking boys entered as Ross and Angus, two gentlemen ushered their families out of the theatre in disgust.

For the first time in her career, Kalyani broke character.

"Wait," she screeched. Those fleeing stopped in their tracks; one of their children, a small girl, whimpered. "Don't you want to know how I became king?"

She looked over her shoulder, and the terrible little witch arrived to usher them back into their seats, ignoring the protestations of the two gentlemen and ladies. When one of them raised his voice, she hooted with a laughter that silenced him. The stage went dark and the curtains dropped.

"If we should fail?" came a voice from the darkness.

"'We fail! But screw your courage to the sticking-place, and we'll not fail,'" the voice answered itself. The audience only saw her now, gleaming teeth and loose hair; whether the rest of the troupe had managed to escape or were cowering in the sidelines, they did not know. Kalyani was playing both Macbeth and Lady Macbeth, hidden in the shadows, her crystalline tones ringing through the small theatre.

A soft light before the curtains, the glint of steel. Macbeth stood staring at a dagger. "Art thou not, fatal vision, sensible to feeling as to sight?" she asked it, with a feverish smile. Two people struggled at the doors by the boxes; a woman shouted, "It's bolted from the outside!" A low hum started in the theatre, the hum of people speaking in urgent voices. A group of people tried to pull open the main exit door. It was locked.

The waif returned, using surprisingly long, elegant hands to indicate that they should return to their seats. A man tried to threaten her; she merely smiled. "The show will be over soon, sir," she said in a low voice. He sat back down, fuming.

Sitting in the total darkness waiting for the play to commence, knowing they would see no one other than the woman wearing black, finally, they fell silent. If some held and squeezed each other's clammy hands, no one saw.

Her clear, cold voice rang out from behind them.

"O horror, horror, horror! Tongue nor heart cannot conceive nor name thee!"

She streaked toward the stage, holding a head in her hands, raining blood over the fine silks and leather and the trembling, stunned faces. She howled, mourning her exasperating mentor, her hate and love pouring out of her like lava.

She spoke while she cried, something about hands, but no one could hear anymore.

*The premise of the theatre built upon a broken promise is based on a real-life historical event. Beadon Street was the hub of Calcutta theatre in the 19th century, and the famous actress and memoirist Binodini Dasi was promised a theatre that she was instrumental in building would be named after her, but it wasn't.*

# SEALING THE ROOM

## André O. Hoilette

*Cothilda / flame woman*

she posed as a well-wisher after the

baby was born. got into the house by

wearing the skin of a sour

woman from the church.

the woman would be found

dead in a day or two, but until then

Cothilda used the skin suit to travel

the sunlit hours.


she decided to stay here

after she saw the baby.

Cothilda has been here every night since

to hear the infant coo

and play with her when

babies should be sleeping

Cothilda watches the infant breathe,

the way her chest rises

baby breath spilling out like a hydrant

sweet and flowing unlike her

still, stale breath.


in the nighttime hours

where the minutes hurry

then slow,

inhale then exhale,

she tries to hold her,

wills her to be her own,

unravelling with her in the wind.


she can't remember her own

baby's face, long dead,

whose children are now

grandmothers themselves.

André O. Hoilette

*Fitzie / obeahman*

Fitzie's been sent for, in a panic.

he stops only to dig a three-foot-

deep hole outside by the hibiscus bush.


he has seen her in his dreams

knew she was somewhere close

in the town. he has been

praying on it.


baby's breathing has stopped

her eyes, fixed black marbles

loose in their sockets.


Fitzie sends the mother outside.

draws hard on his cigar,

the leaves sticky, blows smoke,

closes his eyes to see what is hidden.

he finds it in the corner

lapping the infant's face

a shredded, lavender spectre.


sealing the room

she's been eating baby's spirit

like thread off the spool


Fitzie calls on those gathered

to hold hands and pray.

he seals the room.


pungent splashing of jamaican

white rum across the threshold,

on the windowsills

and empties the bottle

on the perimeter


saying a prayer at each

    *"tek hold a di dragon, di old serpent"*

he lights frankincense

    *"cast 'im inna di bottomless . . . "*

in the northern corner

and myrrh in south and drinks

star oil in the center of the room.

he knows what words to say.

André O. Hoilette

for extra measure Fitzie calls on

jesus to loosen Cothilda's grip

and cast her out. with each breath

he shrinks her form, shackles

her with his commands.


he's brought a kid goat

into the woman's house

calls them to bring it in

its hooves clattering against the tile.

Between the rolling of bones,

prayers and offerings,

he casts the weakened

flame woman into the goat.


now the baby draws its

first strong breath, and again

and again and begins a good

strong wailing.

# SUFFICIENCY

*Excerpt from "Beauty Series"*

## Shalewa Mackall

Enough to become ancestors
to be remembered sideways in crooked poems
to be trotted out on holidays, to be argued over
by folks whose broken lineage is sutured
by your name—a half-remembered talisman—
whose belonging to is shared like your flat feet

> The people, they keep jumping
> till the only way is a prayer

and each other. A projection, a mirror, a window
a wild dance in my messy bedroom—the portal
gave you life anew—remembered enough
to dance on this page—like Grandpa said
*they can only get you if you believe*
so I choose to live empirically in disbelief.
I try to sleep by candlelight. You visit
the dreams of believers more willing than I

> The people, they keep jumping
> till the only way is a prayer

with messages for me, whisper *enough!*

Refuse to remain lost, and land shadowed
in some side-eye corner of consciousness, barely legible
in the sooty essence collected on the thick lips
of glassed candles. Enshrined on my altar
decked in roses, Beauty, you are home

                                The people, they keep jumping
                                   till the only way is a prayer

# CANON

## Sarah Sophia Yanni

if you say          *Lord have Mercy*
     along with the choir
     you will have performed
     a ritual

if you chant          *To Thee O Lord*

     you will have touched
     a byzantine god

priest says          *Christ is Risen*
room bellows         *Truly He is Risen*

     and I tear into my thumb-skin
     saying nothing at all

*Praise the Lord, O my soul!*      praise my blistered body.
*I will praise the Lord*          I will cleanse this body
*as long as I live;*           as long as I have it;
*I will sing praises*          I will douse it in cold

*to my God*
*while I have being*
*Put not your trust in princes,*
*in sons of men in whom*
*there is no salvation.*
*When his breath departs he returns*
*to his earth;*
*on that very day*
*his plans perish.*

then hot then cold
to teach adaptability.
I will not put my trust in others,
in the bodies of those
who offer crowns.
when I breathe it is heavy & the
earth air ruffles;
upon every exhale
I let the stories go.

| | |
|---|---|
| *I believe in one God* | I believe in lungs |
| *the father almighty* | those heaving sacks |
| *the maker of heaven* | giving me breath |
| *& earth* | & purpose |
| *& of all things* | & these purple parts |
| *visible & invisible* | sinewy insides |
| *& in one lord* | & in hands |
| *jesus christ,* | yes, bitten things |
| *the son of god,* | those makers |
| *the only begotten* | a genetic assemblage |
| *before all worlds* | of mothers past |
| *light from light* | small but resilient |
| *very god from very god* | mirroring grace |
| *begotten not made* | tools to make |
| *in one essence* | an essential newness |
| *with the father* | a new morality |
| *by whom all things were made* | of matriarchs & dust |
| *who for us men* | which has no space |
| *& for our salvation* | for weighty rules |
| *came down from heaven* | & heavenly threats |
| *& was incarnate* | & dances beneath |
| *of the holy spirit* | the seat of the guards |
| *& the virgin mary* | expelling tradition |
| *& was made man* | & man-made, ancient |
| *& was crucified also* | rites of bay leaves |
| *for us* | & fear |
| *under pontius pilate* | under sinful pretense |
| *suffered &* | no more suffering |
| *& was buried* | & burial songs |
| *& on the third day* | & I squash the past |
| *he rose again* | rising from shame |
| *according to the scripture* | according to the clergy |
| *& ascended into heaven* | & ascend into honest |
| *& is seated* | belly feelings |

Sarah Sophia Yanni

*at the right hand of*       slightly adjacent to
*the father*       godless canon
*& he shall come again*       & I become
*with glory*       the black sheep
*to judge the quick*       no quick judgment
*& the dead*       & looming death
*whose kingdom*       instead a checklist
*shall have no end*       of unending empathy
*I believe*       I believe
*in the holy spirit*       in this churning agenda
*the lord & giver of life*       of trying & failing
*who proceedeth from*       proceeding from ethics
*the father*       but erupting
*who with the father*       with space
*& son together*       dreaming of movement
*is worshipped*       forming the sacred
*& glorified*       this glorified bounty
*who speaks by the prophets*       of audible sighs

*I believe in one*
*holy catholic & apostolic*
*church*
*I acknowledge one baptism*
*for the remission of*
*sins*
*I look for the resurrection*
*of the dead*
*& the life of the world*
*to come*
*amen*

I believe in dirt
& water
possibility
I acknowledge
the griefs from which
we operate
I look for guts
& minds cracked open
& the genuine bits of
bodies working in tandem
amen

Sarah Sophia Yanni

O Lord our God , who dwellest on high and regardest the humble of heart, who
hast sent forth as the salvation of the race of men Thine only-begotten son and
God, our Lord Jesus Christ. Look down upon Thy servants the catechumens, who
have bowed their necks before Thee, make them worthy in due time of the laver
of regeneration, the remission of sins, and the robe of incorruption. Unite them
to Thy Holy, Catholic, and Apostolic Church, and number them with Thy chosen
flock.

(I suppose there is something left to wish for, in trees or even secular
cosmology. I am looking at a dark sky because it is too drowned by
light here. my heart is not filled quite the way I would like. but there
is something about routine disappointment that makes you a humble person. I'd like to think so, at least. whatever is up there, if you
want to, take a look at what we've done. or maybe don't. or maybe
look with one eye, half blinked, squeezed a little shut. what can we
do to be worthy? I'm sorry that we burned your growings down. I'm
sorry that the air does not smell like fruit here. it smells like dirt and
petroleum and in fall time, fire. ash clouds deposit themselves on
the hood of my car. as I unite with this machine I rescind from any
possibility of you. I turn my music up high and revert to a hopeless
drift, unphased.)

# THE LONGEST STRETCH

*between Ruby Jewel Aid (Mile 29)*
*and Clear Lake Aid (Mile 39)*
*an excerpt*

## Lucien Darjeun Meadows

Sugar rush into a clearing     sudden the light
     we are all pink and blue and gold and violet inside
                I can never be color-blind
       I will always be looking
          for another Native face
             for a bird like you     *bird O choose-it*

I will always be wanting
     to not go into the night alone
            I could use a father right now

The way this sky shivers high on the saddle my feet lost in the snow
                I feel the world
       could break open and I could break too
    tell me there is summer past the next hill
       tell me I can be alone and still do anything
           tell me I am      not

    I want to take off all these masks
      press my face to the direct mystery of it all
     but what if even these hands are
       this face is    *this I is*    a mask too

I want to remember everything

the flickering of the backlit leaves this morning
                    the breath of these runners passing by    lifting
          a hand
this basket of warm air cannot last forever

                    there is no *we* without an hour
                              *now* out of flower

# DOWNRIVER

## Melanie Merle

I find in crowds the same warm and cold spots I find in the ocean.
In the dream, we sit
    your VW Bug parked on a sandbar at the river.
From the passenger seat, I look forward, my gaze fixed.
There is only river and sky,
    white like winter, fingertip ends of a tree branch reach into the frame.
Smell of rotting wood mingles with sun-cracked vinyl and dust,
    laced with cigarette smoke.
Other dreams send bees or bombs,
    a catalogue of sound and violence.
This one is different even when it is the same.
I wish for the water to rise up and swallow us, car and all.
I wish the fish to swim by the windows,
    curiously silent traffic,
    the gar with his alligator snout and the freshwater drum.

I want to say *save me*, but I can only think of the word *eraser*.
I form the word *decision*, but it comes out *diversion*.
I try *division*, but what comes is *dimension*.
I think *bad luck*, and hear an *umbrella open*, so I say *thank you*.
It looks as though snow is falling, but it's the cottonwoods.
Cotton would gather in great drifts.
Caught on wood, it floats downstream.

Caught on wood.

Cot on wood.

My mind sticks in the wooly places.

There are narcissus on the riverbank in wild yellow clusters,
    vanity run amok.

My teeth are bulbs screwed in tight and I am dizzy with their taste.

The dream can only end with my waking.

But upriver, the beaver shapes a new world.

# DATE: POST GLACIAL

## dg nanouk okpik

A fern curls and drinks     water next     to the Chana River;
she/I engrave/s     with drill bows     the tattoos

     layered     on the backside of a gray whale,
Polish     with cotton in circles     to bring out the design.

Over the sea black-whales     arch and span,
     while four-sided sabers     guard the processing

     barge—a city atop the sea.

Pollen lands     where the air is good.     Dig for chert bone.

Find an antler.  Reel in the velvet     make a map for trade.

Small wooden faces     flat     with skin-lined splinters ask:
     *Should we prune*     *more trees or tag and replant?*

We     the Red Stone people
     Keep our millwork central.
In the New Stone Age     don't let the paddlewheel rust.

Around our chins     tie the knitted     musk oxen hat
with ivory toggles     firm and fixed.

     dg nanouk okpik

Kiln powder in beveled pools                    on beetle rust greens.
    The talc settles              no rain in seventeen days.

Invent a fan to blow          the north wind        to cool the ivory bone etch.
The tall grass

calls bent birch                snowshoes to make tracks. *Do we run*
*a tap dry of soot*              *and sludge to forge roots?*

How many drink        wild tea, dip blubber in seal oil?
From the horizon  she/I watch/es fire opals   come from

molten rain,     the clay mass                    returns to
                full grass baskets.

# THE PASSING

## Daniel José Older

Something is very wrong. When I wake up, the knowledge is waiting for me, lurking. All my bones scream it. My gut is clenched with it. It's all over me.

Outside, the sky is still gray. A little light comes in through the window, hits the bare tiled floor. I sit up in bed, feel these old muscles groan with the sudden effort. At first I think maybe this wrongness is in me, with my own collection. I try to steady my mind. Lay back down, close my eyes and go inward to check. All the stories are there, hovering around peacefully, and I breathe a happy sigh. There's hundreds of them, but I know the ins and outs well enough to know at a glance when something's off, and it's not. Not with me anyway. But there it is, that nagging something-or-other. A very terrible thing is happening.

I ease myself up again, slower this time. Drop my legs over the side of the bed. The cold floor sends little gasps of surprise up through the bottoms of my feet. The day is breaking behind the skyscrapers across the river. The city wakes up all around me. I am alive.

But this badness pursues me out of my bedroom, hangs over me while I brush my teeth and sit on the toilet for my morning tinkle. In the shower it recedes some, but then it's back when I'm putting the coffee on. Slithering around my ankles. Crawling up my spine. Diablo. I fight off restlessness while I eat my mushy stuff, because that's not good for digestion. My kitchen is pale and bathed in sunlight. I can smile for a moment,

Daniel José Older

appreciating the bright geometry my windows create with those rays, but only for a moment. Then the feeling's back.

From somewhere inside, a story rises. It was an old guajiro back in Cuba. 'Simpático' is the best word for him. It means 'nice' in English, but nice is such a pathetic word. Nice. It just lives and dies in one breath. Simpático is a whole story unto itself. It has panache. This old man was simpático until the day he died. You know, I think he had a thing for me? I was already very old at the time, and this was way back when, understand, but Tomás had his eyes all over me and that hunger radiated off him in hot waves.

His story—it was about his first love. He was old now, and alone, but he carried it with him everywhere he went, and not in a bad way. It walked along beside him like a faithful friend, that story. Never held him back or distracted him from the present tense, but just remained, a gentle reminder that his heart was alive and well, in spite of whatever hardship may come. Sometimes, before going to sleep, he would think of it and smile his old wrinkled smile. I came to him late at night. Inhaled all that fresh earthy perfume of the countryside breathing through the big open windows in his little house. Put my hand on his forehead and out it came: A whole wily early-twenties romance, complete with messiness and passion, but all in all quite tidy and to the point. I thanked him, and he smiled at me with sleepy eyes.

They always smile when I'm done. They must know that their stories will live on long after they do, that they're sharing a little part of themselves with the great patchwork quilt of humanity, and it must be very pleasant indeed.

Old Tomás's story winds through the chaotic finale and then slides back into the ether and I'm done with my mushy stuff and almost done with my café and the icky feeling is back. Fine. It is here to stay, apparently, so I will investigate. That's all that negativity wants anyway: a little attention. I don't usually pay it much mind because when you do, it feels good and keeps coming back for more. But this is . . . different. It's someone else's shit, first of all, so I don't know why it's come to trouble my morning.

If it's not my shit, it must be one of my sisters'. I admit I've been a little out of touch recently. It's just that I like it up here in my twenty-first-floor apartment, with its cold linoleum floors and the burner that you have to ignite four times before it finally lights, and the occasionally leaking faucet. Most mornings I wake up and am simply content. I have my stories; stacks and stacks of them. Plus I have many memories of my own to wander through. I've been married six times and I still get letters from the offspring I've left scattered around the world. Sometimes different friends or family members stop by for obligatory visits that I can will to be suddenly fascinating tête-à-têtes. Yes, I can still be surprising after all these years. I'm still profoundly in love with life even for all the death I've seen. It still gives me a thrill to feel the cold floor against my bare feet every morning and know that I am alive.

So I don't trouble much with the others. They're fine, I'm sure. They have their occasional meetings, every few decades or whatever, and sometimes I pass through, but mostly, eh, I could go without. There'll be a day when we're all together again, I'm sure. Whatever it is we're holding these stories for will come to pass and we'll convalesce and compare notes. Until then, though, I'll just make my café, eat my mushy stuff, and mind mine, thank you very much.

At least, that's what I would do, if I could shake this feeling. Okay. I rise, supporting myself with one hand on the table, and pad across the apartment. I say pad because I'm wearing these slightly frayed pink slippers, and when you walk around in slippers, you're padding. I hear the dust shuffle beneath them and think I'd better sweep up soon. When I reach the window, the one next to the couch, my mind starts moving fast.

I scan the rising and falling buildings beneath me and realize that whatever's gone wrong, it's gone wrong with Hyacinth. It's a fact I'd been actively trying to ignore, but when I let my mind relax over the cityscape the knowledge just swims right to the surface. Hyacinth is my elder by decades. She's prim and proper to a fault, down and dapper with all the protocols. She's unshakable. I'd say it's even come between us some over the years; I simply tired of her being so thoroughly *her* all the time,

Daniel José Older

and I'm sure she feels the same about me. Truth is: We're probably too much alike to be around each other for very long, but there was a time I damn near worshipped that woman. Anyway, she's the last of my sisters I'd think would fall prey to some simmering ridiculousness. Or whatever this is . . . What I need is a way to see things that are going on in Hyacinth's real physical world, because all this psychic-ether shit is great but only takes you so far.

Beside me is a desk with a computer on it that my niece brought me and I never bothered to set up. Really, what am I going to do with it? I don't type. I have no need for company that's not flesh and blood. I thanked Janie profusely—it was very touching how she said, "Now we can keep in touch!" all excited like—but then I never set it up. My bad, as they say.

Now though, I eye the sleeping contraption with new interest. They have ways of doing things these days, I know. This Internet is full of surprises. Perhaps I could send an email of some kind and find out what's going on. Or whatever it is people do on those universal airwaves. Twit? Twat? It doesn't matter; it might work, and right now I don't have much else to go on.

Juan-José is standing there when I open the door of my apartment. He's wearing that beat-up old Yankees cap and the same humongous headphones and wraparound sunglasses as always. He's got a little plastic yellow flower and he holds it out to me, trying to smile with that toothless caved-in gap where his mouth should be.

I really don't have time for this. I crane my neck and yell "Mirta!" toward the next floor up. "Miiirtaaa!"

"¿Qué pasó?"

"Juan-Jo se escapó."

"¡Ay carajo! ¡Me cago en la madre de Dios!" Mirta yells back. Then she punctuates with a curt: "¡Coño!"

I step past Juan-José as Mirta's flip-flopped feet storm down the stairwell.

*

Benjamin is on the phone when he opens the door, probably with one of his boyfriends back in Wisconsin or wherever. When he sees me he wipes the irritated look off his face very quickly and says, "Hold on a sec, babe." Then he furrows his eyebrows. "Fine! Look . . . I said hold on. Can you . . . can you wait? For two seconds, please, my neighbor just . . . Look!" He looks down at me apologetically. "Look, just hold on. Can I call you back? No? Fine, then hold on."

"It's okay," I say, and turn to shuffle back to my apartment. Maybe I sag my shoulders a little more than necessary. Perhaps I frown some and shake my head.

"No, wait. Babe, I'm going to call you back and we'll finish this later, okay? Fine. Yes. Goodbye." He lets that irritation slide out in a long sigh while staring at the cell phone and then composes himself. "How are you, Ms. Cortázar?"

"I'm fine, Benjamin. I'm sorry to trouble you, but I remember you said once that if I ever needed help setting up that computer I should come knocking?"

Benjamin wears a puffy vest over a Superman T-shirt. He's got light-brown skin and light-gray sweatpants. I was wary of him when he first moved in, mostly because he wears vests and sweatpants at the same time, but he's a genuine enough soul with his little greetings in the hallway and nervous politeness. He looks puzzled for a second. I can see his mind wavering back and forth between me and the cell phone and finally he scrunches up his face and says, "Sure, hang on one sec. Lemme just send a text." He taps away at the keypad, disappears the phone into one of his vest pockets, and follows me across the hall to my apartment.

After the pleasantries and obligatory offering of coffee, Benjamin gets this very serious look on his face and sets to work. He's a computer something-or-other, it's what he does, and you can see that even a simple task like this grants him a certain determined vitality. While I watch, another story surfaces. It's a difficult one, and I wonder briefly if it's a foreboding sign before giving myself over to it. A young girl, Brazilian, who'd had a very terrible childhood. She's killing, systematically

Daniel José Older

killing people who hurt her, one by one, but none of the peacefulness she'd hoped for comes when it's all over. She's just empty. There's something at the end, before it fades out, a little glimmer of hope there, some hint of her new life, but it's fleeting and when the story's over I feel empty too, and very sad.

"You okay, Ms. Cortázar?"

I snap out of it. "Of course, Benjamin. How's it looking?"

"Um, almost done actually."

It's impressive: A whole cascade of wires goes from the screen to the keyboard to the big bulky box on the ground and then a few more connect to a smaller black box with lots of blinking lights on it. "That was quick."

"Well, you know." He looks pleased with himself. "It's what I do." Then a little buzzing noise erupts from his vest and he scowls and pulls out his phone. He taps another message into it, frowning, and apologizes without looking up.

"It's fine. You sure you don't want any coffee?"

"No, thanks, Ms. Cortázar."

"Benjamin?"

"Hm?"

"Do you think, will I be able to be connected to the Internet, when it's all set up?"

He laughs a little and puts away his phone. "Of course! It's already mostly done and what I can do . . . " He slides into the wicker chair I'd set up by the desk and reaches down to flip a switch somewhere. " . . . is set you up with your own wireless network. Let me see . . . " The computer lets out a heavenly chime and blinks to life. How sweet!

"This network setting-up thing, it would take a while? I hate to be impatient but there is actually something with some urgency I need to deal with."

Benjamin turns around in the chair to look at me. "Is everything okay?"

"Yes yes, just a friend of mine. She might be in trouble. It's complicated."

"I see." Of course he doesn't, but okay. "Well, then, I can connect you through my own wireless and that'll be quicker, since your router is already set up."

"Okay." Whatever that means.

*

I used to be so proud when people would mistake Hyacinth and me for sisters. We didn't even look that much alike, but we're similarly complected and both slender and have a spry quickness. I didn't really understand who she was or why she seemed so interested in me at first, I was just awed by her easiness with the whole world, that supernatural calm she carried. Then came the Night of No Return.

I don't remember a lot about it except there was so much music playing and I was surrounded by women. More women than I'd ever seen. They were all shapes and sizes, so many glorious shades of brown and speaking so many different languages. I remember feeling smooth, ready for whatever may come, and realizing I had clicked at least momentarily into Hyacinth's perpetual state of elegant ease.

I'm sure I knew somehow that nothing would ever be the same after that night, and I'm sure I didn't care. I felt those tambores radiating through my body, whispering their secrets. The guitar let out an ocean of notes, dancing with me as I strode through the crowd behind Hyacinth. An enormous woman was playing a horn of some kind; it let out raw, guttural moans that sounded like the swoons of lovers in the act.

We came to a chalk circle where the crowd had cleared some space. A very, very old woman lay propped up on some pillows on a cot in the middle of the circle. She was smiling, watching the beautiful tide of womanhood swirl around her, and when I approached she winked at me and said something in a language I didn't understand. No one had to tell me the old one was dying—it was written, in the most peaceful way possible, all across her wisp of a body.

"Lay down," Hyacinth said, nodding at an empty cot beside the woman. "This is how it all begins."

Ben says, "Ha!" which apparently means I'm connected to the Internet and now fully a part of the 21st century. A page appears on the screen with little animated characters and colorful letters.

"So this is the world wide web I hear so much about," I mutter.

"You should be all set, Ms. Cortázar." I let a moment pass and Benjamin turns around. "Unless you need something else done?"

"I do. But I don't know how to explain it. I'm sorry to trouble you, I know you have other things going on."

"Oh, it's no trouble at all." He takes out his phone and makes a face at it. "Just drama, you know. What do you need to do?"

"Well, I have a friend . . . " Already this sounds like one of those horrible stories you tell a late-night call-in show that's really about you. " . . . And she's in trouble. I think. Well, I know someone's in trouble, and I think it's this one friend of mine."

"Oh."

"Sorry to be so vague."

"How?"

"What?"

"How do you know someone's in trouble?"

Because the knowledge is a cancer creeping through my insides. Because I know things. Because it's true. "Ah. It's hard to explain. Maybe one day. But my friend: if I could somehow, I don't know . . . Check on her. Is there an email that could do that for me?"

Benjamin does some things with his face that I assume mean he's trying not to laugh. Nice kid. "Not an email, necessarily, but maybe an app." He turns back to the screen, his eyebrows arching in concentration. "I wonder . . . "

"Maybe the app could ask someone else's email if she's okay?" I suggest. He's too deep in thought to answer that one so I just let him do his thing.

"There's this one app," he says, a few hmms later. "It not only links up with satellite imagery of a particular location, that's pretty basic Google Maps shit, uh . . . excuse me."

"Oh, it's fine, Benjamin, I curse all the time."

He visibly relaxes. "Oh. You can call me Ben, by the way, only my mom calls me Benjamin anymore."

"Ben, okay. Do you want a beer?"

He chuckles. "It's nine o'clock in the morning."

"I know that."

"Well . . . Sure."

"Go on," I say as I pad across the room to the fridge.

"Oh, well this app, it's super secret actually but I know some of the guys developing it. Still pretty new and probably vastly illegal, but anyway, it hacks into all the security cameras in the vicinity and can actually give you a semi-complete 3D map of what you're looking at. Pretty amazing shi—stuff, uh, shit." He finishes with an awkward giggle.

German really fucked up the English language. A beer? I mean, it's simple, so that's nice. But nothing compares to cerveza with its mischievous regality. Cerveza. It's dignified. I hand Ben a cerveza, a Presidente in fact, which perhaps is not the most dignified of them all, but not bad. He nods and takes a sip. When he finishes a crown of foam ejaculates from the spout and spills onto his sweatpants. "Oh, shit," he says, "I'm sorry."

"They're your pants, not mine," I laugh, padding back to the kitchen for some paper towels.

"Alright, let me see if I can bring this app up."

I give him the paper towels and the address of Hyacinth's Queens apartment, and he clacks away for a few minutes.

I'm getting itchy. The terribleness trembles along my spine; it's a jagged clanging that won't go away. Deep breath. Stifle impatience. Breathe.

"Pow!" Ben yells. There on the screen is a whirling image of Hyacinth's building. I say whirling because it looks as if a helicopter is circling the place, panning every possible angle with startling accuracy.

"Amazing," I gasp. "Tell your friends they have made a very excellent app."

Ben laughs. "I will." He gets out of the chair and I sit, narrowing my eyes at the screen. Hyacinth lives on the third floor, I believe. Her living room window had a fire escape outside and view of the . . . There! I lean even closer to the screen and the image becomes blurry, full of fat, ungainly squares. But there's something there.

"Can you, Ben, can you make it clearer?" Not so frantic. The poor boy will get scared.

He leans forward and does a few things with the mouse. The image stops rotating and swooshes forward toward the spot I was glaring at. First it's still all messy and then, by some means of that weird digital magic, it resolves into a crisp, perfect picture.

"My God," I whisper. Probably, Ben doesn't see it. It's just a tiny sparkling sliver, like a thread of silver caught in the sunlight. It outlines the form of a man standing perfectly still on the fire escape outside Hyacinth's window. A taker. This one would be the lookout. That means that at least one other is either on the way or already inside. This is much, much worse than I thought.

"What is it?" Ben asks.

"Nothing," I say. The lie is plain, though. Ben reads the horror on my face but doesn't say anything.

I stare at the screen for another few seconds, making sure I saw what I saw. "What's the quickest possible way to get to Queens?"

"The G train, I guess, but you'd have to take a bus to the station. Um, you could take a cab but it'd be pretty expensive I think." New York City public transportation is really a world unto itself. Ben considers something and then says, "Or we could take my super-scooter."

I'm a little put out that an adult man has something called a "super-scooter," but listen, I'm in point A to point B mode, so I don't really give a crap what he calls it as long as it moves faster than the B48. And then we're downstairs in the basement storage area and Ben is pulling a tarp off something quite huge and there it is in all its glory. If a Harley Davison had its way with a prehistoric swan, nine months later you'd have a Super Scooter. "Technically, it's a personal hovercraft," Ben is saying as he once-overs it with an old rag. "But you know, they call it the Super-Scooter I guess 'cause it sounds cool."

"I didn't know such a thing even existed." I'm trying not to sound like too much of an awed schoolgirl, but the thing is amazing.

Ben looks around and cranes his neck toward me. "Technically, it doesn't yet. But I know some people who know some people in the tech world, and . . . this is basically a prototype of something that'll be on the market a few years from now. I'm not really supposed to have it at all, just holding it as a favor for a guy. And I kinda swore I wouldn't ever go joyriding on it, but . . . you said this was an emergency, right?"

We just stare at each other for a couple of seconds and then I nod ever so slightly.

"Well, hop on." He sits on the cushiony seat and pushes forward to the edge so there's room for little me. I am frail, older than anyone imagines. Still, there's some room for thrill-seeking left in me. I'm both terrified and feverishly exhilarated by the thought of putting my life in this strange, skinny fellow's hands. I put my own wrinkly old hands against his torso to steady myself while I mount the thing. It hums and vibrates like a living animal beneath m—not an altogether unpleasant experience, I have to admit. Ben clicks a button, the metal gate crunches open and we swoosh out into the sunlit streets.

At first I can't breathe. Or maybe I don't want to breathe, or just plain forget. Everything is moving so fast around me, these streets I know so well just blur past and are gone. And then I realize I'm smiling. Hugely. I must look ridiculous, the wind flushing through my old face, my gray-and-white hair dancing miraculously behind me. I'm zooming through the streets of Williamsburg at Mach 10 clutching a 6'3" 130-pound brown boy from Wisconsin, holding on for dear life. The universe does indeed bring you to strange places.

"You must have wonderful joyrides on this thing with your boyfriend," I say once I catch my breath.

"Oh. I'm not gay."

For a few moments all we hear is the wind whipping alongside us, the occasional horns of midday traffic. "Oh."

"That was my girlfriend Diana I was, um, talking to on the phone earlier."

"Of course."

Maybe it's better if I don't speak. We zip alongside streets and alleyways 'til we're in Polish Green Point, mostly quiet little houses and occasional butcher shops and bakeries. Then, very suddenly, we're flying, literally flying across the Pulaski Bridge. It's a tiny one, as far as New York bridges go. There's some industrial business going on down by the canal, along with the obligatory declaration of love and territorial dispute graffiti. The water is crisp in the midday sun and all the factories and parking lots sparkle dazzlingly along the surface. And then it's all over because we're in Queens, blasting past some warehouses and then cutting through traffic beneath the 59th Street Bridge.

Stories are rising up inside me. They're agitated; maybe they sense the danger. Whatever it is, they need to stop. I can't concentrate when I keep getting whiffs of chocolate, whispers of rain against a window, stomach-clenching jolts of passion and indignation. I close my eyes and will them to back up off me for a bit, smile as the scattered threads of life settle back into place.

"Ms. Cortázar?"

"Yes, Ben?"

"We're here."

*

The door to Hyancinth's apartment is ajar so I ease it open and poke my head in. It's much worse than I thought. The room is a mess, but not the kind you find after a struggle. There are piles of food-crusted dishes, discarded tissues, crumpled-up papers. The blinds are pulled and the whole place seems dusty and grim, like you have to wade through the air. Hyacinth has been wallowing. I step in, bracing myself against the fetid smell of neglect, and gingerly cross toward the bedroom.

There are three of them. They're just barely visible, more glinty flashes of silver thread in the half-light. The lines describe three tall bodies crouching along the floor. Hyacinth lies on her back in the middle of them, her mouth open, her breath coming in irregular bursts like a dying fish. The takers have their hands on her, holding her old body down, although she's so far gone I don't even think they have to. Their heads are nestled against her ribs like suckling pups. They're sucking her stories out, emptying poor Hyacinth of all the hard work she's done over the centuries.

I don't bother being quiet. Anyway, the rage is in me; I don't think I could creep if I tried. The first one rises, all sluggish from so much feeding but still fierce like a cornered street-hound. I narrow my eyes, find where the glimmering contours insinuate something solid and drive my open hand into it. Catch the thing full across the throat and hear it gasp. Those invisible hands reach out toward me so I throw myself forward, feeling my old body crackle and grumble as I go. The taker is thrown off balance and we collapse across one of its still-feeding companions.

On the way down, my leg brushes against Hyacinth's. It's cold and I know if she's not gone yet, it won't be long. I can't be troubled with that now. The two takers are pinned beneath me; it feels like a horrible breeze, writhing up from the floor against my chest. They're pathetic, these wraiths, given over to their gluttony and barely able to stand, let alone fight off a nice old lady like me. So they don't put up much struggle when I place my hands over their faces. Then, with whispered, fevered prayers, I press down with my palms and let all my power to destroy flow through my arms and out into these squirming ghouls.

They squirm, twitch, begin to give over to nothingness. I feel the last raging gasps reverberate through my slender body. An echo clatters along my bones, rattles me, and then they're gone. The third one has wrenched itself away from Hyacinth and is stumbling toward the door. There's so much crap on the floor, the taker has to keep throwing his weight from one side to the other to sashay around things. I walk slowly toward him, watch as he pitches forward and lands in a nebular heap.

It's so easy, I almost feel bad. Then Hyacinth gasps again. The rage wells up inside my chest, a red rising tide. It swooshes through my arm and explodes out my hand and into the back of the taker's head and annihilates him instantly. I rise, scan the piles of laundry and old newspapers. I'm about to take care of Hyacinth when a tingling voice in the back of my head whispers one word: *Window.*

The lookout. I turn toward the window as it cracks and then shatters. I hear the bedroom door swing open behind me and like an asshole, I turn around. Of course it's Ben. But when I realize that, it's too late: The lookout is on me. He's not fatigued and fatted out like his brothers. Those long arms hold me fast from behind and his cold lips are on my skin.

"Ms. Cortázar!" Ben is frozen in the doorway. I must look like a crazy person; I'm sure he can't see the taker. I open my mouth but a sudden shock of pain erupts through me. The taker has sent some sliver of itself inside, is burrowing through those precious stacks of stories. I wait for the panic but instead an unsettling complacency comes over me. The pain subsides and a pleasant haziness takes its place.

"Ms. Cortázar?" I'm sure my eyes have glazed over. I'm not really focusing on anything in particular, because why bother? Everything is taken care of. The boy in front of me suddenly looks at the floor and gasps, "Oh my god!" He runs past me. I think I might turn, at a leisurely pace. Maybe see what the excitement is about. I do, slowly because I'm a little dizzy and the room becomes a blur when I move too fast. Something heavy is weighing on my back but I'm very, very content.

A foot. A woman's bare foot, gray-brown and calloused, with overgrown toenails. It's all I can make out because Ben's crouching over the rest of her. He turns, in slow motion, and shoots me a terrified glance. That's when I see the woman lying on the ground. The whole situation seems so familiar to me, like I saw it in a movie once. Or perhaps it was a story someone told me as I fell pleasantly asleep. Then I see her face.

*Hyacinth.*

Just a whisper. That voice. That's my voice. My whisper. *Hyacinth.* I know her. She is my friend. My sister. Just then, the sad old face trembles slightly and a hoarse breath escapes her open mouth. *Hyacinth.* And I see it: she's full of stories. Well, not full anymore, but there are still some, dancing in there like children left at school after all their classmates have been whisked away.

I have stories in me. Sweet Jesus!

That weight on my back. The taker. The situation flashes back to me and I'm suddenly consumed by panic. Ben is standing, staring with wide eyes. I drop to my knees, my arms are flailing. No. No flailing right now. I will my arms to reach behind me, find the thing, the . . .

Everything is so pleasant. My hand catches something in the air behind my head. A form. I'm sinking toward the floor. Ben reaches out to me. Behind him is Hyacinth, my sister.

This old hand finds its mark and my brain shoots a trembling blast of death through the taker. And something releases inside of me. Terror floods back up; the room is suddenly crisp. I wrench myself free of the taker's grasp and whirl around, still on my knees. He's shaking his head, trying to rally for another grab at me. I put my hand on him and when he looks up I let the death out, let it crease through him, watch him crumble and dissolve at my knees.

"Jesus!" Ben says. "What the fuck is going on?"

I try to stand but it's not working. This combat shit wore me out. Ben offers his arm and I clutch it, pull myself up. Hyacinth takes another breath. I kneel beside her, my whole body trembling, and have a look. She's mostly gone, my sister. As I gaze over that unkempt, tragic body, her withered hair and dry skin, I understand. They've been here for a while now, weeks maybe. That gnawing wrongness I woke up with was just Hyacinth's death knoll. Too late. She didn't even have any fight left in her. The takers found their way in, poisoned the air with that sweet-sensation morphine-type stuff they have, and feasted on poor Hyacinth's stories at their leisure.

Amazingly though, there's still quite a few stories in there. I can sense them twirling and tingling as I get close to her sad old face. She's been around a lot longer than I have. I can't even imagine how much traveling and collecting she's done. The sorrow of the moment suddenly rushes up on me. Hyacinth, for all her pain-in-the-ass perfectionism, taught me so much. There was a time that she was the one I went to when the pressure of all that living felt too burdensome to bear. Her face would crease into a smile and those eyes would glint a little and she'd spit out some silly old aphorism, more potent for its tone than meaning, and I'd feel somehow revived. I'd walk out fresh and the air would seem chilly and crisp around me and the world wouldn't be closing in anymore.

I let it pass. This isn't the time for century-old recollections. Hyacinth really only has another couple of moments left and I need to figure out what to do with her stories. I can't keep them all, I know that for sure. The suddenness of that overload, the two collections colliding, would be a shock to my system that I might never recover from. I could just let them go: as soon as her mortal body expired it would release them like spores out into the world. Most would evaporate. Some might carry off into the early autumn wind and become dreams or fits of inspiration. But all that work, all that collecting . . . It seems a shame to let them go.

"Should we call 911?"

Ben is crouched across from me, staring intently at my face. I must have let my sadness slip out. "No, Ben. There's nothing they can do for her."

He nods like he understands. I suppose, in some way, he must've figured out by now that I'm not your average abuelita next door. I study his face for a second, blocking out all the chaos and carnage around us.

It's an intriguing third possibility, but I have my doubts.

He is, after all, a man. Never seen one of those keep stories. They don't often have that same impulse toward nurturing the inner garden, so to speak. But that's too easy, really. I always assumed there was a tradition or protocol of some kind. If there is, it's buried so deep that it never reached these old ears.

It's not just that though. He's very flimsy, Ben. I don't know if that little body could handle the sudden influx of stories. Even then, long-term, there's no telling what would happen.

"What is it, Ms. Cortázar?"

He's genuine, I'll give him that much. Not trying to be anything but his own strange little self. Maybe, over time, he could develop some more spine and grow into the tremendous responsibility. Maybe. It's cruel, in a way, but crueler things have been done for much worse reasons.

"Ms. Cortázar? Why are you smiling?"

"Lie down, Ben." I say very gently. "Here, next to Hyacinth. This is how it all begins."

# CONTRIBUTOR BIOS

**Aerik Francis** is a Queer Black & Latinx poet based in Denver, Colorado, US. Aerik is the recipient of poetry fellowships from Canto Mundo and the Watering Hole. Aerik's writing can be found at *phaentompoet.com*.

**Alton Melvar M Dapanas** (them/they) is author of full-length hybrid collection *Towards a Theory on City Boys: Prose Poems* (Guildford: Newcomer Press, 2021), assistant nonfiction editor of London-based Panorama: *The Journal of Place & Travel*, Iowa-based *Atlas & Alice Literary Magazine*, and editorial reader for *Creative Nonfiction* magazine. (*https://lnktr.ee/samdapanas*).

**André O. Hoilette** is a Jamaican-born poet living in Denver, Colorado. He is a Cave Canem alumnus and the former editor of *ambulant: A Journal of Poetry & Art* and former assistant editor of *Nexus Magazine*. He earned an MFA in Fiction and Poetry from Regis University's Mile-High MFA program, and his work earned a 2020 nomination for a Pushcart Prize. His work has previously appeared in *Role Call, Stand Our Ground, Bum Rush the Page: A Def Poetry Jam* and Cave Canem 10-Year Reader anthologies and journals: *Inverted Syntax, Cultural Weekly, Rigorous, milk magazine, Nexus magazine, South Broadway Press* and *Burrow Press*.

**Brian K. Hudson** has done many things to earn a living: programming, washing dishes, providing tech support, welding, and shelving library books, to name just a few. His current and longest-held career has been teaching

English at the college level. His short stories can be found in *mitewaci-mowina: Indigenous Science Fiction & Speculative Storytelling* and a special issue of *Lightspeed Magazine,* PEOPLE OF COLO(U)R DESTROY SCIENCE FICTION!, which won the 2017 British Fantasy Award for Best Anthology. He teaches digital storytelling and Native Studies in Albuquerque, New Mexico.

**Cindy Juyoung Ok** teaches creative writing and translates from Korean. A MacDowell, Lambda Literary, and Banff Centre Fellow, her recent poems and stories can be found in *The Margins, The Nation,* and *The Yale Review.*

**Daniel José Older**, a lead story architect for *Star Wars: The High Republic*, is the *New York Times* best-selling author of the upcoming young adult fantasy novel *Ballad & Dagger* (book 1 of the Outlaw Saints series), the sci-fi adventure *Flood City*, and the monthly comic series *The High Republic Adventures*. His other books include the historical fantasy series Dactyl Hill Squad, *The Book of Lost Saints*, the Bone Street Rumba urban fantasy series, *Star Wars: Last Shot*, and the young adult series the Shadowshaper Cypher, including *Shadowshaper*, which was named one of the best fantasy books of all time by *TIME* magazine and one of *Esquire*'s 80 Books Every Person Should Read. He won the International Latino Book Award and has been nominated for the Kirkus Prize, the World Fantasy Award, and the Mythopoeic Award. Find more info and read about his career as an NYC paramedic at http://danieljoseolder.net/.

**George Abraham** (they/he) is a Palestinian-American poet and author of *Birthright* (Button Poetry)—a Lambda Literary Award finalist and winner of the Big Other Book Award. They are a Kundiman fellow, a Radius of Arab American Writers board member, and a Litowitz MFA+MA Candidate in Poetry at Northwestern University.

**dg nanouk okpik** was born in Anchorage, and her family is from Barrow, Alaska. She earned a BFA at the Institute of American Indian Arts and an MFA at the University of Southern Maine's Stonecoast College. Her debut poetry collection, *Corpse Whale* (2012), won the American Book Award. Her work has also been featured in *Effigies: An Anthology of Indigenous Writing from the Pacific Rim* (2009) and *Sing: Poetry from the Indigenous Americas* (2011). A recipient of the Truman Capote Trust Scholarship, she has taught at the Institute for American Indian Arts and has served as a resident advisor for the Santa Fe (New Mexico) Indian School. She lives in Santa Fe.

**Jennifer Elise Foerster** is the author of three books of poetry: *Leaving Tulsa* (2013), *Bright Raft in the Afterweather* (2018), and *The Maybe-Bird* (The Song Cave, May 2022). She served as the Associate Editor of the recently released *When the Light of the World Was Subdued, Our Songs Came Through: A Norton Anthology of Native Nations Poetry*. She is the recipient of a NEA Creative Writing Fellowship, a Lannan Foundation Writing Residency Fellowship, and was a Wallace Stegner Fellow in Poetry at Stanford. Her poetry has recently appeared in *POETRY London*, *The Georgia Review*, *Kenyon Review* and other journals. Jennifer currently teaches at the Rainier Writing Workshop and is the Literary Assistant to the US Poet Laureate, Joy Harjo. Foerster grew up living internationally, is of European (German/Dutch) and Mvskoke descent, and is a member of the Muscogee (Creek) Nation of Oklahoma. She lives in San Francisco.

**Juan J. Morales** is the son of an Ecuadorian mother and Puerto Rican father, which inspired many of the poems in his poetry collections, *The Siren World* and *Friday and the Year That Followed*. He is also the author of *The Handyman's Guide to End Times*, winner of the 2019 International Latino Book Award. His poems have also recently appeared in *Pleiades*, *Crazyhorse*, *Copper Nickel*, *PANK*, *Poetry*, *terrain*, *Salamander*, *Collateral*, *Acentos Review*, *The Laurel Review*, and the anthologies *Dear America* and *Breakbeats Vol. 4 LatiNext*. He is a CantoMundo Fellow, a Macondo Fellow, the editor of

*Pilgrimage Magazine*, and the Chair of English and World Languages at Colorado State University Pueblo.

**Kenji C. Liu** (he/him/his) is the author of *Monsters I Have Been* (Alice James Books, 2019), finalist for the California and Maine book awards, and *Map of an Onion*, national winner of the 2015 Hillary Gravendyk Poetry Prize (Inlandia Institute). His writing is in numerous journals, anthologies, magazines, and two chapbooks, *Craters: A Field Guide* (2017) and *You Left Without Your Shoes* (2009). An alumnus of Kundiman, the Djerassi Resident Artist Program, and the Community of Writers, he lives in Los Ángeles.

**Kenzie Allen** is a Haudenosaunee poet and multimodal artist, and a descendant of the Oneida Nation of Wisconsin. She is a recipient of a 92Y Discovery Prize (2021) and a James Welch Prize for Indigenous Poets (2021), and fellowships from Vermont Studio Center and Aspen Writers' Foundation. Kenzie's work can be found in *Narrative Magazine*, *Boston Review*, *The Adroit Journal*, and other venues. Born in West Texas, she currently lives and teaches in Toronto.

**Lucien Darjeun Meadows** was born and raised in the Appalachian Mountains of what is now sometimes called Virginia and West Virginia to a family of English, German, and Cherokee descent. An AWP Intro Journals Project winner, Lucien has received awards from the Academy of American Poets, American Alliance of Museums, and National Association for Interpretation. His debut collection, *In the Hands of the River* was published in September 2022 by Hub City Press.

**Lynn C. Pitts** was born and raised in the small bayou town of Houma, Louisiana—down at the "bottom of the boot." She received her bachelor's degree in drama and communications from the University of New Orleans and an MFA in fiction from Sarah Lawrence College. In her spare time she has attempted, with varying degrees of success, to juggle writing advertising copy with writing novels and short stories. She calls the Fort Greene neighborhood home, loves magical realism, fancy food, good wine, train trips, mountains by the sea, July on Martha's Vineyard, people who love her back, and mosquito-free environments. She doesn't eat Creole or Cajun food north of Baton Rouge and is bitter about the popularity of boneless chicken breast and cropped wide-legged pants; feel free to ask her about that and other topics that annoy her on Twitter @LynnTalks2Much.

**Mary Lou Johnson** is an aspiring playwright who explores how art can be used as a vehicle for social change. She holds a BA in Sociology from Spelman College and a MA from NYU–Gallatin School of Individualized Studies (Cultural Heritage and Identity and Public Policy). Her writing is inspired by this quote from Nina Simone: *You can't help it. An artist's duty, as far as I'm concerned, is to reflect the times.* Currently, she is working on other pieces to reclaim the narrative of lost voices. Originally from Newport, Rhode Island (US), she lives in Paris with her husband and daughter.

**Melanie Merle** is a writer, a teacher, a caregiver. Her first work was published by *Poetry Northwest*, as a finalist for the inaugural James Welch Prize in 2021. She works for the Lighthouse Writers Workshop in their outreach program, teaching Writing to Be Free to a group of women in a community incarceration facility.

**Pedro Iniguez** is a speculative fiction writer and painter from Los Angeles, California. His work has appeared in *Nightmare Magazine, Helios Quarterly, Space & Time Magazine,* and *Tiny Nightmares,* among others. He can be found online at *Pedroiniguezauthor.com.*

**Ra'Niqua Lee** has an MFA from Georgia State University. Her work has appeared or is forthcoming in *Cream City Review, Indiana Review, Passages North,* and elsewhere. She was a participant in the Tin House and the Kenyon Review summer workshops. In 2021, the Georgia Writers Association awarded her the inaugural John Lewis Writing Grant for fiction. Her flash collection *For What Ails You* is forthcoming from ELJ Editions in 2023. Every word is in honor of her little sister Nesha, who battled schizoaffective disorder until the very end. For her always.

**Ruth Ellen Kocher** is the author of *Third Voice* (Tupelo Press, 2016), *Ending in Planes (*Noemi Press, 2014), *Goodbye Lyric: The Gigans and Lovely Gun* (Sheep Meadow Press, 2014), *domina Un/blued* (Tupelo Press, 2013), winner of the Dorset Prize and 2014 PEN/Open Book Award, Green Rose Prize winner *One Girl Babylon* (New Issues Press, 2003), *When the Moon Knows You're Wandering* (New Issues Press, 2002), and Naomi Long Madgett Prize winner *Desdemona's Fire* (Lotus Press 1999). She has been awarded fellowships from the Cave Canem Foundation and Yaddo. She is a Contributing Editor at *Poets & Writers Magazine* and Distinguished Professor of English at the University of Colorado where she teaches Poetry, Poetics, and Literature.

**Sarah Sophia Yanni** (she/her) is a Mexican-Egyptian writer, editor, and educator. She is the author of the chapbook *ternura / tenderness* (Bottlecap Press, 2019) and was a Finalist for *BOMB Magazine*'s 2020 Poetry Contest, Poetry Online's 2021 Launch Prize, and the *Hayden's Ferry Review* Inaugural Poetry Contest, and the Andrés Montoya Letras Latinas Poetry Prize. She serves as Managing Editor of TQR and holds an MFA from Cal Arts.

**shakirah peterson** is a writer, collagist, and photographer from Los Angeles, California. Her work has been supported by Clarion West, the Hurston/Wright Foundation, VONA, *Obsidian*, and *Epiphany Magazine*, amongst others. She received her MFA in Creative Writing from Louisiana State University in May 2022.

**Shalewa Mackall** is an artist and educator dedicated to liberatory creative practice. A Brooklynite, Garifuna woman, Gen X-er, midcareer choreographer, mother, daughter, cancer survivor, pie maker, and Deep House-head, Mackall is currently developing projects engaging memoir, move ment, and poetry. Her poetry is forthcoming in *Obsidian* and has been included in *Peregrine Journal*, *Mom Egg Review*, *African Writer Magazine*, *The 50in50 Project* in New York and Los Angeles, and the 2019 Visible Poetry Project. Mackall has developed her craft as a 2019 Poets House Emerging Poets Fellow, four-time VONA alumna, The Watering Hole Fellow, at Tin House, and in Cave Canem workshops. Mackall currently teaches dance and Black Studies at Saint Ann's School, in Brooklyn.

**Sheree Renée Thomas** is an award-winning fiction writer, poet, and editor. Her work is inspired by myth, folklore, science, and the genius of the Mississippi Delta. Her fiction collection, *Nine Bar Blues: Stories from an Ancient Future* (Third Man Books) was a Finalist for the 2021 Ignyte, Locus, and World Fantasy Awards. Other books include *Sleeping Under the Tree of Life* and *Shotgun Lullabies* (Aqueduct Press). She also is a co-editor of *Trouble the Waters: Tales of the Deep Blue* (Third Man Books) and *Africa Risen: A New Era of Speculative Fiction* (Tordotcom), and edited the World Fantasy Award-winning anthologies, *Dark Matter: A Century of Speculative Fiction from the African Diaspora* and *Dark Matter: Reading the Bones* (Grand Central). She is an associate editor of *Obsidian* and helms *The Magazine of Fantasy & Science Fiction*. A former New Yorker, she lives in her hometown, Memphis, Tennessee, near a mighty river and a pyramid. Visit www.shereereneethomas.com.

**Shreya Ila Anasuya** is a writer from Calcutta, India. Shreya's fiction has appeared or is forthcoming in *Strange Horizons*, *The Magazine of Fantasy and Science Fiction*, and in the anthologies *Magic Has No Borders* (HarperTeen), *Magical Women* (Hachette India), and *A Case of Indian Marvels: Dazzling Stories from the Country's Finest New Writers* (Aleph Book Co). Her work in creative writing, journalism, and editing has won the Toto Award, a Sangam House Residency, several UNFPA/Population First Laadli Media Awards, and the Otherwise Fellowship. They are a PhD candidate in cultural history and writing at King's College London. For more, please visit www.shreyailaanasuya.com.

**Soham Patel** is the author of *all one in the end/water*—(Delete Press, 2023), *ever really hear it* (Subito Press, 2018), winner of the Subito Prize, and *to afar from afar* (The Accomplices, 2018).

**Thea Anderson** is a writer and astrologer. She is the assistant editor at *Triangle House Review* and the Director of Production at CHANI. Recent astrology writing has been published by *The Mountain Astrologer*. She is currently working on her first novel. Past workshops/fellowships include Tin House and Kimbilio.

**Thirii Myo Kyaw Myint** is the author of a novel, *The End of Peril, the End of Enmity, the End of Strife, a Haven* (Noemi Press, 2018), which won an Asian/Pacific American Award for Literature, and a book of creative nonfiction, *Names for Light: A Family History* (Graywolf Press, 2021), which was the winner of the 2018 Graywolf Press Nonfiction Prize. She is an Assistant Professor of English at Amherst College.

**Tonya Liburd**'s work has been used in Nisi Shawl's workshops, and in Tananarive Due's UCLA Black Horror course, both to demonstrate 'code switching'. She has been longlisted for the 2015 Carter V. Cooper (Vanderbilt)/Exile Short Fiction Competition. Her website is *https://www.tonya.ca*; she's on Twitter at @somesillywowzer.

**Wendy Chin-Tanner** is the author of the poetry collections *Turn* (SRP, 2014) and *Anyone Will Tell You* (SRP, 2019), co-author of the graphic novel *American Terrorist* (AWBW, 2012), co-editor of *Embodied: An Intersectional Feminist Comics Poetry Anthology* (AWBW, 2021), and author of the novel *King of the Armadillos* (Flatiron Books, 2023).

**Yohanca Delgado** is a 2021–2023 Wallace Stegner Fellow at Stanford University. Her writing has appeared in *Story*, *The Believer*, *One Story*, *A Public Space*, *The Paris Review*, and elsewhere. She holds an MFA in Creative Writing from American University and is a graduate of the Clarion and VONA workshops.

# NOTES & ACKNOWLEDGEMENTS

An excerpt from "canon" by Sarah Sophia Yanni was included in *Mizna*, Fall 2021. Reprinted with permission of the author.

"Digital Medicine" by Brian K. Hudson was included in the *People of Colo(u)r Destroy Science Fiction!* special issue of *Lightspeed Magazine*, Issue 73, June 2016. Reprinted with permission of the author.

"DownRiver" by Melanie Merle was included in *Poetry Northwest*, Vol XVI, Issue 1, Summer & Fall, 2021. Reprinted with permission of the author.

"From Senegal to Senatobia," excerpted from "Shanequa's Blues—Or Another Shotgun Lullaby," was included in *NINE BAR BLUES: Stories from an Ancient Future*, by Sheree Renée Thomas. © 2020 Sheree Renée Thomas. Published by Third Man Books. Reprinted by permission of the author.

"Hello, Ghost" from *to afar from afar* by Soham Patel. © 2018 Soham Patel. Published by The Accomplices. Reprinted by permission of the author.

"The Sacred Interrupted" by Mary Lou Johnson is excerpted from "The Sweetest Moment Ever," performed in Paris, France in 2018.

"Mile 22—" by Lucien Darjeun Meadows was included in *American Poetry Journal*, Issue 18.2, 2021. Reprinted with permission of the author.

"One week away and the forest has changed" and "The edge of descent, digression's highway" by Jennifer Elise Foerster appear in *The Maybe-Bird* (The Song Cave, May 2022) and are published with permission of the author.

"OskΛnu·tú" by Kenzie Allen was included in *Poetry Northwest*, Volume 16 Number 2/Summer & Fall 2021. Reprinted with permission of the author.

"Post-Glacial" and "She Sang to Me Once at a Place for Hunting Owls" from *Corpse Whale*, by dg nanouk okpik. © 2012 The Arizona Board of Regents. Reprinted by permission of the University of Arizona Press.

"The Last Kingdom" from *Bright Raft in the Afterweather* by Jennifer Elise Foerster. © 2018 Jennifer Elise Foerster. Reprinted by permission of the University of Arizona Press.

"The Longest Stretch" by Lucien Darjeun Meadows was included in *you are here: a journal of creative geography*, Volume 22, 2021. Reprinted with permission of the author.

"The Passing" from *Salsa Nocturna* by Daniel José Older. © 2012 Daniel José Older. Published by Crossed Genres. Reprinted by permission of the author.

"Transmigrations" by Kenji C. Liu features the lyric "Lonely lonely lonely whale" from the song "Whalien" by BTS.

"Violet" by Lucien Darjeun Meadows appears in *In the Hands of the River* (Hub City Press, 2022), was first included in *Ecotone* (Spring 2016), and is published with permission of the author.

"Yangon" from *Names for Light: A Family History* by Thirii Myo Kyaw Myint. Copyright © 2021 by Thirii Myo Kyaw Myint. Reprinted with the permission of The Permissions Company, LLC on behalf of Graywolf Press, Minneapolis, Minnesota, www.graywolfpress.org.

# READING & TEACHING GUIDE

## The Editors, Khadijah Queen and K. Ibura

This section of the anthology is meant to help readers, instructors and students tease out themes and hold robust discussions about the work herein. We hope the guide can foster engagement with and deepen understanding of the authors' creative works individually and in relation to one another. We trust that folks will feel free to adjust and adapt the questions and writing exercises according to their needs.

### *Editorial Interrogations*

In the anthology's introduction, the editors discuss human relationships, quoting lines from the anthology's poems and stories. After reading the introduction, what do you think the title *Infinite Constellations: Speculating Us* means? Not every text in the anthology is futuristic or fantasy-based. What do you think speculating means in the context of this anthology? Write an essay in response to the introduction, pulling lines from three or four pieces in the anthology, explaining the role speculating plays in the anthology. How do the anthology's contributors use imagination, memory, and relationships to speculate? What are they speculating about?

*

"Oskʌnu·tú" by Kenzie Allen opens the *Infinite Constellations: Speculating Us* anthology. Pair up with one or two other students and explore why you think "Oskʌnu·tú" may have been selected to introduce the anthology.

Using your conversation as a guide, write a page arguing why you think "Oskʌnu·tú" was or was not a good choice to begin the anthology. Following your argument, choose three lines from the poem and pair or juxtapose the lines with specific stories and/or poems in the anthology. Describe the literal, emotional, and philosophical meaning of each line—and explain how the story or poem you are pairing it with aligns with or rejects the line. Suggested lines include:

- You are not that kind of wolf who would / devour the world.
- I don't know what it looks like, / peace, I say, except / for the outline of where it's been
- An island / where we all are well-fed

*

In "Red Green Blue," Cindy Juyoung Ok introduces "the idea of the party within the party: that in any group of people formed for any amount of time, there is always an inner core." This can be the same for bodies of work. *Infinite Constellations: Speculating Us* contains a range of literary styles, forms, and themes. Take on the role of the editor and choose three to five pieces from the anthology to represent the "party within the party"—works that you believe speak as the core of the anthology. Write an essay of three to five pages. Start by introducing the works, then describe the relationship between them, and argue why you believe they are the inner core of *Infinite Constellations: Speculating Us*.

### Thematic Analysis

"The Swan" by Lynn C. Pitts, "Antelope Canyon" by Thea Anderson, and "Mermaid Names" by Ra'Niqua Lee deal with transformation in parallel ways. Transformation is also a theme in "on bended knee" by shakirah peterson; however, the transformation follows a different arc. Map the arc of transformation over the course of each story, then compare and contrast the stories' approaches to the theme. How do these stories address the body and an individual's agency over their body? In the case of

"The Swan," "Antelope Canyon," and "Mermaid Names," transformation is forced on the characters, whereas in "on bended knee," one character is the source of transformation. Do the stories provide differing perspectives on transformation? What are the liminal spaces expressed in each story and how do those liminal spaces interact with the real world?

*

In "Plink" by Yohanca Delgado, the world is turned inside out and the familiar has become unfamiliar. The story introduces a shift in a relationship between a daughter and a mother. "Letter to a Hiring Manager" also documents the shifts in roles between a mother and a daughter. Both stories hint at a danger in the spaces between these relationships. What are some of the elements of danger introduced in each of the stories? What personal experiences have you had where a close familial relationship suddenly shifted and you found yourself playing an unexpected role?

*

In both "Digital Medicine" by Brian K. Hudson and "The Passing" by Daniel José Older, an older member of a community passes important cultural knowledge on to a younger member of a community. What moments in each of the stories provide insight into what draws the older and younger characters together? Compare and contrast the missions of older characters in "Digital Medicine" and "The Passing." What is at stake in these stories and what will it mean if the older characters have been successful in their missions? What role does technology and culture play in each story—and how do technology and culture intertwine in the plot, possibility, and meaning in each story?

## Textual Conversations

"She Sang to Me Once at a Place for Hunting Owls" by dg nanouk okpik, "Dream of a Space Tattoo" by Juan J. Morales, and "reflection on spices" by Sarah Sophia Yanni are all prose poems. Look up the definition of a prose poem. What poetic elements stand out to you between these three prose poems? The poems contain a range of literal and metaphorical meanings. What comparisons can you find between the literal meaning of the three poems? What alignment or echoes can you find in the metaphorical or metaphysical meanings of the poems?

*

In the poems "One week away and the forest has changed" by Jennifer Elise Foerster and "Date: Post Glacial" by dg nanouk okpik, nature is a full-fledged character, sometimes overwhelming in scale when compared to the speaker of the poem. In each poem, the speaker is questioning—sometimes appearing to be lost and sometimes appearing at home in the wilderness. Interrogate the friction and union between each poem's speaker and nature as described in the poems.

*

Possession and desire are themes of both "sealing the room" by André O. Hoilette and "Playing MacBeth at the Electra Theatre on Beadon Street" by Shreya Ila Anasuya. In both texts, the main character is overtaken with the desire to attain something she does not possess. What are the ways that the two themes parallel and diverge from each other? How does possession lead to mortal danger in both texts? What are the cautionary messages that can be drawn from each story?

## Form and Device

"Carville National Leprosarium, 1954" by Wendy Chin-Tanner and "Hello, Ghost" by Soham Patel both interrogate a second-person character. One of the poems addresses the "you," and the other poem narrates the actions of the "you." Compare and contrast the way the authors employ the use of second person. Does the second person create more or less intimacy; more or less distance between the reader and the people in the poems? How do both poems deal with the space and distance between people, history, and memory?

As a form, plays do not include long descriptive sections or narration; consequently, playwrights must include all the information in dialogue that is spoken by actors. In "The Sacred Interrupted" by Mary Lou Johnson there are few set descriptions or stage direction, yet the environment and location of the play's three characters is very clearly drawn. How does the author bring to life the characters' environment and interactions? Which lines describe the type of home environment the play is happening in? How are the characters' relationship to each other revealed through the actions they take throughout the excerpt? What family rituals are core to the main character's memory and how does it inform the lens through which the character views the parents?

*

Beyond language, poems also use form and structure to communicate meaning. Two poems that enter into conversation with religious texts break the poem onto opposing sides of the page. Why do you think George Abraham in "Against Allegory (I = Eve & Satan)" and Sarah Yanni's in "canon" chose similar forms? How do these forms help impart layers of meaning to the poems? Do you think anything is buried in the breaks between the poems? As a reader, did you fill in the breaks with your own thoughts, musings, and connections?

## Reading Between the Lines

In "Sufficiency" by Shalewa Mackall, the author writes: "The people, they keep jumping / till the only way is a prayer." In "From Senegal to Senatobia" by Sheree Renée Thomas, the author writes: "The blues burst from the will to overcome sadness, to overcome anger, bad luck, exploitation, pain." Imagine these two pieces in conversation with each other. What life outlook does "Sufficiency" express? Does "From Senegal to Senatobia" express the same outlook or a different one? How is the theme of resistance expressed in each text? What historical events or realities may have informed each text?

*

"Violet" by Lucien Darjeun Meadows, "Returning" by Aerik Francis, and part 18 of "Transmigrations: A Future History of Multiple Bodies of Water" by Kenji Liu take an intimate view of nature and the environment. What are some ways that each text personifies or animates nature? How do the authors interpret nature's perspective in the texts? Identify some of the descriptive terms each text uses to describe nature, and create a personality profile for nature as presented in each text. Then imagine what relationship humankind would have in interacting with nature in the form described in the text. Would some relationships be gentler or more threatening? More confrontational or more symbiotic?

*

In "Ways To Use Silhig Lánot" by Alton Melvar M Dapanas and "A Final Song for the Ages" by Pedro Iniguez, inanimate objects are the conduit for human connection. Which objects connect the characters to their loved ones? How is the connection activated? What objects exist in your life that hold resonance, memory, or a connection to someone you love?

## Creative Interpretations

"how to battle" by Ruth Ellen Kocher is an instructional poem. It structures the messaging through direct instructions throughout the poem. The instructions are not for a literal task, but rather a deeper approach to life. Think about a larger approach that helps you navigate life and write your own instructional poem. Pay close attention to the metaphorical language Kocher employs in lines such as "widen your stance / collect your splinters of regret" and "assume the empirical formula of ancestors / so they taste your breath." Be sure to include metaphors and descriptive language with plenty of movement.

"Yangon" by Thirii Myo Kyaw Myint interrogates family history and connections to home in a series of reflections grounded in childhood memory. Explore an area of your family history and hometown that interests you. Instead of writing one long piece, structure your reflections in separate sections that are connected by theme. Like in "Yangon," the sections do not need to be chronological, and can dive into different aspects of the theme. End your piece with some element of nature, science, and/or travel.

*

"Above Ground" by Melanie Merle, "My Mother Told Me I Am Under Shango" by Tonya Liburd, and "Red Green Blue," Cindy Juyoung Ok reflect on heritage. "Above Ground" focuses on the physical environment and experiences of childhood. "My Mother Told Me I Am Under Shango" relates clothing to traits inherited from or gifted by the speaker's mother. "Red Green Blue" interrogates ways in which our birth cultures influence us. What are some of the memories, qualities, habits, perspectives, and behaviors you have inherited from your family lineage? Embody your familial inheritances in a poem.

# ABOUT THE EDITORS

**K. Ibura** is a writer, editor, visual artist, and traveler from New Orleans, Louisiana—which is the original home of the Chitimacha Tribe. She writes across genres, publishing essays about identity, race, and gender and fantastical short stories about mystical happenings, ancient histories, and future imaginings. She is the author of two speculative fiction collections: *Ancient, Ancient*—winner of the James Tiptree Award—and *When the World Wounds*. Her debut novel *When the World Turns Upside Down* is a middle grade book about the COVID crisis and the fight for social justice. She is currently working on a speculative YA series about a teenager with mysterious powers and a life-changing legacy. She supports writers through workshops, her Patreon page, and her Notes from the Trenches e-book series. You can learn more about her work at kiburabooks.com and kibura.com.

**Khadijah Queen** writes in every genre. She is the author of six books of innovative poetry, most recently *Anodyne* (Tin House 2020), winner of the William Carlos Williams award from the Poetry Society of America. A zuihitsu about the pandemic, "False Dawn," appeared in *Harper's Magazine* and was selected as a Notable Essay by Best American in 2020. Her verse play *Non-Sequitur* (Litmus Press) won the Leslie Scalapino Award for Innovative Women's Performance Writing; the Relationship theater company staged a full production at Theaterlab NYC in 2015. Individual poems and prose appear in *American Poetry Review*, *The New York Times*,

*The Poetry Review* (UK) and widely elsewhere. She holds a PhD from the University of Denver and her first book of criticism, *Radical Poetics* (Univeristy of Michigan Press), is forthcoming in fall 2023.

**SHEREE RENÉE THOMAS**

I am a daughter of rivers and of the rich, black earth. My people on both sides of my family are from Sunflower County, Ruleville, Mississippi, and Memphis, Shelby and Fayette Counties, Tennessee. My family lived and worked once as bondspeople and then as freedmen in the homeland that was the Chickasaw Nation. My ancestors once lived in Beaufort, South Carolina, and Virginia. The oldest part of our lineage is shared with the Mende people of contemporary Sierra Leone.

**RUTH ELLEN KOCHER**

I identify as she/her. My people are from ancient places.

# I AM

●

# WE ARE

**THEA ANDERSON**

I am Black, and my people are from Texas, Illinois, and Tennessee.

**SARAH SOPHIA YANNI**

I am the first-gen daughter of Mexican and Egyptian parents.

**TONYA LIBURD**

I identify as Black, and my people are multiracial, from the Caribbean.

**PEDRO INIGUEZ**

I am Latino and my people are from Mexico.

**RA'NIQUA LEE**

I identify as a Black woman, raised by amazing Black women, and we are from Georgia, occupied Muscogee Creek land.

**WENDY CHIN-TANNER**

I identify as a woman and my people are Chinese American.

**SHALEWA MACKALL**

I am a Black woman who is a member of the first, third, and at least sixth generation of people in my familial lineages born in the US. These lineages are Garifuna, Caribbean, Latin American, Enslaved and Free.

**THIRII MYO KYAW MYINT**

I identify as Asian American and Burmese American, and my known ancestors settled in villages, towns, and cities along the Irrawaddy River.

**YOHANCA DELGADO**

I am a Latina of African, Indigenous, and European descent. My people are from Cuba and the Dominican Republic.